BAD
INTENTIONS

CHARLEIGH ROSE

ISBN-13: 978-1717449429
ISBN-10: 1717449425

BAD INTENTIONS
Cover Designer: Letitia Hasser, RBA Designs
Cover Model: Cauê Amaral
Cover Photographer: Juan Espana
Interior Formatting: Stacey Blake, Champagne Book Design

PLAYLIST

"Monsters"—Matchbook Romance

"Sweet Dreams"—Marilyn Manson

"Heaven"—Julia Michaels

"Wrong Way"—Sublime

"Him and I"—Halsey & G-Eazy

"In My Blood"—Shawn Mendes

"Sally's Song"—Fiona Apple

"Sparks Fly"—Hey Violet

"Bad at Love"—Halsey

"Bittersweet Symphony"—The Verve Pipe

CHAPTER ONE

Lo

SAME SHIT.
Different day.
Different climate.
New start.

Or, at least that's what I'm telling myself as I dig through my still-packed bags, searching for a clean sock—it doesn't even have to be a matching one, just a clean one—in the tiny shoebox of a bedroom at Henry's cabin. Henry is my father. The father whom I haven't seen since I was eleven years old. The father who bailed on our family long before that. The father whom Jesse barely even remembers, seeing as how he was only seven when our dad left for good. The father who reluctantly agreed to let Jess and me stay with him when shit hit the fan back home. All out of options, I unfolded the scrap of paper I'd managed to keep hidden from Mom all these years—the one with my dad's address and phone number—and made the call. We went from the shittiest part of Oakland to River's fucking Edge, Nowhere, USA. Population: us, and like three other people.

I grab one of Jesse's socks and bring the dingy, off-white thing to my nose before deciding that it smells clean enough. I throw on my old pair of black army boots that hit just below my calf over my black leggings, button up my oversized flannel, and pull on my gray beanie over my messy hair. I make a mental note to buy us some actual winter clothes with my first paycheck. You'd think it would still be warm in October—granted, it's practically November—but you'd be wrong. When people think of California, they think of palm trees and beaches. But here? Way up here? There's nothing but mountains and pine trees. Which, I'll admit, is part of its charm, and I'd probably be in heaven if it weren't for the fact that I'm fucking freezing and Henry already lectured us not to turn the heat above sixty.

I stand with my hands on my hips, scanning the room for an acceptable hiding place. The mattress sits on the floor next to a busted old nightstand. The closet is overflowing with storage and trash bags full of God knows what. It's not that I have anything of value to most people in this particular bag—besides the few bucks I have left to my name—but it's all I own. My entire life has been reduced to three duffle bags. And if I've learned anything from growing up with an addict for a parent in Oakland, it's *always hide your shit*. I bend over to zip my bag shut before wedging it between the nightstand and the mattress. It will have to do. Henry says River's Edge isn't like The Bay Area, and while that's clear, I'd argue that people are the same at their core, regardless of their zip code. We're all flawed, selfish humans doing what it takes in order to survive. Myself included.

I suck in a fortifying breath, taking in my new life, and mentally preparing myself for what today holds. I have to enroll Jesse in school, fight with him to get him there first, then apply to anywhere and everywhere in this one-horse town so I can pick up a job. Henry said he could try to find something for me to do at his auto shop once a week until I find something else, but what the hell do I know about cars? I mean, I could probably hotwire one, but I don't know anything about maintenance. Plus, I need to work more than one day a week. I walk out of my new room, kicking the door shut behind me.

"Jess!" I yell once I enter the living room, only to find him still asleep, with one arm and one leg hanging off the edge of the couch. "I told you to get up twenty minutes ago!" I nudge him in the ass with my foot until he groans and rolls over.

"Why the fuck won't you let this go?" Jess mumbles, pulling the blanket over his eyes. "I'd be more help getting a fucking job than wasting time with school."

"It's your senior year," I argue, tugging the blanket off his face. "You can't quit now." I won't let him. Where we come from, it's a rarity to even make it that far. Myself included. I dropped out my junior year to work full-time and take care of him. I don't regret my choice, but I want more for him.

Jess rolls his eyes and snatches an old cigarette out of the ashtray on the coffee table and lights it up before taking a drag. He stands and pulls on his crumpled-up jeans from the night before and throws on his beat-up brown boots, not even bothering to tie the laces.

"Happy?" He shrugs. "I'm dressed. Let's fucking go."

"It's cold out," I scold him, but I smile when he grabs his jacket and backpack off the recliner next to him.

"You're bossy. Anyone ever tell you that?" He plucks his trusty skateboard that sits next to the front door, holding it under his arm.

"You love me anyway." I knock him with my shoulder, eliciting another eye roll, but he can't hide his smirk.

I open the door, pulling my jacket up to my chin. *Holy shit, it's cold.* We don't even take two steps outside before we both stop short.

"How are we getting there?" Jess asks, arching a brow.

"Fuck."

Jess huffs out a laugh before turning back for the door. "I'm going back to bed." In The Bay, we could walk almost anywhere we needed to go, and for anywhere else, we had BART. Somehow, I don't think that's going to work here.

"Wait, Jess," I say, jerking my chin toward the old, shitty 4Runner with silver paint oxidized from the sun. It sits on the far side of the driveway, halfway in the yard. It's a long shot. It might not have gas or even run. It's old enough to be hotwired, though. Definitely an early nineties model.

"Worth a try, right?" I shrug, and Jess reluctantly makes his way over to the run-down SUV to check it out. I follow. He opens the door, and the sound of metal screeching against metal assaults my ears.

"The keys are in it," he says, sounding about as baffled as I feel, but my face, along with any hope I had, falls because we both know what that means. There's no way anyone would leave the keys in a working vehicle. He tries them anyway, and to both our surprise, the engine roars to life. "No fucking way."

"Eeek!" I squeal, hopping in as he slides over into the passenger seat.

"Good old Henry was right. This place is nothing like The Bay."

"And look," I say, pulling my phone out of my jacket pocket. "We still have time to get you to school."

"You know, on second thought, this *is* stealing…" Jess says.

"And you suddenly have a problem with that on the day you start school?" I ask with an arched brow.

"I'm just sayin'. We might not want to steal from the person letting us live with him. Don't bite the hand that feeds you and all that."

"Fuck him." I laugh. "He has years of making up to do. And this piece of shit doesn't even begin to cover it." I slide the seat forward as far as it will go and put the car in reverse. "This is the first day of our new life, little brother. Don't screw it up."

"You're not his legal guardian?"

"No, ma'am. He's my brother, though, and I've never had a problem enrolling him before." God knows I've done it enough times between moving and Jess getting kicked out.

"That's fine, as long as he does live with you and you both live within the district. You'll need to fill out the Custodial Statement and Agreement forms, then come back with your proof of residence, and, if at all possible, a parent's signature. He will be able to start as soon as we have that information," the lady in front of me explains. She looks young. Maybe thirty, with blonde, stringy hair and a pair of black-framed glasses perched on her petite nose.

"Listen…" I start, leaning my forearm on the desk in front of me, my eyes locking onto the name on her desk plate, "Lacey. I will get you everything you need. But Jesse has already been out of school for two weeks. It's his senior year. He's going to have trouble catching up as it is." It's a damn lie. Jess is brilliant. The only way he won't catch up is if he doesn't try. The sooner I get this over with, the sooner I can look for a job. "I'm sure I don't have to tell you that every day he misses is another day he'll fall behind."

Lacey worries her bottom lip, looking over at Jess who gives her his best innocent, underprivileged boy face.

Lacey sighs, and I know we've won. "Fine. He can start. Fill out these forms now, then bring me your proof of address and a parent's signature tomorrow at the latest."

"Thank you!" I say, slapping my palms down on her desk a little too enthusiastically, causing her to jump in her seat. "Really, thank you. We need more people like you working in the public school system."

Lacey beams with pride, and Jess snorts out a laugh at my bullshitting before disguising it as a cough.

"I'll let your guidance counselor know you're here so you can set up your schedule."

"Thank you," Jess says in a low voice with a dip of his chin, and I swear she blushes.

"Don't even think about it," I warn once she rounds the corner and is out of sight. "Don't fuck this up. We're going straight. No hacking. No backtalk. And absolutely no seducing the faculty. Not even flirting," I stress. "This is our last shot, okay?" This is a small town with one high school. We can't just enroll him into another school if he gets caught having an inappropriate relationship with a teacher's aide or smoking weed in the bathroom. Like I said, Jess is brilliant, but that doesn't mean he isn't also kind of an idiot.

"What?" Jess asks, feigning innocence. "I wasn't doing anything."

"Mhm," I say, thumping him on the forehead with the palm of my hand. "Behave."

I sit down and scribble in the blanks, agreeing that I'm the responsible party for the "child" and that I'll be taking over parental duties and giving the school permission to contact me for any reason, *blah blah blah*. It takes all of two minutes. Lacey returns, looking over the forms.

"Everything here looks good. You can see Mr. Hansen now," she says to Jess. "Just get me the rest of those forms tomorrow," she adds, looking in my direction.

"I will. I promise."

Jess picks his backpack up off the floor and shrugs it onto one shoulder.

"See you at home," he says.

"How are you going to get there?"

"I'll find a way," he says, lifting a shoulder. "If not, I have my board."

"Good luck," I say, and then he's walking out the door, but not before tossing a wink in Lacey's direction.

Jesus Christ.

The bad thing about small towns is that it's near impossible to find a place that's hiring. I've been to every damn grocery store, café, and little clothing boutique in a twenty-mile radius. No luck. I swing into a parking lot near what I guess would be considered the *downtown* area, right on the Nevada border. A couple of shitty casinos, some restaurants, a bar, and a tattoo shop. *Hmm. A tattoo shop.* I've had a lot of jobs in my twenty-one years of life, but I've never worked in a tattoo shop.

I walk toward the neon pink sign flashing on the glass door that reads *Bad Intentions.* I push it open, and the door dings, announcing my arrival. There are two guys tattooing, and one holds up a finger, letting me know someone will be with me shortly before he goes back to his client. The other one doesn't even look up.

I decide to check out one of the portfolios on the coffee table in front of two black leather couches. I sit down on one of them, flipping through the pages of tattoos. These are gorgeous. I mean, there are the run-of-the-mill zodiac signs and tramp stamps, but some of these are so intricate and…beautiful. Most of the tattoos I've seen are the kind you get in prison or your friend's basement. This shit is art.

"Can I help you?" a deep, aloof voice asks. I snap the book closed and stand before looking up at the man who greeted me. He's wearing a black hoodie pushed up to his elbows, exposing two tattooed forearms, black jeans, and a slouchy beanie that hangs off the back of his head. His eyes are ice blue and intense, cutting right through me, framed by thick eyebrows the color of coal that are pulled together expectantly. Or maybe that's irritation I detect.

He lifts a brow, waiting for my response. *Shit.*

"Hi," I say, snapping out of it, extending my hand and pasting my brightest smile to my face. He pulls off his latex gloves, tossing them into the trash can next to the front desk, but doesn't take my hand. "I'm Logan."

"Sorry, no walk-ins today. All booked. We have a couple openings next week if you want to leave your name with Cordell," he offers, jerking his chin toward the guy tattooing an elaborate rose onto some girl's calf as she white-knuckles the edge of the table she's lying on.

"Actually, I was looking for a job. You guys hiring?"

"You an artist?"

"No, I mean, like answering calls or something. Anything, really. I just moved here, and I'm a quick learner."

"Definitely a *no*, then."

I should take the rejection and leave, but I'm desperate. And clearly, they could use the help. I'm sure potential clients would feel awkward, wondering what was expected of them if no one was there to greet them and give some direction. Especially if they've never gotten a tattoo before. I know I would. "Come on, you guys need someone at your front desk," I say, all false cheer and good-natured.

"There's the door," he says, pointing two fingers in the direction of said door. The counterfeit smile melts off my face, and the irritation that's been brewing all day finally comes to a boiling point.

"Aren't small-town folk supposed to be welcoming, and I don't know, *nice*? You don't have to be a dick about it."

"Okay."

"*Okay*?" *Who the hell responds with* okay? His lackadaisical response only frustrates me further.

"Okay," he repeats. "I'm a dick. You're an asshole who can't take no for an answer. Glad we've established that. Nice to meet you. Now, if you'll excuse me…" He dips his head and walks away. The other guy—Cordell, I think—snorts and shakes his head. There's no bite or malice in his tone. He basically just told me to *fuck off* with a polite smile on his face.

I blow out an exasperated breath before turning for the door, and right as I'm about to walk out, he speaks again.

"Oh, and welcome to River's Edge."

I flip him the middle finger and push the door open. I'm supposed to go pick up the spare key Henry said he'd make for me, but I'm starting to think I might have to take him up on the offer to put me to work. I was really hoping I wouldn't have to resort to working with him, but it's not looking good. I don't want to feel like I owe him anything. I'm already staying at his house.

Just as the door is closing behind me, a girl stumbles out of the place next door, almost face-planting onto the sidewalk. I throw out my arms in a useless attempt to catch her before she goes down.

"Holy shit," she breathes, catching her balance and smoothing out the mat in front of the door with her foot. I look up to see the sign that reads *B.B.B.* with *Blackbear Bar* written underneath—a silhouette of a bear behind it.

"Drunk already?" I laugh. "It's like two in the afternoon. My kinda girl."

"I wish," she mumbles, leaning against the wall before opening a pack of cigarettes and bringing one to her lips. "I always trip over that damn mat. I keep telling my boss to get one that doesn't bunch up. Want one?" she asks, holding out the gold and white pack as she takes a drag.

"Nah, I don't smoke." Pretty much everyone in my life does, but I've never seen the appeal. I can't tell you how many times I was made fun of as a kid for smelling like cigarettes at school. I hated my mom for smoking inside—though that was nothing in comparison to her crack habit. But, in my selfish twelve-year-old mind, the drugs didn't affect me, at least not my social life. The smell of smoke *did.* My hair, clothes, everything, always reeked. You spend money to kill yourself and smell like an ashtray in the meantime. No thanks.

"Yeah, I don't usually, either. It's one of those days."

I nod. "I'll take a job, though. Got one of those for me?" I'm half-joking, but if it works, it works.

She blows out a cloud of smoke and looks over at me, eyeing me up and down.

"What's your name?"

"Logan," I say, holding out my hand, and unlike the guy next door, she shakes it. "But everyone calls me Lo."

"I'm Sutton. You new in town?" She tucks a strand of hair behind her ear. She's gorgeous with straight jet-black hair that doesn't quite hit her shoulders and is slightly longer in the front.

"Yep."

"Are you here for good or just temporarily?"

"For good...ish," I answer honestly. We'll be here until summertime at the very least. Who knows what the future holds after Jess graduates. I don't see us going back home anytime soon.

"We do need someone, but not if you're going to bail in a couple weeks or a month. It's slow now, but we're about to hit our busy season, and we'll need you till at least March."

"Sold."

"Do you have any experience bartending?"

"Bartending, serving, closing, opening, cooking, hosting, bussing...you name it, I've done it."

"Can you work weekends?"

"I can work whenever you need me."

"I'll talk to my boss, but no objections to working weekends and a great rack to boot? Pretty sure you're Jake's dream employee. Got a number where I can reach you?"

Sutton puts out her half-smoked cigarette then holds out her phone. I program my number before she pockets it back into the tiny apron tied around her waist.

"Thanks. You're the first nice person I've met here."

"Don't thank me yet. This is the calm before the storm."

It's meant to be a warning, but what she doesn't know is that this job is already a million times better than anywhere I've ever worked. I can tell that much without even stepping foot inside. The uniforms aren't skimpy, for one. Black leggings and a white tee with the Blackbear logo on the right breast. Beats the last bar I worked at that required me to have my tits and ass on display for every drunk asshole to grope. I can handle the long hours and tired feet.

"Challenge accepted."

CHAPTER TWO

Dare

"I'VE GOTTA GET TO THE CAR SHOP BEFORE THEY close. You good to close tonight?" I ask Cordell, who's finishing up on his client. It's a weekday, so I usually stay until at least twelve. Sometimes as late as two a.m. on weekends to catch the crowds at closing time, but tonight, Cord is closing up shop for me.

"I got it."

"Thanks, man."

I pull my hood onto my head and step outside. It's the end of October, which means two things. One, winter is coming. Two, *tourists* are coming. Well, it's always tourist season here—with the lake and the river for the summer and the snow for winter sports—but December and January are notoriously brutal. Good for business. Bad for my whole *not liking people* thing.

I jog over to my truck, needing to be at the shop before it closes in—I check my phone—six minutes. *Fuck.* I can make it, as long as I don't hit any traffic. I fucked up my tire on a pothole, and this place is the only one in town that carries the right tires for my truck. Driving on it is sketchy, but I had to be at Bad Intentions for a twelve o'clock appointment.

I jump in, throwing it in drive, and haul ass toward the shop. The sun is already setting over the lake, and I squint my eyes against the rays peeking through the pine trees that stab at my vision. I pull up with a minute to spare and hope that the old bastard didn't decide to close early. Businesses here run on River's Edge time. Which means, you can't fucking count on anything to be open when they're supposed to be. If they're not busy—or if they want to pack it up and call it a day early—they can, and they will. I like money too much to run my shop like that. More than that, I know what it's like to have *none*. And I don't ever plan to go back to that life.

The door chimes when I walk in, but it's not Doris, the eighty-year-old smart ass that usually works the front desk that I see. It's someone much younger and, I'll admit, much better looking. It's the chick from the shop earlier, and she's standing with her arms folded across her chest, facing the door behind the desk. I can see her profile, not missing the generous curve of her ass in those tight pants, but she doesn't notice me.

"Well, that was fast," I say, pushing back my hood, then tugging the beanie off my head and running a hand through my hat hair. Her head whips around, and her scowl deepens at the sight of me. *So she remembers me. I'm flattered.* "Found a job already?"

"No," is all she says. Before she turns back around, I see the tan-ish purple ring around her eye that I didn't notice earlier. *Who gave this chick a black eye?*

"Okay, then. Is Henry in?"

"*Definitely* no," she says, throwing my words from earlier back at me.

"Touché."

14

Henry walks in from the back, wiping his perma-greased hands onto a grimy white rag.

"I see you've met my daughter, Logan," he starts, shooting me a look that says not even he knows what he got himself into.

His daughter? Fuck.

"I didn't know you had a kid."

"Neither did he, apparently," she mutters.

"Don't listen to her. I have two, but it's been…a while since I've seen them."

"Ten years. Time just gets away from you, huh, Pops?" Logan deadpans.

My eyebrows shoot up to my hairline, my eyes bouncing between them like I'm watching a tennis match. They go back and forth for a minute before I chime in and ask about the tires. I decided to get a whole new set since I have to replace the one, and they're getting pretty bald anyway. Henry, thankful for the interruption, lets me know that they did come in.

"But my guy called in sick, and I've been all booked up, so we'll squeeze you in first thing in the morning. What time does your place open?"

Awesome. Note the sarcasm.

"Noon."

"Since my darling daughter here helped herself to one of *my* vehicles, she can repay me by giving you a ride home. You can leave your truck here, and I'll have it done by ten thirty, eleven tomorrow."

I almost say no. But Logan's eyes beg me to do just that, and for some reason, I want to do the opposite. Plus, I need to get this done as soon as possible.

My lips slowly stretch into a wide smile.

"Deal."

Logan takes an angry swipe at the keys on top of the counter and storms outside.

"My chariot awaits," I say with a shrug.

"Good luck," Henry mumbles under his breath. "And try to be nice to her, will ya? She hasn't had the easiest life. If you think she's crazy, you should meet her mother."

I give him a nod and hand him my keys before turning to leave.

I jump into the passenger side of the only other vehicle besides Henry's and mine, but she doesn't speak, or even look at me. I take her in, *really* looking at her for the first time. Long, wild, dark hair. Porcelain skin. Tiny frame. Her big, innocent, hazel eyes betray her caustic front. I haven't spent more than five minutes with this girl, but I can already tell she's the type of crazy I need to stay far away from. This morning, she was all sunshine and rainbows when she came into the shop, but it didn't take much for her true colors to come out.

"You gonna tell me where to go or…?"

Right. She doesn't know where I live.

"Go left, then left at the light."

She does.

We drive in silence for a long while. No music, because we can't even get a radio station to come in clearly up here. I notice that she's shivering with only a thin flannel to keep her warm. If she's already this cold, she's in for a rude awakening in another month or so.

I lean forward to turn the heat on, but her fingers land on mine for a brief second, intercepting me before turning it back off.

"Heat doesn't work. And it smells."

"Might want to have your dad fix that or you're going to need a thicker coat in a couple weeks."

She scoffs, like that's out of the question, but doesn't respond.

"How far am I taking you? I didn't realize this was going to be a road trip."

"I live outside of town. A few more miles."

"You live alone?"

"Yep."

"Not a fan of people?"

"Nope."

She gives me a sidelong glance, and she's silent for a beat. Assessing. Then she speaks.

"It must be nice to live on your own."

It's small talk, which doesn't seem like something this girl does often. Her words are intentional. So, I play along.

"You don't?"

She shakes her head. "Never have. Staying with Henry for the time being."

"How old are you?"

"Twenty-one," she says defensively.

"I didn't mean anything by it." I'm surprised by her age, though I shouldn't be. She looks young, but something about her feels much older.

"My mom was never home. By the time I was old enough to move out, my brother was just starting high school, and I knew if I left, there'd be no chance of him graduating." Logan looks over at me with wide eyes, probably hating that she just divulged so much about herself. I know that look because I have the same aversion to sharing.

"I pissed the bed until I was twelve," I blurt out in an

attempt to even the score. Tell her something embarrassing about me to get the focus off her. And it works, because her expression goes from horrified to surprised, and then her cheeks puff out as she tries to hold back from laughing. She loses the battle and something between a laugh and a snort slips out, and even I can't help but chuckle.

"Why would you admit that? To anyone? *Ever*?"

I shrug. I haven't told anyone that before, for obvious reasons.

"Turn up here," I say, gesturing to the left with my finger. "Follow this road until you see a cabin on the right."

"You weren't kidding when you said you lived alone," she says, taking in the pine trees that line the narrow winding road. "You're *really* secluded out here."

"I like my privacy."

"I guess so."

Logan pulls into my driveway, and she looks over at me as she comes to a stop. She wets her lips with the tip of her tongue, and my eyes can't help but follow the movement. She swallows, and her throat moves with the action. I have the urge to take her inside and see what those hazel eyes look like when she's on her knees for me, what those puffy lips look like wrapped around me. But the last thing I need is to hook up with someone who isn't just passing through, and it's only a matter of time before she hears about me from someone in town and decides to stay far the fuck away from me. As she should.

Instead, I force myself to open the car door and get out. I prop my forearm on the doorframe, duck my head down, and say, "See you tomorrow."

"Tomorrow?" she questions, her eyebrows tugging together in confusion.

"Yeah. I'll need a ride back to the shop. Pick me up at nine."

"It'll cost you," she warns.

"Naturally. How much?"

"Fifty bucks."

"Fifty bucks," I repeat. "I could get a fucking Uber for less than that." She doesn't need to know that Ubers don't come all the way out here.

"Take it or leave it." She shrugs, expecting me to say no.

"See you at nine."

She raises an eyebrow, surprised by the fact that I'll actually pay her fifty dollars for a ride, I'm not sure. Maybe both.

"I don't even know your name."

"You never asked."

"*Well*?" she asks expectantly.

"It's Dare."

I pat the top of the rattletrap she calls a car and walk away, hearing her drive off behind me.

Lo

Dare. That's not a name. That's a warning. And I've been with enough bad boys to heed the warning. *I think.* Then again, the last time I tried going for someone different—a straight-laced suit, someone who appeared to be a good guy with a good career—things got ugly. Sometimes the nicest guys have the darkest sides.

Either way, I can't deny that he intrigues me. He looks like he'd know his way around a woman's body. But this is our new start. And I can't fuck it up by hooking up with the first boy I see, even if he does have the prettiest, bluest eyes known to man and a smirk that I felt right between my thighs. This is a small town. People talk, and the last thing I need is to be labeled the town whore. I just need to keep my head down, get a job, and get Jess through school.

My phone vibrates in my pocket, and I fish it out, only to see *Private Caller* flash across the screen. Unease prickles my spine. This is a brand-new number. Eric, my ex-boss and part of the reason I left, bought my old phone. He didn't like not being able to keep tabs on me, but I threw the phone away just before I left town. I used most of the money I had saved to buy myself a new one and added a line for Jess. They had a deal, and I ended up getting him a phone for ninety-nine cents.

There's no way Eric would know my number. The only people who do know it are Jess, my mom, and now Henry. But I can't shake the feeling that it's him. It's not like I'm afraid of Eric. He'd never physically harm me—psychological manipulation and intimidation are more his style—but the thought that he somehow got my number is…unnerving. I roll my eyes at my dramatics and shove my phone back into my pocket. There's no way it was him. Probably a solicitor.

"Lo?" Jess asks with a cautious lilt to his voice. "Everything okay?"

Jess may be my kid brother, but he worries about me like a parent would. That's what happens when your mom is a deadbeat and your dad is MIA. We are all each other has.

"I'm good!" I say, maybe too cheerily, because he casts me a suspicious look. "How was school?" I ask around a bite of my eggs, if only to change the subject.

Sometimes we have what I call Upside-Down Days, where we have pancakes and eggs for dinner instead of breakfast. I made it up when Jess was a little younger. It was more fun than saying, "Listen, we are too broke for real food, and all we can afford are eggs and pancake batter, if you're lucky." Years later, we're still broke as shit by most people's standards, especially at this moment, but it sort of became our thing. Even when I was working for Eric, making enough to support us and still have leftover spending money, we still had Upside-Down Days.

Jess walks over to the sink to fill his cup with tap water before taking a drink and wiping his mouth with the back of his hand. "Got head in the girls' bathroom at lunch, so I guess you could say it was a successful first day."

I scrunch my nose. "What did I tell you? Play it straight, and for God's sake, keep your pants zipped. Just for eight more months."

"Relax, we didn't get caught."

"*Yet*," I warn. "I guess I should just be glad it wasn't the school secretary."

"I never said it wasn't Lacey," he says mischievously.

"Jesse, I swear to God…"

"I'm just fucking with you. It was some girl from my math class. Who called your phone a minute ago?" In true Shepherd fashion, he flips the topic back to me to take the heat off him.

"What?" I ask, clearing my throat.

"Was it him? Eric? Is he fucking with you again? I swear to God, if you go back to him…"

I get his concern. Every single time he warned me about Eric, I brushed it off. At first, it was the money. He had it, and we needed it. He gave me whatever I needed. But then, it became more complicated. Lines were crossed, and morals were blurred. It wasn't pretty, and I'm not proud, but I *am* done. I never want to be the person I was when I was with Eric again.

"Nah, I think it was one of the places I applied to earlier."

"Weird, because you got that same panicked look in your eyes that you get whenever that piece of shit is involved."

"It wasn't him," I say firmly. I stand abruptly, causing my chair to scape across the cheap wood flooring. "Why is it so goddamn cold in here?" I change the subject once again, pulling my shirt closed. "I gotta take a hot shower. My tits are going to freeze off."

Jess shakes his head, and he doesn't believe me for a second, but he doesn't say a word as I make my way up the steps.

Once I peel off my clothes and stand under the scalding hot water, my mind drifts back to the hot guy with tattoos. And I allow my fantasy from earlier to run wild, in the privacy of this bathroom, because it can't happen in real life.

The buzzing under my pillow cuts through my dreams, forcing me into reality. I open one eye, waiting for the sleep to clear to be able to focus on the words on the screen.

You're late.

Late? It's from a local number. It takes a minute for my brain to catch up and remember that I'm supposed to pick Dare up. *How the hell did he get my number?* Tired eyes drag up to the time displayed in too-small numbers on the top of my screen. It's nine twelve. *Shit.* Jess is late for school. I scramble out of bed and dig through my bag, only to realize I don't have any clean jeans. Or leggings. Or underwear. Or anything, really. I really need to ask Henry if he has a washer and dryer. I haven't seen one, and this place isn't exactly a palace, so it doesn't look promising.

I have no choice but to go in what I'm wearing, which happens to be rumpled gray sleep shorts and a white tank top. I end up throwing on fuzzy striped socks that go up to my knees and Jess' oversized hoodie that fits me like a dress. I run down the stairs and into the living room, skidding across the floor, expecting to find Jess comatose on the couch.

Instead, I see a piece of paper on top of his pillow that reads *Henry took me to school. No, you're not being punked. He offered, and you looked tired.*

Henry took him? *Huh.* Maybe coming here was the right move.

I walk over to the table and grab my purse and keys. As I'm slinging the tattered brown messenger bag over my shoulder, I notice the paperwork with Henry's signature that Jess was supposed to take back to school.

"Dammit, Jess," I mutter under my breath before swiping it off the table. I tuck it inside my bag and add it to my list of shit to do today. I'm starving, but I don't have time to eat, so I take a bite of a piece of toast that was left out from someone's breakfast, stuff my feet into my boots, and then I'm gone.

"You didn't have to get all dressed up for me," Dare jokes as he takes in my wild hair, baggy sweater, and face free of makeup. He's amused with my ragamuffin state, but then his eyes land on my bare thighs, and I swear his nostrils flare at the sight. I'm tempted to spread my legs a little farther just to push him. To gauge his reaction. But I don't do that.

"Only the best for random strangers who force me to be their chauffeur," I say snidely instead as I pull out of his driveway and head toward Henry's shop. Dare's eyes, still locked on my thighs, snap up to meet mine. They're filled with something I can't put into words so much as *feel*. It's not transparent, overt lust like most men. But something...*more*. Something intense. And I want to know what it means. But before I can decipher it, he schools his expression and looks away.

"How did you get my number?"

"Your dad gave it to me."

"How nice of Henry to give my number out to strangers."

"Stop calling me a stranger. I've known Henry longer than you have," he points out.

"Touché," I say, nodding, because what else can I say? Other than *ouch*. He's not wrong. He may have known him longer, but he does know him better than I do.

"That was a dick move," he says after a minute. "Sorry."

He chokes out the word *sorry* like he's swallowing a handful of nails. As if the word is foreign to him, and he's never had to apologize for anything in his whole life. It almost makes me laugh.

"Nah," I shake my head, aiming for nonchalance, "it's true. So, why am I picking you up so early?"

"Need to eat. There's a restaurant next to your dad's shop."

Ignoring the weird feeling that comes from someone referring to Henry as my dad again, I ask, "Are you asking me out for breakfast?"

"No, I'm telling you to drop me off next door, so I can get a bite to eat. My fridge is empty."

Oh.

"But if you need to eat, too," he continues, scratching at the back of his neck in an uncomfortable gesture, "I won't stop you."

"I'll pass." I laugh. I might be hungry, but I don't have the time or the money to waste. Not that my pride would ever let me accept that non-invitation anyway.

"Suit yourself." He shrugs.

I drive in silence, my freezing legs bouncing, trying to get warm. Dare is quiet, too. His legs are spread wide, sitting like a fucking king in this piece of shit car, one arm propped on the door as he gazes out the window. I like that he doesn't feel the need to fill the silence with meaningless words.

"Pull in here," he says when we're close to the shop. I do as he says, swinging into the narrow parking lot of a place called Sissy's that sits next to another one named Belle's. He doesn't hesitate. Doesn't ask me to join him.

Dare reaches toward me, and my breath catches as his cold fingers slip between my thighs. Goosebumps prick my skin, and my nipples tighten almost painfully. Dare's bottom lip is trapped between his teeth as he tosses me a

25

cocky look.

"Thanks for the ride," he says in a low voice, and then he's gone.

I look down at my lap to find what he left tucked between my legs. A fifty-dollar bill. *Jesus.* I didn't think he'd actually pay me.

After dropping the forms off at Jesse's school, I went home to change and found the washer and dryer in the garage, so I tossed a load in. Then, I drove around aimlessly, applying for any place I may have missed, before I got a call from Sutton—the girl from the bar. She told me I got the job, and to come in next Thursday. When I asked if I needed to fill out an application or come in for an interview, she laughed like that was the craziest thing she'd ever heard. I'm just glad she called.

Feeling optimistic for the first time since we got here, I decided to use some of Dare's money—which I plan to pay back as soon as possible, which will be easy since I'll be working next door—to pick up some pizza and beer for dinner tonight after grabbing Jess from school.

Henry stuck around after he got off work, and for the first time in over a decade, we had dinner with our dad. It was…weird. But a nice weird. He wasn't like Mom who'd ramble on about being watched through cameras in the buttons of people's jeans, how everyone was out to get her, and she couldn't trust anyone. *Paranoia at its finest.* Dinner with Henry was almost *normal.* I've never had normal, but I've seen it on TV.

We're still sitting at the table, drinking our beer. The pizza has been demolished, and the grease-stained box is full of crust, crumpled-up napkins, and bottle caps.

"So, you guys going to tell me why you're here yet?" Henry asks after taking a swig of his Budweiser. I gave him the bare minimum when I called him. I told him we needed to get out of town, but I never mentioned Mom or Jess or Eric or any of that. He doesn't need to know about Eric, and the look that Jess sends me tells me that he doesn't want him knowing about his trouble, either, but I have to give him something. I decide that telling him about Crystal would be safe, and the most relevant to him.

"Mom was getting really bad," I start. Henry's eyebrows pull together in concern as he puts his elbows on the table, listening intently. I don't know why, but it bothers me. How can he act concerned when he threw us away like yesterday's trash? "She hadn't paid the bills in years," I continue, pushing my irritation aside. "She was almost never there. She disappeared for months, and Jess and I always scrounged together whatever we could from our jobs. But that was fine. We managed. We preferred when she wasn't home. It was easier that way. Calmer," I clarify, nodding to myself. "But then she got another shitty junkie boyfriend. This one didn't have his own place to stay, so Mom suddenly remembered she had a home."

"He was nasty as fuck, too," Jess chimes in, absently spinning a quarter on the kitchen table. "That fool never showered. Stole my shit. Ate all of our food—well, whenever they were too broke to get high and actually had appetites."

"They wouldn't leave. Brought their lowlife friends around. Then it all came to a head when Mom's boyfriend

27

beat the shit out of Jess because he wouldn't give them our last twenty bucks. She sat there and watched him hurt her son, and then me, and didn't do a single fucking thing about it."

Jess' fists clench, and I know he's thinking about what happened that day. He was half-asleep when our mom's boyfriend, Darrell, attacked him. He's lucky, too, or Jess would've killed him. He told him to fuck off when he asked for money, and then *bam*. Darrell went off. And once I tried to pull him off, he turned on me. Jess was swinging blind, blood in his eyes, while Mom screamed. For *Darrell*. Not her children. She let him beat on her, but I thought, maybe, some sliver of mother's instinct or love was still inside her. You hear about panicked mothers lifting cars off their trapped children. I'd have settled for one word. Just one word. *Stop*, is all it would have taken for me to know she was in there, somewhere. That was the day I knew my mother was gone completely, not that she'd ever been the best parent. But she was ours, and she was all we knew.

"Christ," Henry says, rubbing at his forehead. "I don't blame you guys for getting the hell out of there."

"There's more," Jess says, and the crease between Henry's eyebrows deepens.

"I called the cops. When they showed up, asking about a disturbance, Mom stood out of sight, shaking her head, silently begging me to turn them away. I didn't. They had warrants. Lots of them, for things we didn't even know about. Long story short, they're both in jail." If she gets lucky, she'll do court-ordered rehab instead of doing time, and then probation. Whether it's jail or rehab, I know she'll be fed, sheltered, and sober. I don't care how it happens.

I still remember the way she looked at me. How I held

her stare, resigned, as I slowly swung the door open wide, and did what you never, under any circumstances, do in a neighborhood like mine. You don't rat out anyone, ever. *Especially* not your blood.

But as I looked at Jess, swollen, bloody, and humiliated, I knew he needed me to show him that someone would love him like he deserved. Stand up for him. Protect him. That *I* loved him like a mother and a sister and a best friend, and *I* would always do what's best for him, even when she wouldn't. And I did it for Crystal, too. If she has any chance of living a normal life, or even a *sober* life, then maybe jail was the best and safest place for her.

So, I'll be the rat. The snitch. I'll be whatever the fuck you want to call me, and I won't regret it. Not even for a second. That doesn't mean we wanted to stick around to see what happens on the off chance they get off easy, though. Plus, with Jess getting caught hacking into the school's system, changing grades, his beef with the piece of shit dealers he was stupid enough to get involved in, and me finding out Eric lied about everything, it was the perfect storm. We needed to get out before it swept us away. There was no other choice.

Henry sits there quietly, his features twisted into something I can't decipher. Guilt? Anger? Or maybe it's discomfort, because he can't really defend her, knowing he failed us, too.

"Well," he says, clearing his throat. "You kids are welcome to stay here until they kick me out." Henry mentioned on the phone that his lease was up soon. The owner is selling the place, but I was too desperate to care. "I'm not here a whole lot, though. I'll keep the lights on. You two will be responsible for your food. All that I ask is you respect my house, and maybe leave me a plate of dinner every now and then."

"And the 4Runner?" I ask, hoping I'm not pushing my luck. Henry sighs and pinches the bridge of his nose.

"Why not. Bring it by the shop. I'll give it an oil change and make sure it's in decent condition."

That was easy. Too easy. Experience tells me I should be wary, but my gut tells me he's being genuine.

"Thank you," I say, and I mean it.

He stands and gives me a nod before he walks away. He pauses after a few steps and hesitates before speaking.

"I, uh, know I left you kids…" He trails off, seemingly uncomfortable. "Truth is, I was as bad as your mother back then. I won't pretend to be a saint. Not now and sure as hell not then. But I'm sober. Have been for years, save for the occasional beer," he says, jerking his chin to the empty on the table. "I know the chaos that surrounds your mother better than anyone, and you won't find that here. That's one thing you can count on."

He forgets that I was old enough to know what was going on. Even in my ten-year-old mind, I could see that my mother was poisoning everyone around us, including him. His intentions were good, but the execution was bad. And then he left. He'd left before, but that time, he never came back. Our mom spiraled. The little care we did have was gone. No one made sure we had food to eat or clothes to wear. No one made sure the light bill was paid or that we got to school. So, I did what I could to raise us both while harboring bitterness and resentment toward Henry for leaving.

Jess is quicker to forgive. He puts on a front of holding out, either because he doesn't want to admit it or maybe he just doesn't want to disappoint me, but I can see it in his eyes. He's ready to have a dad, and I don't want to get in the way of that. He was too little to understand when Henry lived with us. Maybe he wasn't a doting father, but he was there when our mom wasn't. He never hit us. Never yelled. And I felt like he liked us well enough. Then, he left. I don't know what's worse—remembering that you once had a parent who cared, at least a little, and then losing them, or not having much memory of it at all.

I don't feel sorry for myself. It's just the way things are. I'd venture to say a good eighty percent of kids in our hood live the way we did. It wasn't anything out of the norm, but it doesn't mean I don't resent my parents for their choices. For the life Jess and I could've had if they had their shit together.

Jess looks to me as if to say *can we trust this?* And I give him a slight nod of encouragement.

"Thanks," Jess mutters to Henry, and then he pulls a tattered book out of his backpack, walks to the couch, and plops down, where he will most likely stay all night. Henry walks upstairs, where *he* will most likely stay for the rest of the night. I sit down next to Jess. Wordlessly throwing an arm over his neck, I lay my head on the side of his shoulder before lifting the cover of his book to see what he's reading, even though I already know what I'll find. *The Outsiders*. I've never read it, but he once joked about being a modern-day Ponyboy.

"You okay?" I ask.

"I'm good," he replies easily.

"Have you heard from anyone back home?" Jess still keeps in touch with some of his friends and one of our neighbors, who is supposed to let us know if Mom shows up again.

"Nope. You?"

"No. I didn't even tell anyone I was leaving."

"Savage," he says, his eyes still on the pages of his book.

"I'm not taking any chances." I don't elaborate, but he knows what I mean. I'm not risking Eric finding me and trying to drag me back into his fucked-up world. "And you shouldn't, either," I add, jabbing a finger into his cheek. He jerks his face away.

"I'm not an idiot. I only told Mel and Danny." Danny and Melanie are his two best friends, the latter being his sometimes girlfriend. Danny is trustworthy. The jury is still out on Mel.

"I know you aren't. I just want you to be careful."

I want a good life for him more than I've ever wanted anything in mine. This is his shot—our shot, and I can't help but feel like it's going to be ripped away from us at any moment.

Jess assures me that he will and goes back to his book while I opt for watching Jimmy Fallon, and it's not long before I feel myself drifting off to sleep.

CHAPTER THREE

Dare

I

T'S MIDNIGHT BEFORE I GET HOME, HANDS CRAMPING due to a combination of a long session and my tendency to choke up on my grips when I'm tattooing. All I want to do is crash, but when I open my door, I see my buddy's girl, Briar, standing with her arms crossed, and Asher Kelley sitting on the couch. He only shrugs when I shoot him a look.

"You know how she gets," he says by way of explanation.

"Dammit, Dare. When are you going to realize you have people who give a shit about you?"

"What's she pissed about now?" I ask tiredly, tossing my keys onto the counter and bracing my palms on the edge of it.

"You missed dinner," Kelley says, an amused smirk on his face.

"Shit, my bad."

Briar seems to think I'm going to self-destruct at any moment. She has this rule that I go to their house once a week for dinner, but "dinner" is really code for *make sure Dare has some social interaction that doesn't involve a client and has at least one meal that doesn't come from a microwave per week.* In the two years that I've known her, she's somehow weaseled her way into my life, bringing my friend count up to a total of four. Five, if you include Adrian, Briar's friend who is even more intent on befriending me than she was for some fucking reason. The guy doesn't even live in River's Edge, but you'd think he does by how often he's here, in my shop, in my *house*. Why is it that the few friends I do have are always in my space, completely oblivious to my propensity to be a loner?

Briar gives me a sad shake of her head. I don't like disappointing her. She's like a little sister. An annoying sister, but a sister nonetheless.

"I've been distracted between my truck, and there was this fucking girl—"

"Girl?" Briar asks, perking up, and I roll my eyes. "There's a girl? What girl?"

"Jesus Christ." I should not have said a damn word.

"Dare, did you meet a *girl*?" Briar asks again, coming to stand next to me in the kitchen.

"Like, one you don't have to blow up first?" Ash chimes in from his place on the couch.

"Fuck off. She's just some chick who came in looking for a job."

"Hmm," Briar says, cocking her head to the side, looking for any sign of deception. "But she's distracting you?"

"Drop it, Briar. There's more chance of me dating *you* than this girl." That earns me a pout from Briar and a death glare from Asher. It's true, though. I don't date, as cliché as that sounds. I fuck when porn and my hand lose their appeal. And I'm selective about *who* I fuck. I prefer them to be tourists for a few reasons. They're never here for long, therefore can't, or *shouldn't*, rather, expect anything long-term—but that's not to say I don't get the occasional clinger.

For the most part, though, they come into town, the good girls looking for a night with the bad boy, and then go back home to their Ivy League boyfriends, feeling like they got something out of their system. Tourists also don't know my history, which is an added bonus. I don't like *anyone* knowing my business. Not even Kelley knows the extent of my past, and he's the closest thing I have to family and the one person who would understand, given his own similar past. I've hinted at what happened when he was going through his own shit, but I don't talk about it. Cordell and his brother Cam know because we were friends back then, but they know better than to bring it up. It's an unspoken rule. I relive that shit in my head every single night. I don't need to be reminded of my mistakes out loud.

"For the record, I don't believe you. But I'll let it go. *For now.*" She tacks the last part on, narrowing her eyes and pointing her finger at me in an attempt to look threatening. It's hilarious, really, considering she's about as intimidating as a pet bunny. "And you can make it up to me by coming to my party next week," she says, blue eyes big and hopeful.

I groan. I hate parties. I'm already mentally preparing myself for our work Halloween party. All the surrounding shops have one big costume party at Blackbear. If I was the only owner who didn't participate, I'd look like an even bigger asshole, and I'd never hear the end of it. I'd rather choke on a bullet than go to two parties in the same month.

"Come on, you know I wouldn't ask you unless it was important to me," she whines, and I shoot her a look. She invites me to every goddamn thing she attends.

"Okay, so I *would* invite you, but you know I wouldn't push."

"Briar passed her midterms," Kelley says, coming up behind her, squeezing her hip and looking at her with his eyes full of pride, and she beams up at him. It's still weird to see this side of him, but that's the Briar Effect.

"Four people were dropped this semester alone. And passing is a big deal. I just really want the people I love to be there."

"Wouldn't miss it," I say reluctantly, but I mean it.

"I love you, too," Briar says before smacking a kiss onto my cheek. Ash walks over, scoops her up, and her legs wrap around his waist.

"Now get out of my house." I've spent enough time with these two to know what comes next.

"He's just mad because he hasn't been laid in weeks," Asher mumbles into Briar's neck as he carries her toward the door.

"Leave him alone." She giggles as he reaches back to close the door behind him.

He isn't wrong. I haven't fucked anyone lately, and it's making me a moody son of a bitch. It isn't because there's a shortage of willing females, either. I just haven't found someone worth the trouble.

My thoughts immediately turn to Logan. Her bare milky thighs. Her full lips. Her porcelain skin. I could probably fuck her. I *want* to fuck her. But I won't, because girls like her—the beautiful ones with daddy issues—are pure chaos. And chaos is my kryptonite.

I push away thoughts of Logan and decide to shower. Afterwards, I'm too tired to sleep, as if that makes any fucking sense, so I sketch out some tattoo ideas. Drawing always relaxes me. It started as a coping mechanism when the guilt and intrusive thoughts became too much to bear.

After turning to drugs and alcohol to numb the pain, I turned to creating art. Art is a generous way to put it. It was far from it when I first started, but now, it's my lifeline.

I tried other career choices. Even started my own roofing business. I saved enough money to start Bad Intentions, then had Asher take over the roofing company when he moved back. I still technically own it and take jobs on the side every now and then, but creating keeps me grounded and sane in a way that even roofing can't. It worked at first, because I was fucking angry, and it was a good outlet—throwing myself into physical labor, hammering away at shingles all day, getting my aggression out—but I'm not angry anymore. I'm resigned. I know what I did, and I'll pay for it every single day for the rest of my life.

I sketch at the high-top counter in my kitchen for maybe thirty minutes before giving up on the three staggered pine trees in front of me. The same ones I have on my forearm, and the same ones I find myself drawing over and over again. I throw my pencil down at the drawing like it offended me. And it has. This was supposed to help me feel calmer, to clear the fucked-up thoughts in my head. To quiet the guilt. But not even the pine trees can help me tonight. I can't pinpoint why I'm feeling so off, but I can't shake my weird mood, so I stand from my barstool and punch the light switch with my fist before heading upstairs to bed.

I don't even make it to the top of the stairs before I hear a knock at the door. *Which idiot is it now?* My bet is on Cordell. Cam is too busy being a dad and Asher was just here, so that leaves one person. Except when I swing open the door, it's not Cordell's face I see.

"Hey, roomie," Adrian says with a big stupid smile on his face that has women dropping their panties for him despite the fact that he's a goofy bastard. I take one look at the backpack on his shoulder and the suitcase in his hand before slamming the door in his face. He throws out a palm to stop it from closing.

"I'm just playin'! Kelley won't let me in. And judging from the noises coming from inside their house, it's going to be a while."

On one hand, I don't want to do anything to encourage him. Adrian's like a fucking fungus. He's grown on me. A little. But I won't admit that to anyone. On the other hand, I just want to get some fucking sleep.

"One night," I warn. "I mean it. Take the couch." I jerk my chin toward the living room behind me. I have rooms upstairs. Asher's room is even furnished, but I like my space, and knowing Adrian, he'll take it as an invitation to move in if I let him have his own room.

"You're the boss, applesauce."

I shake my head, and he walks past me, kicks off his shoes, drops his pants, and plops down on my couch like he owns the place.

"Make yourself at home," I mutter, grabbing a blanket off the back of the recliner and throwing it at him. He takes the hint, covering his shit up.

"What, you sleep with pants on?" He scoffs.

"In other people's homes, I sure as fuck do." I turn back for the stairs. "I'm going to bed."

I'm warm. Uncharacteristically warm. Those are my first thoughts when I wake up. Then I remember that Adrian's here. He probably turned up the heat. Eyes still closed, I kick off my blankets, ready to doze back off for another hour, but then my foot hits something hard. Something that grunts.

"I swear to God, if you don't have pants on, I'm going to fuck you up."

I don't get a response, and I turn, as if in slow motion, to see Adrian sleeping, head on my pillow, without a care in the world. I kick him hard enough to roll his ass out of my bed and onto the hardwood floor. He lands with a *thud*.

"*The fuck?!*"

"My thoughts exactly. Who sneaks into another man's bed?!"

"It was fucking cold! You left me with a tiny ass blanket that wasn't even big enough to cover my balls."

"So, you didn't think to take Ash's old room, or I don't know, wake me up and *ask me* for another blanket?"

"Why are you making this such a big deal?"

"Because I don't like people in my fucking bed. Especially ones with dicks."

"Noted," Adrian grumbles, and when he stands, I see that he's wearing sweats. Thank fuck for small miracles.

There was no sleep to be had after waking up to Adrian's mug in my face. Instead of getting an extra hour of sleep, I dragged my ass to the shop early. Bad Intentions is my home away from home anyway. I have everything I need here, including the few hours of peace and quiet before we open that I can't seem to get at my own home.

As I'm checking out the schedule for today, I see Logan across the street. She's getting out of her dad's 4Runner, then looks both ways before running across. At first, I think she's coming here, but she's heading for the place next door. When she drops her keys and bends over, I have to admit, she's got the best ass I've seen in a long time. Tiny waist, thick thighs, and a fat ass. *God bless yoga pants*.

Blackbear isn't open yet, so she knocks on the door. Logan steps back, rubbing her upper arms and bouncing in place as she waits for someone to open it. Her tits jiggle, and I bet if I were closer, I'd see her hard nipples through her shirt. As if she can hear my thoughts, she turns toward me. We lock eyes through the window. It's too late to act like I wasn't staring now. She holds my gaze, the wind blowing a strand of her dark hair across her face, neither one of us backing down.

The door opens, breaking our staring contest, and out comes Jake. She smiles at something he says, and then he holds the door open for her, checking her out as she walks in. I can't fault him when I just did the same thing, but I will anyway.

Ignoring her presence was supposed to be easy, and it would've been. I would've forgotten all about her by tomorrow, had she not gotten a job right fucking next door.

40

Lo

I break Dare's icy stare as my new boss greets me. I paste a smile onto my face as he opens the door for me.

"Logan?" he questions, and I nod. "My bad, I was in the office in back. Come in."

His voice is easy and friendly, and he's much younger than I thought he'd be. He looks somewhere between twenty-five and thirty with dark, floppy hair under a backwards baseball hat, brown eyes, and tanned skin. He looks like a surfer type. Not exactly what I was expecting.

"I'm Jake," he says, extending his hand to shake mine. His grip is firm, but gentle and his hands are warm.

"Logan. But you just said that, so you already know. Everyone calls me Lo." *I'm gonna shut up now.*

He laughs, still holding on to my hand, shaking it up and down. I snatch my hand back when I realize I'm still hanging on like a creep. Way to make a good first impression.

"What brings you to River's Edge?"

I hesitate, thrown off by the question. How does he know I'm not from here?

"It's just that usually the only people to come here either have family here or are tourists," Jake clarifies upon sensing my confusion.

"Is it that obvious that I'm an outsider? Do I have a sign on my forehead?" I laugh.

"Nah. But you're not a tourist if you're looking for a job, and if I had seen you around before, I'd *definitely* have remembered."

Is he hitting on me? Or am I reading into that?

Jake clears his throat. "I mean, I never forget a face."

"Actually, my dad lives here," I say, letting him off the hook.

"No shit?"

"Shit," I say, nodding. "And my little brother goes to school here now, so I'll be here for the foreseeable future."

"That's what's up," he says, reaching over to grab a pile of papers off the bar top. I think this might be the most casual interview-slash-orientation I've ever had. I don't feel nervous or like I have to put on an act. Jake is warm and inviting and easy to talk to.

"Have a seat," he says, pulling out a stool for me. "I just need you to fill these out, and I'll grab your uniform."

I fill out the application, and Jake brings me two white T-shirts with the Blackbear logo on them—one with long sleeves, one with short—and an apron. I change in the bathroom, then Jake takes a photo copy of my ID and shows me around a little. Before long, Sutton shows up, cheesing from ear to ear once she sees me.

The rest of the day goes off without a hitch. There's a steady flow of customers, but not too busy, so we have a lot of time to bullshit and get to know each other. I learn that Sutton is hilarious and kind of a badass. Sometimes you can just tell right when you meet someone that they're just *good* and *genuine*. That's Sutton. I learn that Jake is probably a solid eighty percent of the reason this place is in business, because his admirers come in all day long, taking up tables, hanging around far after their meal is finished only to stare and take the occasional stealthy picture when he's not looking. I guess he's a big deal around here, but I haven't figured out why that is yet.

It's six p.m. by the time my shift is over, but the sun

has already set, making it feel much later. I offer to pick up another shift, because the night shift is always where the money is, but Jake laughs at me and tells me to go home. I think he thinks I'm joking. I'm not.

I count my tips in the break room, pleasantly surprised by the amount I made for a Thursday afternoon. Ninety bucks isn't bad at all.

"What's up with Jake?" I ask Sutton, who's sitting in a chair with her feet kicked up onto the small table in front of us. "He some kind of celebrity around here?"

"He used to be a pro snowboarder."

"Huh," I say, perplexed. This place is *so* not Oakland.

"Oh, by the way, you're coming to our annual company Halloween party next week. It's mandatory," Sutton informs me.

"Can I throw on some cat ears and call it my costume?" I don't have the money or the desire to figure out a legitimate costume.

Sutton gasps, looking deeply offended. "Absolutely not! Come to my house after work next Friday. I think my sister still has her Sally from *The Nightmare Before Christmas* costume. Either that or a giant hotdog. Your choice. I can grab it for you."

"Sally it is," I say, laughing. "I love that movie." It's one of the only good memories I have with both of my parents. Henry rented it around Christmastime, which sparked a heated debate on whether it was a Christmas movie or a Halloween movie—my vote is both, by the way—and we made a pallet on the floor, all four of us cuddled up, eating popcorn and candy, while we watched. Jess was still a toddler. I was probably seven or eight. Looking back, our mom was most likely coming down because she slept most of the time. Regardless, for some reason, I've never forgotten that night.

"So, it's settled then. We'll have some drinks and get ready together," Sutton says, clapping her hands excitedly.

"Can my brother come, or is it employees only? To the party, I mean. Not your house," I clarify.

"Your brother is in high school, right?"

I nod.

"I think it's supposed to be twenty-one and over, but no one really enforces it. Just tell him not to be a dumbass and try to order a drink."

"He's not an amateur." I laugh. Jess will probably come toting a water bottle full of vodka or some shit, but he's not stupid enough to try to order from the bar. Though, I bet it's harder to get your hands on stuff here than in Oakland. He has older friends back home, but even if he didn't, there's a homeless man on every corner looking to score a beer or a few bucks in exchange for buying booze.

To be honest, I give Jess shit, but he really is a good kid with a big heart. He smokes weed and drinks, but that's our normal. I don't know one kid in Oakland that doesn't. I'm just glad he's not a pillhead or a smackhead…or a crackhead or a cokehead. None of the bad *heads*. Just a pothead. I can live with that.

Jake taps his knuckles on the doorframe, and I look over at him from my seat at the table. "Good job today," he says with a smile. "A few more days of training and I'll put you on the night shift where I need you."

"She's already better than half your staff," Sutton says, rolling her eyes.

"True. I just have to go through the motions, so I don't piss anyone else off. Everyone wants the night shift."

"Oh, thank God," I say, tucking a strand of hair behind my ear.

"We work the same shift again tomorrow. Wanna come in a little early and have a late breakfast? Jake makes the best pancakes on this side of River's Edge," Sutton says, bumping his hip with hers.

"That's bullshit. I make the best pancakes on the entire lake and you know it."

"Debatable." She shrugs.

"But yes. By all means, I'll come in an hour early and cook breakfast for you two princesses. I don't have a life or anything."

"Damn right you will," Sutton says before heading back to tend to her remaining tables before she clocks out. "See you at ten!"

"You don't really have to do that," I say once she's gone.

"No, you should. It's my pleasure. I just like to give Sutton a hard time."

"Yeah?"

"Yep. In fact, I'll fire you if you don't."

I cross my arms. "Is that so?"

"Okay, no. But it was worth a try."

I laugh, rolling my eyes. I know he's teasing, but there's a little sliver of...*something* that crawls up my spine. Not exactly suspicion, but it leaves a bad taste in my mouth. It's not him. It's Eric. His brand of manipulation started off playful, just like this. And I never would've guessed things would end up the way they did. Not even for a second. And now, I'm suspicious of everyone, even harmless guys with floppy hair and kind eyes.

"If you insist," I say, ducking under his arm that's braced against the doorframe.

"If I have to be here early with Sutton, then so do you."

"I heard that!" Sutton yells from somewhere in the kitchen around the corner.

"See you then."

I'm in the middle of the street, halfway to my car, before I remember that Dare is next door. I stop in my tracks, looking behind me. The Bad Intentions sign glows pink in the night sky, and I can see that the shop is busy, but I don't see Dare.

I jog back across the street and pluck a fifty-dollar bill from my pocket. I open the door, and a guy with gauges and suspenders walks toward me, smiling, but I wave him off, letting him know I'm not a customer. There are a couple of other guys tattooing, one I recognize from the last time I was here, one I don't. Dare is sitting on a stool near his station, with his hands behind his head and his legs spread wide.

I walk right up to him, and when he finally sees me, he doesn't react. Doesn't seem shocked by my presence. I bend over, getting close to his ear, and whisper, "I don't need your money." His eyes widen slightly, but he doesn't move a muscle, hands still clasped behind his head. I take it a step further than he did and tuck the money inside his jeans, and under his boxer briefs. He raises a brow when my fingers touch the warm skin of his lower, *lower* stomach.

I pull my hand back and walk away without another word, hearing a *damn* and *who the hell was that* mixed with a low whistle and some laughs. I don't know what Dare's reaction is, because I don't look back.

When I get home, the house is empty. I decide to shoot Jess a text.

Me: Where are you?

Jess: Studying.

Me: Liar.

Jess: Well, she does give good brain.

I'm confused for half a second before he sends me a picture of a girl's blonde head bent over a book with a notebook and pencils scattered around her, unaware that Jess has taken the photo.

Me: Don't be creepy. By the way, I left a few bucks for you on the counter for lunch tomorrow. I'm probably going to pass out early. Be safe.

Jess: I will. Pleasantville is hella sketchy after dark.

Me: Shut up.

Jess: I'm gonna need a gun if you expect me to survive these streets.

Me: I'm going to bed, now…

Jess: Make sure you lock the door. I hear home invasions are on the rise here.

Such a jackass. I laugh at his ridiculousness, tossing my phone facedown onto my bed. I start to pull my shirt over my head, but my phone rings a second later.

"If you're calling to tell me you've been kidnapped and need ransom money, tell your kidnapper he took the wrong kid. We're poor."

"You wouldn't have to be poor if you'd come back to me."

My stomach twists at the voice from the other line, and even though I know exactly who it is, I pull the phone away to check the screen, but it doesn't show the number that I've had memorized for the past year. It reads *Private*.

"How did you get this number?"

"That's all I get? No, *Hello,* Eric. *I've missed you*?"

"What do you want?" I ask, trying to sound assertive

and unaffected. I don't want to let him know he can still affect me in any way. He can sniff out when someone is intimidated, and he feeds off it.

"I want you back here. In my house. In my bed."

I can't help but laugh. He is literally insane.

"That ship has sailed, Eric. Besides, your bed is big, but it's not big enough to share with your *wife*."

"She's gone."

"Bullshit," I spit.

"She's...*away*, getting help. Then she's going to get her own place once she's well again."

I hope that's the truth, but I can't believe a word out of Eric's mouth.

"Where's Cayden?" I ask quietly.

"He's here. With me, of course."

My heart physically hurts when I think about Cayden. At twelve years old, he's the only innocent in this fucked-up scenario. My throat gets tight when I think about how he must be feeling without his mom. I know better than anyone. The hardest part of leaving Eric was leaving Cayden.

"He misses you, baby. We both do," Eric says in that soft tone. The one he saves for times like these, when he knows he doesn't have the upper hand. But sweet-talking won't work this time.

"I miss him, too," I say, voice cracking before I steel it. "But you're fucking delusional if you think I'd ever come back to you." I hang up the phone before he can respond, and then I stare at the dirty carpet, sucking in a deep breath, trying to escape the guilt that threatens to swallow me whole.

I had an accidental affair with the married father of the child I nannied. There were many casualties, but the one I regret most is Cayden.

CHAPTER FOUR

Dare

"SO, A FINE ASS FEMALE COMES IN HERE AND sticks money down your pants like you're some stripper, then you continue to stare out the window every day for almost a week straight, just to catch a glimpse of her, and there's nothing going on between you two? That's the story you're sticking with?" Cordell asks sarcastically as he cleans his station. Logan paid me a visit last week, and my dick is just now calming down. I was waiting for a client when she came in and stuck her hands down my pants, which made for a very uncomfortable session. Lots of adjusting going on. Lots of distracted thoughts.

Fuck that girl for getting into my head.

"Yep," I say shortly. Even if it wasn't the truth, this isn't teatime gossip.

"So, she's fair game then?" Cord asks, testing me.

"Go for it," I say, picture of ambivalence.

"Bullshit." He laughs.

"What the fuck do you want me to say? Is she hot? Hell yeah. But I don't even know the chick."

Cordell looks at me with a puzzled expression, like he doesn't even know who I am. "You don't *know* her? Since when has that been a requirement for you?"

"That's not what I meant." He's right. I don't exactly flaunt my hookups, but everyone knows I don't make "lasting relationships". One-night stands work best when you don't have to see the other person on a regular basis.

"Okay…" he says in a way that tells me he's not buying it.

"Anyone left on the books tonight?" I ask, done with this topic.

"Nope. You ready to go?"

"Might as well." Matty and our piercer, Alec, are closing up tonight, so we can go to Briar's get-together.

"Let's roll."

We walk into Ash and Briar's house, late enough that no one's paying attention, but not so late that I piss them off. They're all used to my antisocial ways. I usually slip in once everyone is already liquored up and dip out without a word an hour later.

"You came," Briar says when she sees me, voice soft. She leaves Asher's side to walk over to me, then throws her arms around my torso, hugging me tight.

"I said I would," I say, tussling her blonde hair. She pulls back, hair all mussed with a cheesy smile on her face.

"Thank you."

"Congratulations," I say before making my way over to Ash. He gives me the bro handshake with the one-armed hug while Briar greets Cordell. Adrian gives us a nod as he picks a roll from the plate on the counter, shoving the entire thing into his mouth. I say hi to everyone: my buddy Cam—Cordell's brother—his girl, Mollie, and their kid River, who's toddling around in a Burton beanie. I'm surprised to see Briar's brother, Dash, and her mom, Mrs. Vale, here, too.

"What, no girl distracting you tonight?" Ash says sarcastically.

I flip him off instead of telling him to fuck off for Briar's mom's benefit.

"What girl?" Adrian asks around a mouthful of bread, just as Sutton rounds the corner…with Logan. We lock eyes, neither one of us expecting to see each other. She's wearing a long-sleeved T-shirt almost the same shade as her porcelain skin that fits snug against her tits and the curve of her hips, tight, black pants, and black boots.

"Oh, hey," Sutton says when she notices me. "This is my new friend, Lo."

"Yeah, we've met," I say, trying not to stare.

Logan gives a wave.

"Are you serious?" Sutton says, looking between the two of us. "Why does this keep happening to me? Can't I have one friend to myself?"

Everyone snickers, remembering how Cam and Mollie were in a situation like this one not too long ago. Except theirs was much more complicated.

Fucking small towns.

"All right, now that we all know each other, let's eat." This comes from Adrian. I've never been grateful for his big mouth until this moment.

We stack our plates full of lasagna, salad, and bread, and I'd bet my shop that Briar planned it on purpose, knowing it's my favorite, though she'd never admit it. This is a get-together to celebrate *her*, yet she makes *my* favorite meal. That's just how she is. Her thoughtfulness used to make me uncomfortable, still does sometimes, but I've mostly learned to accept it by now.

Everyone finds a seat wherever they can. I opt for the couch, and Ash sits next to me, while Briar sits at the kitchen table with her mom, brother, Sutton, and Logan. Cord, Cam, and Mollie sit at the counter while River, who refuses to be contained to her seat, plays at their feet as they bribe her to eat her lasagna, bite by bite.

"How's married life?" I ask Ash. They're not married yet, but they for damn sure act like it. I met Ash when he was just a fucked-up kid. He was in a bad place, I gave him a job and a place to stay, and we've been family ever since. Truthfully, he reminded me of myself. The only difference is Ash's guilt and self-loathing is misplaced, whereas I'm one hundred percent responsible for the mistakes that plague me. There's no way around it.

Asher is only a few years younger than me, but he seems to think I have my shit together. I do on the outside, but inside? I'm more fucked up than he knows. I just don't care to show it.

"Can't complain." He shrugs, picture of nonchalance, as always, but I speak fluent Asher, and I know that really means life couldn't be better. He's fucking crazy over that girl, and he almost fucked it up. *Several* times.

"Her dad still a piece of shit?"

"Pretty much." He leans forward with his elbows on his knees and tosses his wadded-up napkin onto his plate. "I don't think anyone really hears from him much, unless it's Christmas or someone's birthday. He did offer Dash a job, though." Ash huffs out a sardonic laugh. "I don't know why the fuck he thought that would go over well."

"What about you? You doing all right?"

Ash's head is down, eyes on the floor, and he nods his answer. We don't usually do this whole girl-talk thing, but I feel it's my duty to check in on him every now and then. Especially since his dad passed a couple of years ago. They, like most families, had a dysfunctional relationship, and I know he feels guilty for how things went down at the end. I never met my parents—have no idea if they're alive or dead—but regardless, we're in the no parent club together.

Logan laughs at something Briar says, catching my attention. She tosses her head back, laughing loud and unfiltered, just like her. She sits surrounded by all my friends, completely at ease, and if you were on the outside looking in, you'd probably guess that they were lifelong friends and I was the outsider.

"What's up with you and that one?" Ash says, flicking his chin in Logan's direction.

"That…was the distraction."

"It's like that?" Ash asks, his eyebrows rising.

"It's not like anything. She came in looking for a job, then she gave me a ride home when my truck was at the shop. She's Henry's kid," I add.

"No shit? I didn't know Henry had a kid."

"That's what I said. He's got two, apparently. I don't think they're close, though."

"Do we know anyone with normal parents anymore?"

"A few, maybe." I shrug. "I think it's more normal to be fucked up these days."

"We're normal as fuck then."

"Agreed."

Dash walks over with three bottles of beer in hand,

sitting on the couch on the other side of me, then sets a bottle in front of each of us.

"So, who's the new girl?" he asks in a hushed tone.

"Dare's distraction," Asher answers.

"Would you shut the fuck up? I liked you better when you were miserable."

Adrian approaches, nudging Dash, making us all move down, and then we're all four crammed onto one couch.

"Sutton looks pretty fucking hot tonight," Adrian says, not bothering to lower his voice.

"I can hear you," Sutton deadpans, and Logan tries and fails to smother her smile, shaking her head at Adrian.

"All right," I say, slapping both palms against the tops of my knees before standing. "This is a little too close for me."

"We're out," Cam announces, lifting River into his arms before wrapping a blanket around her. "Congrats, again, Bry." He gives Briar a hug, and she kisses River's cheek. Mollie hugs her, too, and Briar thanks them for coming. Cordell decides to catch a ride with them, too.

Mrs. Vale stands and makes her way to the hook that holds her coat and purse. "It's getting late. I should be getting back to the hotel. Dashiell, will you be sleeping here?"

"You're both welcome to stay, Mom," Briar says. "You don't have to go." Briar shoots a helpless look toward Asher, and the rest of us take that as our cue to give Briar and her mom some privacy.

I go to take a piss while everyone else heads toward the kitchen. When I come out, Mrs. Vale is gone. Sutton is standing in between Dash and Adrian, Ash and Briar are still in the living room, huddled closely on the couch, speaking in hushed tones. And Logan? She's sitting back at the kitchen table fucking with her phone, staring at it like it's a Rubik's Cube that she can't solve.

"Having trouble there?" I ask, taking a seat next to her. She tosses her phone into the bag at her feet with an annoyed expression.

"I was trying to figure out this music app my brother downloaded, but technology is not my friend."

"That's refreshing. Most girls' phones are an extension of them."

"Not this girl. I don't even know where it is half the time." She laughs before something across the room catches her attention. "Which one do you think is interested? I can't tell." I follow her gaze to see that she's focused on the Sutton sandwich.

"My bet is on both. It's kind of their thing." I watch her carefully to see her reaction.

"You mean, like…" Lo pauses and looks between them, putting the pieces together.

"Yep. They've been known to share from time to time."

"Well, all right," she says before lifting her beer to her lips.

"Does that make you uncomfortable?"

"Not even a little. If they're all on the same page, why not? Everyone's always so worried about what other people will think," she says, throwing me off. I never know what this girl is going to say, and it intrigues me. *She* intrigues me.

"Is that something you're into?"

"Nah," she says, lifting a shoulder, her finger circling the rim of her bottle. "Not my thing."

"What is your *thing*?" I ask. I shouldn't ask. Not because it's too forward, but because I'm almost afraid of her answer. If she gets specific, I know I won't be able to get the image out of my head. She licks her lips, her finger pausing its movement.

"I don't know. I have lots of *things.*"

Her eyes fall to my hand that's wrapped around my beer bottle, practically white-knuckling it from the sudden sexual tension.

"I have a thing for hands and forearms, for one."

"That's specific," I say. Logan's tiny hand reaches toward mine, peeling my fingers off the bottle before laying it flat on top of her palm. She uses her other hand to ghost her fingertips over the ink on my arm. She grabbed me with the familiarity of an old friend or a lover, and the way she traces the lines of my ink is almost…reverent.

"Do these have a special meaning?" she asks, her curious eyes lifting to mine.

"Nope. I just like them."

"Good a reason as any. They're beautiful." Logan seems to realize she's still holding on with one hand and stroking me with the other, and she pulls away, sitting a little straighter, and my palm drops, slapping against the wooden table.

I'm so focused on Logan that I don't even notice Briar and Asher approaching until they're already sitting at the table next to us.

Briar rolls her eyes, looking in her brother's direction. "It's like they don't even try to hide it anymore."

"What's the point? Everyone knows." Ash shrugs.

"The point is that he's my brother, and Adrian's practically related to us, too. I don't want to know about their sex lives. And I still can't believe you knew and never told me."

Asher shoots me a baffled look, and I just smirk.

"You *just* said you didn't want to know," he points out.

"Well, yeah, but she doesn't want you to keep things from her, either," Logan chimes in.

"Exactly," Briar says, pointing a finger at her. "I like her."

"Fucking girl logic," Ash says, shaking his head. "I thought Nat and Adrian had something going on. Or was it Dash? Or both?"

Nat is Briar's friend. I met her a couple of times—all sarcasm and dark, red hair—but she doesn't come around much. Adrian, on the other hand? Can't get rid of him. And Dash comes up on the odd holiday or three-day weekend.

"Don't even ask. All three of them get weird whenever it comes up, and Nat has a boyfriend now. She was going to come up, actually, but she ended up having to work."

Sutton walks away from Dash and Adrian and comes to stand in toward Logan. "You ready to go home?"

Adrian shakes his head behind her, and Logan goes along with it.

"I'm good," she says, lifting the beer that she's been nursing.

"Are you sure?"

"You guys can stay here," Briar offers.

"I should get home to my little brother at some point."

"I can give you a ride, if you want," I say, leaning closer to Logan. I don't know why I offer. I don't usually go out of my way to be near anyone. Even with the girls I do hook up with, the conversation is always kept to a minimum. But here I am, doing the exact opposite of what I know I should be doing.

"Thanks," Logan says, a smile spreading across her face. "But I'm going to call my brother for a ride."

I notice that the purple around her eye has all but disappeared, leaving only a faint trace of yellow near the inner corner. It makes me wonder how she got it in the first place. My hand tightens around my bottle of beer as my mind runs wild with different scenarios.

"Suit yourself. I'm going to take off soon, if you change your mind."

She gives me a nod.

A few minutes later, she says her goodbyes, then she's gone. I wait a few minutes, not wanting it to seem like I'm only leaving because she did, but when I finally walk outside, she's still here. She's sitting cross-legged at the foot of the driveway, hands braced on the cracked asphalt behind her, chin tipped toward the night sky.

I kick around the idea of joining her in my mind, and the thought surprises me. I don't know what makes this girl any different from anyone else, but she piques my curiosity. Ultimately, I decide against it, but for some reason, I don't get into my truck and leave, either. Instead, I hang back in the shadows near the porch while she waits for her ride, oblivious to my presence.

The shitty Toyota pulls up and Logan stands, wiping her hands off on her thighs. She rounds the vehicle and gets into the passenger side, and I watch as they speed away before making my way to my truck.

CHAPTER FIVE

ℒ𝑜

"**H**OW OLD IS YOUR SISTER, SUTTON? SEVEN?" I ask as I stand in front of her full-length mirror, trying to stretch the material of the tattered, patchwork dress that fits more like a miniskirt past my ass cheeks. If I had known I'd end up in a dress the size of a Band-Aid, I would've worn underwear today. When I tug it down, it shows more boob. When I pull it up, it shows more butt. See my conundrum?

"She's nine," she says with a straight face.

"Are you kidding me?" I whip around. "Why would you think that I could fit into a nine-year-old's clothes?" When she told me that I could wear her sister's costume, I didn't think she was talking about a *child*.

"Well, I was right." She laughs with a shrug. "Besides, it's sexier this way."

"And colder," I point out.

"Throw these on. Problem solved."

She balls something up and flings it toward me. I catch it with one hand, letting it unravel. It's a pair of fishnets.

"Oh, cool, these holey tights will really do the trick. I won't be cold at all now," I deadpan.

"They'll help more than you think." Sutton laughs,

running her hands down the sequins of her black irides-cent dress. It fits like a corset around the waist and flares out to look like a mermaid tail at the bottom. She looks gorgeous with her dark hair and sultry makeup with rhine-stones and shiny scales somehow pasted to her cheeks and forehead.

"Why do you get to be all sexy Gothic mermaid and I'm stuck in an actual children's costume?"

"Because I love Halloween and I planned this shit for months. Now shut up and finish your stitches," she says, gesturing to my half-finished rag doll makeup. "You're hot."

If there's one girly thing about me, it's my ability to do makeup like a pro. I spent a lot of my teen years practicing. More makeup meant more attention, and attention meant more tips. Then later, Eric liked to parade me around in front of his rich friends and colleagues, and of course, I had to look the part. Having an affair was one thing. Having an affair with a hood rat from Oakland? Unacceptable.

I put the finishing touches on the stitches next to the corners of my lips, my forehead, and on my neck before painting my lips in a red lip stain. I complete the look with heavy mascara and a smoky eye, giving myself an apprais-ing look in the mirror. *Not bad.* I look intentionally sexy, like a slutty nurse or cop costume—though, I'm not sure that's necessarily a good thing.

"What did you end up doing after I left Briar's thing the other night?" I ask, suddenly remembering. When Sutton asked me to hang out, the last person I expected to see was Dare. This small town really lives up to the stereotype.

"I ended up passing out on her couch." She shrugs.

"Well, that's anticlimactic," I tease.

"Sorry I don't have more excited news. If you looked up my dress right now, I'm pretty sure you'd find cobwebs."

We both laugh, and Sutton grabs her small, black clutch.

"Do you have a jacket I could borrow?" I only have my pullover hoodie and wearing that defeats the purpose of dressing up.

"Nope. You're not covering all that up," Sutton says, wiggling a finger up and down in front of my chest. "Plus, you'll be warm. We'll be inside."

"Fine," I grumble, then snatch my hoodie off her bedpost and tuck it under my arm, just in case. Being comfortable trumps looking good any day.

"If you put that on, I will burn it," Sutton singsongs as we make our way outside.

Tonight should be interesting.

When we pull up to the bar, the entire parking lot is packed, and when we walk through the doors, I don't even recognize the place. The outside was completely dark, no lights or *Open* sign. Even the tattoo shop next door had its windows shuttered in black. But inside, everything is bathed in a purple glow from black lights. Some song I don't recognize blares from the speakers that I didn't even know this place had.

"I thought this was a work party?" I yell over the music.

"It is!" Sutton yells back, bringing her mouth closer to my ear. "It's everyone from here, Bad Intentions, some people from the casino, and the coffee shop. It's sort of like a party crawl, except we can't use the casino for obvious reasons, and the coffee shop is pretty small, so they all pretty much bounce between next door and here!"

I nod, letting her know I heard her. It's one of the biggest party days of the year, so of course they wouldn't shut down the casino for Halloween.

"Let's get a drink!" Sutton grabs my hand, pulling me toward the bar. She's right. I don't need my hoodie. All these bodies have made the place almost uncomfortably warm.

Jake greets us with a flick of his chin as he's filling up a glass with draft beer, and then he does a double take when he realizes it's me. He looks me up and down before shaking it away. Sutton notices it, too, because she bumps her hip with mine, and I roll my eyes.

"What can I get you, ladies?"

"I'll just have a Bud Light draft," I shout.

"She means a lemon drop! Four of them! Plus, a Jack and Coke."

"No." I laugh. "Just beer."

"Fine, but you're taking shots with me, too."

Jake's eyes dart between the two of us, waiting for us to come to an agreement. I give him a shrug, and then a second later, he's sliding a glass of beer and a Jack and Coke across the bar top before turning to make Sutton's lemon drops.

"I don't do shots." Not anymore. I could drink every person in this place under the table without batting an eye when it comes to beer, but liquor is another story.

"They're good," she promises. "They have a freaking sugar rim! Not exactly hardcore."

Fuck it. I haven't let my guard down in a long time.

I haven't had any *fun* for even longer. I tip back the shot, the saccharine sweet liquid barely having a chance to hit my tongue before it coats my throat and warms my belly. I pluck another shot glass out of Sutton's hands and take that one, too.

"These things are dangerous! They taste like candy."

Sutton squeals and takes the two that are left and then leads me through sweaty, carefree bodies to the dance floor. "Monsters" by Matchbook Romance starts to play—I know because one of the few times I could actually afford to buy Jess a birthday present, I got him Guitar Hero, and this particular song was our favorite to play. We start to dance, but I need to ditch my sweatshirt, so I hold up a finger, letting her know I'll be right back. I spot an empty table and shove my way through the crowd to toss it on the back of a chair. Right when I reach the edge of the crowd, I try to take another step, but my shoelace is trapped under someone's foot, and I pitch forward. My arms reflexively shoot out to break my fall. I squeeze my eyes shut and brace for impact. But it doesn't come. Some unlucky bastard breaks my fall, and just when I think I'm going to take us both down, two strong palms steady me by my shoulders.

I puff a strand of hair out of my face and look up at the victim of my clumsiness. He's tall with dark hair, a black tux, and his face painted in skull makeup. He's creepy hot, which is coincidentally my favorite kind of *hot*. And then he lifts a brow, as if waiting for me to remove my hands from the silky lapels that sit on his hard chest and…I know those eyes.

"Sorry," I say quickly and pull my hands back like his suit is on fire. The last thing Dare needs is another girl quite literally falling all over him. I bend over, swiping my hoodie off the sticky floor, and I'm about to walk away, when some girl moves in front of me, blocking my escape.

"Oh my God, Jack and Sally! That is the cutest couples' costume I've ever seen! You guys *have* to enter the costume contest. You'll totally win."

She's wearing a bunny costume, which is fitting seeing as how she's talking a mile a minute like the goddamn Energizer Bunny.

"Oh, I'm not—" I start.

"Yeah, no, we're not—" Dare says at the same time.

"Can I get a picture of you guys?" Energizer Bunny asks, cutting us off. I look to Dare, unsure of how to react. I don't even know her, but if she's here, she has to work at one of the participating businesses, so I assume Dare does. He responds by throwing an arm around my shoulder, pulling me close into his side. My insides flip at his nearness, and his scent, a mix of pine trees, wood, and something else I can't put my finger on, makes it hard to not melt further into him.

I stand, body tense, not wanting him to see how he's affecting me, and he slides his hand down to my hip. He grips it tight, too tight, but it's not painful. He pulls me in even closer, dipping his head down to mine, and then his mouth is at my ear, his breath on my neck.

"Relax. I don't bite. Unless you ask me to." His thumb rubs my hip through the thin material of my dress, and my breath catches, my mouth popping open slightly. I turn my head toward his, but he faces forward, a devious smirk plastered to his face. And then a flash blinds me.

"One more!" E.B. yells over her lens. I expected her to pull out her phone to snap a quick photo, but clearly, I'm mistaken. A guy I didn't notice before stands off behind her to her left, out of costume, toting what I'm assuming is her equipment bag, looking like he'd rather be anywhere but here. She must be an event photographer or something.

"Smile, Logan," Dare says with another squeeze to my side. I do, giving the biggest, cheesiest one I can muster.

Another flash.

E.B. looks at the display on the camera, seemingly pleased with the shots as she nods to herself, and then she's off, her assistant following dutifully behind her.

But Dare's hand is still on my hip, and his eyes are burning into mine. I break away from his hold, making my way back to Sutton, forcing myself not to look back.

Sutton and I dance for a few songs before two guys in Mario and Luigi costumes join us. Mario is hot; Luigi is… well, *not*. But Sutton is into it, so I'm fine being the wing woman. I see nothing wrong with dancing with them… that is, until Luigi gets handsy. The first time he curves his hand around my hip, I brush it away and look over my shoulder to give him a warning glare. But when I feel his erection press against my ass, I'm out.

Before I can swing around to punch this guy, Dare shows up, arms crossed, looking pissed. And for some reason, that turns me on. *A lot.*

"I've been looking for you," he says, eyes narrowed, and it takes me a minute to realize his intentions, my eyes widening with understanding.

Luigi backs up, hands held high in surrender. "Sorry, man. Didn't know."

"Keep your fucking hands to yourself," Dare warns, before turning to me. "Come with me." He holds out his hand and I take it, before he leads me toward the door. I look back for Sutton—who is currently still grinding on

Mario—knowing I shouldn't just disappear. But, I'm powerless to this feeling, and I want to see where it leads.

So, I follow.

Dare

I don't know what the fuck I'm doing. But from the moment I saw her dancing to "Monsters," I couldn't take my eyes off her. She didn't dance for anyone else, didn't care or even notice who was watching. Then, I saw that asshole touching her, and I could see that she wasn't into it, even from where I stood.

I have no business touching Logan, let alone dragging her off to my shop. But here I am, pushing open the door and leading her to the drawing room in the back of the shop. There are a few people hanging out, playing pool in the main waiting room, but most people are over at the bar.

Logan's eyes are wide as she takes in her surroundings. She's never been back here before. The place is deceptively big. When you first walk in, all you see are the front desk, a small sitting area, and some of our shop's merch. You'd never know all this was back here. We have a piercing booth, which is really more of a room, and four stations in the main room. Then, there's the big waiting room, a sitting area with a fireplace, a bar, a pool table, vending machines, the works. Plus, another room for even more stations if we had them, a bathroom, and a soundproof drawing room. Which is where I'm taking Logan.

"What are we doing?" she asks, pressing her back flat

against the closed door.

"I don't fucking know," I say honestly, walking to the other side of the room before I rest my palms on my desk behind me, putting some much-needed distance between us. I'm the one who brought her here. Seeing her in that dress, feeling that soft body against mine…temporary insanity. That's what it was. Except, I still want to pin her to the wall.

"We could play a game?" she suggests innocently, then her teeth dig into her bottom lip, thighs squeeze together. She's…turned on.

"What do you have in mind?" My hands clench the edge of the desk, keeping me anchored to my spot.

"Truth or Dare, of course," she says mischievously.

"Real original," I taunt. "I choose Truth."

"Hmm," she says thoughtfully, her fingertip pressed against her red lips. "What's your real name?"

The question throws me. No one ever asks that. I've always been Dare, and no one's ever questioned it. I haven't been called my given name in years. I decide to tell her, if only to hear what it would sound like from her lips.

"Stefan." It's been so long since I've said that name out loud.

Logan's head cocks to the side, as if I've surprised her. "Really? I would have guessed Darren or Derek or something."

"My last name is Adair. Being the scrawny kid in foster care with a name like Stefan? Not exactly intimidating. But Dare was. One of the other kids started it and it stuck." I shrug. I've been Dare longer than I was ever Stefan, but somehow, it still feels like mine. Like most people would feel about their childhood bedroom or their old favorite song.

"Okay, *Stefan*," she says, emphasizing my name, and fuck if I don't like the way it sounds. She saunters over to me, not stopping until she stands between my spread legs. She brings her mouth close to my ear, her dark hair swinging forward and brushing my lips. "I choose Dare," she whispers, her lips touching the shell of my ear. I feel my dick swell in my suit pants, but I don't move my hands from my desk.

"I dare you to let me kiss you." My voice comes out huskier than intended.

Logan swallows hard, and my eyes follow the movement in her throat. "A kiss? That's it?" she says, challenging, but I see the nerves she's trying to hide and the pulse fluttering in her neck.

My hands are on her in an instant, roughly turning her so we switch places, her ass on the desk, and me in between her thighs. I fist her hair at the base of her head and tug back, just a little…testing, hinting at how I want it. She closes her eyes, letting a little moan slip free. I ghost my lips along her neck, and she waits, eyes still closed, for me to make my way to her mouth.

Instead, I run my free hand from her knee up to her thigh, slowly, to gauge her reaction. When she opens for me, ever so slightly, my dick jumps. *She wants this*. I drag my teeth along the tendon in her neck as my hand moves closer to the heat between her legs, my fingers digging into the holes of her fishnets, clawing through to her flesh on my way up. When I touch her pussy over her tights, she shifts toward my hand.

With that one, little move, all bets are off. I drop to my knees in front of her, roughly grabbing her thighs as I place my face between them. Logan gasps, but doesn't object as my tongue darts out to lick her through her holey tights. Her palms are flat against the desk, her head thrown back as I flatten my tongue and give another long lick.

Logan grabs the back of my head, pulling me into her, then I plant her other foot on the desk, opening her wide for me. She starts reaching for the band of her tights, lifting her ass, struggling to get them off, so instead, I hook my fingers through the holes and *rip*. Logan sucks in a breath, her wet, pink pussy on display for me. I bite the fleshy inside of her thigh hard enough to leave a mark. She flinches, but then she lets out a low moan, tossing her head back, rocking her hips toward my face. *Oh fuck yeah.* Something about Logan brings out my baser instincts. She makes me want to tear her apart, to bite and bruise. To let her do the same to me, to claw her fingers down my back and fuck me up. Because I'd never mar her permanently, but I'd gladly bear her scars.

I sink my teeth into her one more time before burying my face between her legs. Her feet slip off the edge of the desk and she crosses them behind my head. I smooth my hands up the outsides of her thighs to her lower back, bunching her dress as I go. I suck her clit into my mouth, causing her to rub herself against my face. There aren't any inhibitions or shyness in her movements. Just two people making each other feel good. When her legs start to shake, she stops me, pulling at my face until I stand. Her hands shoot out to the fly of my pants, quickly unclasping and unzipping, and then her hand pushes down into my boxer briefs, wrapping around my cock. I groan, my eyes squeezing shut. "Fuck."

Logan grips me so right, so tight. She strokes me a couple of times before placing me at the wet place between her legs. When my cock meets her slick flesh, our eyes meet, maybe for the first time during this entire encounter. Me, silently asking if this is okay. Her, silently nodding her consent. Logan rubs her thumb across my lips and chin, wiping her wetness away, before she brings it to her mouth, seductively sucking it off.

Fuck, this girl.

I bring my hands to her waist, digging my fingers into the soft flesh. I start to push inside of her, but then there's banging at the door.

"What the fuck!" I yell over my shoulder, still positioned right at her entrance. Just barely inside. Not enough. Not even fucking close.

"There's a kid at the bar about to get jumped! Says he's Logan's brother," Cam shouts from the other side of the door.

"Jess?" Logan shrieks, dropping her legs, effectively breaking contact. She shoves me out of the way and hops down, running for the door. She blows past Cam and his perpetually amused expression, tugging her dress back down, not giving him a second look.

Well, that was one hell of a first kiss. And I didn't even make it to her mouth.

CHAPTER SIX

Lo

"**W**HAT THE HELL ARE YOU DOING HERE?!**"
When I finally find Jess, he's being held
back by Cordell, while Jake and some
other guys I don't recognize hold back two preppy looking
assholes as they lunge for Jess.

"I heard there was a party," he says smiling, with a dark
curl of hair hanging in his face, cigarette dangling from his
lip, like he's not in the middle of a barroom brawl.

"Jesus Christ, Jess. What did you do?"

"He sold us this bullshit!" Preppy Douche Number
One chimes in, holding up a plastic baggy.

"Don't be mad just because you can't tell the difference between bud and oregano." Jess laughs. The other guy
lunges for him again.

"We want our sixty bucks back!"

"Just give them their money back," I say. Jess doesn't
make a move, but Dare walks up, standing between Jess
and the other guys.

"Get the fuck out," he says to them. I hear the shocked
gasps and whispers, but I don't understand why.

"Give me my money back and we'll go," the bravest
and blondest one says, crossing his arms across his baby

blue Lacoste polo.

"You're not getting shit. Consider it a sixty-dollar lesson not to buy drugs from a fucking high school kid," Dare spits. Jess smirks triumphantly, and the other guy's pale cheeks burn bright red with rage as he grits his teeth. He wants to argue, but thankfully, he doesn't. I close my eyes and exhale in relief once they're gone.

"What are you thinking?" I yell, slapping Jess upside the back of the head. "What happened to keeping your head down and getting through school? Do you *want* to move back home?"

"They're just some stupid yuppy college kids, Lo. It's not a big deal." Jess tries to play it off because we're in public, but I can tell he's feeling sheepish. I see it in the way he averts his eyes and in the nervous laugh that slips out. Siblings know how to read each other better than anyone else.

"This is our only shot. Stop trying your best to mess it up."

"My bad, Lo. Fuck."

"How'd you get here?"

"My board," he says, gesturing to where his skateboard lies on the floor next to the bar.

"I didn't drive." I rise onto my tiptoes to scan the crowd that has already forgotten about this little altercation and has gone back to dancing and drinking, but I don't see Sutton anywhere.

"I'll take you guys," Jake says.

"It's *your* bar," Dare points out before turning back to me. "I'm taking you. Come on."

Dare places a palm at the small of my back and guides me toward the door. I reach behind me, pulling on Jess' sleeve to make sure he follows. I catch Jake's eyes as I do, and he shakes his head, as if he's disappointed.

Dare opens the truck door for us, and Jess flips the bench seat forward to climb in back. I grip the side of the door to pull myself up, but before I do, two hands grip my waist, lifting me up and depositing me onto the seat. It smells like him in here. Like pine trees and leather seats. Dare slams the door shut and walks over to the driver's side, and Jess clears his throat from the back seat.

"Shut up. You don't get to give me shit about anything right now."

"I didn't say a word," Jess says, holding his hands up in mock surrender.

Dare hops in and looks over at me, his ocean eyes bright under the dome light.

"Your house?" he asks, turning the ignition.

"My car is at Sutton's."

"I'm Jesse, by the way," Jess says, resting his elbows against the top of the bench seat, chin propped on his forearm. "Lo's brother."

"I gathered that," Dare says flatly. "How do you know those guys?"

"I don't." Jess shrugs. "They approached me for some bud when I was skating earlier. Guess I just have that kind of face," he says sarcastically. "I saw an opportunity to make some cash, so I took it. Told them I didn't have it on me, and they told me to meet them over here later. I knew Lo was at the costume party. Guess they followed me once they realized it was oregano."

I roll my eyes, resisting the urge to slap him again.

"They're East Shore kids," Dare says. "They wouldn't do shit."

"That's not the point," I say. I turn toward Jess, and he smothers a smile. "What?" I snap.

"I just know you're about to lecture me again, but it's really hard to take you seriously when you look like that."

I completely forgot I was in costume. I flip down the visor to look in the mirror. My lipstick is smudged, but other than that, I don't look too crazy. Dare looks over at me, his eyes heating as I fix my lips with the tip of my thumb, and I know both of us are mentally replaying how it got smeared in the first place.

If Jess hadn't intervened, Dare would've fucked me on that desk. I don't know whether to hate him or thank him for it. I know it would have been a mistake. A big, fat, glaring mistake. I *know* that, but even now, even after the haze of lust has cleared, I want to do it again.

I shake my dirty thoughts away, turning back to Jess.

"Just…please, Jesse. *Try*. I don't want to go back there. I can't. And if you go back, I go back." I choose my words carefully, not wanting to get too personal in front of Dare, but Jess knows exactly what I'm referring to. Eric. Mom. Everything.

"You're not going back, and he's not getting near you," Jess swears, his voice resolute and intense. I look at Dare from the corner of my eye, and though I can only see his profile, I see his eyebrows tugging together, curiosity piqued.

I nod to Jess and pat his arm before sitting forward in my seat.

"I'm not sure where Sutton lives," Dare says, breaking the silence. "Briar mentioned the area once, but I don't know exactly where."

I search my brain, trying to remember an address or

even a street name, but I can't focus. Maybe it has some-thing to do with the fact that I still have the remnants from his face paint smeared along the insides of my thighs, or the fact that I can still feel his teeth marks there.

"She lives off Lakewood," I say when it finally clicks into place. Dare turns onto Lakewood, and once he sees my dad's Toyota, he pulls up next to it.

"Thanks," I say dumbly, not knowing what else to say, especially with my kid brother in the car, pushing the seat forward so he can slip out first. I'm jostled around from the movement, my palm slapping against the dash. My dress has ridden up, and my tights are ripped almost all the way down to my knees. I clamp them shut, feeling exposed from the cold air that hits my damp thighs. Dare eyes me up and down like he's getting one last look before I leave. His right hand is on the steering wheel, and he lifts four fingers in a wave with a slight dip of his head.

"Later, Sally."

"So, you and Dare, huh?" Sutton asks as she pulls an up-side-down chair off the table as we prepare to open.

"What do you mean?" I ask, playing dumb. I like Sutton. I like her more than anyone I've met here, so that basically makes her my best friend by default. She just doesn't know it yet. But that doesn't mean I want to fess up to what happened with Dare. It won't happen again any-way, so there's no point.

"Don't bullshit a bullshitter," Sutton says, pointing a finger at me and lifting one perfectly plucked brow. "He doesn't talk to anyone. Especially people he doesn't know." Is that why everyone seemed surprised when he jumped to my aid?

"You hooked up with Dare?" Jake chimes in from behind the bar. I shoot a look at Sutton, and she mouths *sorry* with a sheepish shrug.

"I barely know the guy," I hedge, avoiding a straight answer. It's none of his business anyway.

"Just…be careful," Jake finally says, then he and Sutton share a look I can't decode.

"What?" I ask, waving my hand in the space between them. "What was that about?"

"He's…dangerous. I just don't want to see you get hurt."

I scoff. *Hurt*? I don't even know the guy. I'm not sure whether he means hurt in the physical or emotional sense, but either way, I can take care of myself.

"I appreciate the concern, but I think I'll survive."

"You don't know that, Jake. I think he's a good guy." Sutton has a bite in her tone that I haven't heard from her before. It surprises me.

"Say that to his foster family," Jake says, shaking his head. Sutton turns her attention back to me.

"He's misunderstood. Don't believe everything you hear."

Jake makes a disapproving sound before disappearing to the back room.

I go back to cutting up the oranges, lemons, and limes for the garnish tray. I'm dying to ask about Dare, but I don't want to give Sutton more of a reason to believe there's something going on there. So, I stay silent. And, annoyingly, she doesn't offer anything else.

After adding some maraschino cherries to the garnish tray, I check the time on the big wooden clock with a black bear on it that reads *On Mountain Time*. It's two minutes until eleven, so I flip the sign from *Closed* to *Open*.

The rest of the day goes by fast, and my pockets are already fat with tips and I still have two hours to go, so I'm feeling pretty good about life in general. Jake has been weird since earlier, not his usual flirty self, but I don't let it put a damper on my mood.

I walk toward the break room with a little extra pep in my step. But when I hear Jake's irritated voice coming from the small office in the back, I stop in the doorway, the smile melting from my lips.

"Shit," he says under his breath, throwing his phone onto his desk. I tap my knuckles against the doorframe.

"Everything okay?"

"Yeah." He pinches the bridge of his nose.

"What's up?" When he meets my eyes, his expression is sympathetic, as if my cat just died and he doesn't know how to break it to me.

"I have to cut your hours."

"What?" My fingers dig into the doorframe. "Why?"

"That was Sam. The other owner. His pain in the ass niece is coming up for a while, and he told her parents he'd have a job for her. He didn't realize I already hired someone."

"Okay, so make her a hostess or something," I try.

"You know the money is in the tips…"

Exactly. And that's *my* money.

"Okay, so what are we talking here? Like thirty hours a week?"

"More like fifteen. Maybe twenty. Possibly more once

the busy season hits, because I'll need you both."

"This is bullshit," I mutter under my breath, unable to keep my frustration at bay.

"I know it is. Believe me, I'd rather work with you every day than her. I'm not happy about it, either."

He seems to have his own reasons for being pissed, besides just cutting my hours. I know my anger is misdirected, but *fuck*. Fifteen hours? That's nothing. *Nothing*. I exhale through my nose and close my eyes. I give myself a quick mental pep talk. I'm lucky to have a job. It just might take me a little bit longer to save up for a new place.

Jake's looking at me warily, as if I'm a volcano ready to erupt. I give him a terse nod before turning for the door.

"Logan," he says, but I wave him off.

"I'm sorry. I shouldn't have snapped at you. I just need to figure something else out."

My phone rings, but I don't recognize the number, so I silence it, only for it to ring again immediately. I hold a finger up, letting Jake know I need to take it.

"Hello?"

"Hi, yes, is this Logan Shepherd?" It's a woman's voice, assertive, but somehow soft.

"Yes…" I say, but it comes out as a question rather than a statement.

"This is Susan Connelly. The principal at River's Edge High School."

Oh God. What did Jess do? The sinking feeling in my gut multiplies times one million.

"Is Jesse okay?" I ask, plugging my free ear with my finger in an attempt to hear her above all the noise of chattering customers and clanking dishes. I meet Jake's eyes, and his forehead wrinkles with concern.

"He's okay, but he was involved in a fight on campus. I'm going to need you to come in so we can discuss his behavior and the resulting consequences."

"Okay. I'm on my way."

"Shit." I shove my phone back into my pocket and turn to leave. "I'm sorry. I have to go."

"Is everything okay?" Jake asks, standing from his desk.

"No. Yes. I don't know. Jess got into a fight at school, and I have to go meet the principal."

"Do you want me to drive you?"

"No, I have Henry's car. Thanks, though. I'll come right back," I promise.

Jake nods, and I'm out the door.

When I arrive at the high school, I push through the double doors and walk to the same office I brought Jess to the other day. Lacey sees me storming toward her, and she quickly snatches the phone up to her ear and quietly mumbles something into the receiver. I spot Jess in a chair to my right with his head hanging low, and another kid sits a few seats away from him sporting a busted lip.

I hurry over to him and squat down to his level, pulling his chin up to inspect him. He jerks his head out of my grasp, but not before I see traces of a bloody nose.

"You good?" I ask, looking at the other kid out of the corner of my eye. I can't coddle Jess in public. That's the surest way to get him to shut down completely.

"Fine," he says, his lip slightly snarled.

I hear a door open behind me, and a woman's voice follows.

"Miss Shepherd, Jesse. Please, come with me," the principal says. She's tall and thin with her short blonde hair slicked back into a low ponytail. "Stay put," she says, pointing a finger at the other kid. "We're still trying to get ahold of your parents."

I hear the kid mumble a sarcastic *good luck with that* right before the office door closes behind us.

"Have a seat," she says, gesturing toward two wooden chairs with blue padding. There's a man standing off to the side of the room wearing a white polo with the school's logo, a hat, and a whistle around his neck.

"This is Coach Standifer. He's our P.E. teacher. Jesse was in his class at the time."

"Nice to meet you," he says, offering his hand. I shake it and give a wobbly smile before sitting down. Jess takes the seat next to me.

"I understand that you're his sister?" Mrs. Connelly asks.

"Yes, ma'am."

"We usually require a legal guardian for this type of thing, but I understand your case isn't…typical."

Oh, you mean most kids here have parents who actually give a shit? Crazy concept.

I don't respond. I sit quietly, waiting for the gavel to drop.

"Jesse has made quite a stir in the short time he's been here," she says, looking through pages inside a manila folder. "He's been late, missed periods, mouthed off, and today, he was physical with another student. I'm sure you know we can't allow that. The protection of our students is paramount, and it's my job to make this a safe environment."

"Jesse isn't violent," I start. "I'm not sure what happened, but I can promise you it won't happen again."

"It can't. To be frank with you, Miss Shepherd, we have

enough to expel him right now."

At that, Jess finally reacts. His head snaps up. "You can't do that," he says. His voice is steady, but I can hear the underlying panic.

"But," she continues. "I've decided to suspend you for five days."

Jess shakes his head, his nostrils flaring. He angles his face toward the floor, never wanting anyone to see the emotions he wears so clearly on his face. "I'm the first one to admit that I'm a fuckup, but this time it wasn't my fault."

"Did you throw the first punch?" she asks, one eyebrow raised in question.

"Yes," he admits grudgingly. "But—"

"You threw the first punch, Mr. Shepherd. I'm sorry."

"Can we pause for just a minute?" I ask, holding a palm up. I need to know exactly what happened if I'm going to talk him out of this one. "Jess," I say, turning to face him. "What started this? Tell me how it happened from start to end."

Jess rolls his eyes and picks at the strands of ripped thread at his knee. "Doesn't matter."

"Jess, please. I can't help you if I don't know how to defend you."

"Collins was pulling his shit again," Coach Standifer chimes in, surprising me, and from the looks of it, Mrs. Connelly, too. "Kid kept throwing a basketball at Jesse. I fouled him and told him to knock it off. Saw him walk right up to Jesse, point-blank, and throttle that ball right into the back of his head. Before I could react, Jesse turned around and swung."

"Are you kidding me?" My blood is boiling. "It's taking every ounce of *my* self-control not to go out there and pummel that kid. How can you expect Jesse to just let that happen?"

"Mr. Collins will be reprimanded as well. He claims it was an accident, and technically—"

"With all due respect, Mrs. Connelly, it was no accident," the coach says.

"So, what do you propose we do?" she asks tiredly.

"I'm not saying Jesse shouldn't be punished. Physical violence is never the answer," he says, eyeing Jess. He's silent for a minute, assessing, and hope starts to bloom in my chest. "Give him to me for six weeks," he finally says. "He'll join the school wrestling team, as well as the club outside of school. He'll arrive early and set up, stay late to clean up. Two meets a month, minimum. If he misses one practice, you can suspend him."

"Pft." Jess scoffs. "Yeah, I'll go ahead and take that suspension," he says before standing. I jerk him back down by his wrist.

"Don't you dare," I say for his ears only. "You're getting an out. Don't fuck it up." Mrs. Connelly's expression tells me that maybe I wasn't quiet enough.

"Well, Jesse?" she asks, arms crossed. "What's it going to be? Six weeks of wrestling plus a week's worth of detention, or one week of suspension?"

"Where the hell did the detention part come from?" Jess asks, losing patience.

"Watch your mouth. That's the second time you've used foul language. Now, this is the only deal you're going to get. Take it or leave it." She shrugs.

I can tell Jess is about to say something stupid, so I stand and say, "He'll take it." I turn to Coach Standifer. "And thank you," I say with a little more sincerity in my voice.

He gives me a nod. "Jesse?" Coach prods. "You good with this? It's a commitment, and I expect you to show up."

"I'm good with it."

"All right, then. You'll do your detention first, and we'll start the wrestling next week."

"I'm going to send you home for the rest of the day," the principal says. "Come back tomorrow with a better attitude."

Jess gives a reluctant nod and shakes the hand that Coach holds out for him.

"Deal," I say when Jess doesn't respond. *Fucking teenagers.* "Thanks, again." And then I'm dragging Jess out of the office by his sleeve.

"What is your problem?" I whisper-yell once we're in the hall.

"Oh, I'm sorry," he says, voice dripping with sarcasm. "Should I have thanked them for punishing me for defending myself?"

"I know." I pause in the hall and give a heavy sigh. "I *know*. It's bullshit. But we have to play by their rules."

"I fucking swear I'm trying, Lo," he says, the fight leaving his voice, and the guilt in his voice tears me up.

"I know you are." I throw an arm around his waist, and his goes around my shoulders as we walk out of the school. "Try harder."

"Did you have to leave work?"

"Yeah." I shrug.

"I'm sorry."

"I know."

Instead of taking Jess home, I decide to bring him to work with me. I figured I could get back faster this way, and I can probably score him a free dinner. I plan to offer to work an hour later to make up the time I missed thanks to Jess. Right before we walk in the door, I get a call from Henry. I lift the phone to my ear, waving for Jess to go in without me.

"Henry," I greet him.

"Kid," he says, and I almost crack a joke about him referring to us as *kid* because he doesn't know us well enough to remember our names, but I refrain. Barely.

"What's up? I'm heading into work."

"Just wanted to give you a heads-up. Got word today. We're out at the end of the month."

And the remainder of my earlier optimism is gone. Just. Like. That. "Already?"

"Sorry, kid," he says, clearing his throat uncomfortably. "I, uh, I gotta get back to work. I just wanted to give you as much notice as possible."

"Yeah. Thanks," I say quietly before stuffing my phone back into my pocket. Tears prick my eyes, and I squeeze them shut, willing them not to fall. "Fuck!" I yell before kicking the wall. Hard. "Fuck, fuck, fuck." That hurt like hell. I squat down, back against the wall with my elbows propped on my knees, forehead leaning against my steepled fingers.

I hate this feeling. Helpless. Useless. Inadequate. But I'll make it work. We always do. It's just bad timing, and when it rains, it pours.

"What'd the wall ever do to you?"

I don't need to lift my head to know the source of that deep, sarcasm-coated voice. I look up at him for a second, to see him standing a few feet away, all crossed arms and creased brows.

"It had it coming."

He nods, wordlessly walking over and sitting on the ground next to me, ass on the hard pavement with his knees up. He doesn't speak. Just sits in silence, waiting for me to compose myself.

"Jake cut my hours," I finally divulge. Forehead still in my hands, I swivel my head to face him. "I really fucking needed those hours."

"Prick."

"It's not his fault. But yeah."

"He's still a prick."

"Henry's lease is up, too." I don't elaborate. He can put two and two together.

We're quiet again, and if I wasn't so worried about coming up with cash, it might be awkward to be around him. We haven't spoken since Halloween. Haven't so much as exchanged a single text. But I'm too preoccupied to care right now.

"Work for me," Dare surprises me by saying.

"What?"

"Work. For. Me," he says again. "I need an assistant, and someone who can man the front desk. You need the money. It's a win-win."

"Pretty sure I already tried to work for you and you made it clear that you weren't hiring."

"Well, I know you're a local now. We locals gotta stick together, right?"

I want to ask him why he's helping me, because I don't buy that for a second. I don't want pity. And I definitely don't want this to turn into another situation where my boss thinks he can throw money at me and expect me to be his fuck toy at his disposal.

"What happened the other night...it won't happen again." If I'm going to take this job, it has to be said. No matter how much I want to feel his mouth between my legs and his hands on my waist again.

"Maybe." He shrugs. "If it happens, it happens. But anything that does or does not happen won't affect your job. You have my word on that."

"Not happening," I reiterate, raising a brow.

"Do you want the fuckin' job or not?" he asks, exasperated. I do. *Of course, I do.* But this has the potential to get complicated. I make a promise to myself right here and now that I'll bail before anything has a chance to get messy.

"Yes. Thank you," I say sincerely, meeting his icy eyes.

Dare nods. "Meet me after your shift tomorrow. We'll go over everything then." He stands, and I crane my neck to see him as he runs a hand through his thick black hair.

"Okay."

"Okay," he repeats, and then he turns and disappears inside Bad Intentions.

CHAPTER SEVEN

Lo

I STAND IN FRONT OF THE MIRROR IN THE BAD Intentions bathroom and lift the front of my work shirt to my nose. *Ugh.* I smell like cheeseburgers and the beer that a drunk customer spilled all over their table… and me. I strip off my work shirt before digging around in my backpack, thankful that I had the forethought to bring an extra shirt for my first day. I toss my shirt onto the porcelain sink and notice a framed cross-stitch photo that reads *Please don't do cocaine in our bathroom*. Surrounded by flowers, it looks like something someone's grandmother would have hanging on their wall. I laugh out loud and take a picture with my phone to show Jess before I pull my plain black V-neck over my head.

I don't know what I expected, but I'm surprised at how clean everything is here. I've only been inside a couple of times—the last time it was dark, and I was drunk on Dare, so I didn't pay too much attention. I guess a tattoo parlor would need to be a sterile work environment, so it makes sense.

I tie my red and black flannel around my waist before I pull the hair tie from my ponytail. I let my hair fall around my shoulders and shake it out with my fingers.

Good enough.

I leave the bathroom and go back to the front desk, where Dare is waiting for me. I'm not boy crazy. I don't swoon or lose my mind when an attractive guy comes along. Looks don't matter much to me—I know firsthand that some of the most beautiful people are ugly on the in-side—but Dare is on another level. His inky black hair is perfectly disheveled like it was on Halloween, and I have the urge to run my fingers through it. He's tall, probably a good eight inches taller than my five foot three. His eyes seem impossibly blue, his jaw sharp. Thick, black eye-brows. Full bottom lip, the top one slightly thinner.

But the sexiest thing about Dare isn't physical. It's in the way he carries himself. His intensity. His give-no-fucks attitude. I may not be drawn to a pretty face, but like a typical girl, I *am* drawn to a challenge. He's closed off and mysterious and kind of cranky, so why do I want to be the one to crack the shell and get under his skin?

He gives me an appraising look, his eyes lingering on my cleavage for half a second, then clears his throat. I get a sick sense of satisfaction to know he's affected by me, too, if only a little.

"I'm going to warn you now. Your title as a reception-ist? It's a little misleading. What I need you for goes way beyond that."

I arch a brow at him.

"Not that far, smart ass."

I laugh and move behind the counter next to him.

"You'll be in charge of scheduling, answering phones, greeting customers, payments, and all that shit. But what we really need help with is keeping everything clean, ster-ilizing our stations, setting up and breaking down stations, cleaning, offering the clients water or reading material, cleaning, taking photos for our albums, cleaning, grabbing stuff for the artists when we need it, cleaning…"

"A lot of cleaning. Got it."

"A clean shop is a happy shop. No one wants to get tattooed in some haggard ass tattoo parlor."

"Not really a good look," I agree.

"Exactly."

Dare clicks around on the computer.

"This is called InkBook. It's what you'll use for scheduling, client records, online bookings and confirmations, payroll, everything."

He walks me through the program, step by step, telling me it's "just like QuickBooks," whatever that is. I should be writing this down. I'm going to forget every single thing he says in approximately seven seconds. I'm halfway tempted to pull out my phone and record the whole thing, but somehow, I don't think he'd appreciate that.

I can't help but stare at his colorful arms, and his big veiny hand as he grips the mouse, and the way his long, thick finger clicks it, his eyebrows cinched together in deep concentration, the inky black strand of hair that fell in front of his eye, and the tattoo that peeks out from the collar of his T-shirt. *Get it together, Lo.* Have I not learned my lesson? Eric was the last person to affect me and look how that ended up.

After he finishes teaching me how to use the software, he shows me how to set a station up. There are covers for every goddamn thing, and nearly everything is good for one use only. Then, he introduces me to the guys.

"Guys, this is Lo. Lo, this is Alec and Matty. You know Cam and Cordell." Dare points to each one. They're standing around the pool table, not a client in sight.

"Wait, are you…?" I trail off, looking at the one with blond hair that reminds me of the guy from *Sons of Anarchy*, tattoos clear up to his jaw.

"Another fan girl?" the one with the golden-brown skin and backwards fitted hat asks—Matty, I think, and I look to Dare in confusion.

"Nah." Dare chuckles, looking down at me. "Not even on her radar."

"Fan girl? I was going to ask if they were brothers." They look alike, but I didn't realize how similar until they stood next to each other.

"My bad. Cam is a pro snowboarder. And yes, they're brothers," Matty informs me. What's up with this town? Apparently, River's Edge loves snowboarders like Oakland loves the Raiders.

"Ah," I say, rocking on my heels. "And that's like…a big deal?" I don't mean anything by the question, but they all seem to think it's hilarious.

"Little bit," Matty says. "Chicks around here dig that shit." He smirks, twisting the pool stick between his fingers before he bends over and takes his shot.

"Oh."

"I like her," the lean pale guy with plugs in his ears and hair sculpted into the perfect pompadour announces. He's wearing a white tee with suspenders and cuffed jeans. Very vintage. Very rockabilly. The process of elimination tells me he's Alec.

He saunters over and props an elbow on my shoulder. "Everyone's obsessed with fucking snowboarding around here, except for Dare and me. I think even Matty wants to suck Cam off."

"Fuck you," Matty says, but there's no heat in his words.

"I actually met you on Halloween, too. *Briefly*," Cam finally chimes in—not bothered in the least by the way they talk about him like he's not here—a knowing look plastered to his pretty face. My cheeks heat when I realize he was the one who told us Jess was in a fight at Blackbear.

Dare's bottom lip is trapped between his teeth and his eyes lock with mine, as if he's remembering that night, too.

"So, Logan. Ever think about getting a piercing?" Alec asks out of nowhere, inspecting me for any signs of metal, and I'm thankful for the interruption.

"Not really." I shrug. I don't even have my ears pierced. I attempted to pierce my belly button with a safety pin when I was thirteen, but I leave that part out.

"No tattoos, either?"

"Nope."

"You're working at Bad Intentions now, baby. Time to look the part," Alec says.

Matty and Cordell laugh, and Dare knocks Alec's arm away from my shoulder.

"Alec is our piercer. Stay away from him or he'll have you looking like a human pincushion by next week. Hit me up if you want to put some ink on that virgin skin, though," Cordell says, and Dare scoffs.

"What? Her skin is pale as fuck, and completely free of ink. It's an artist's wet dream."

Dare looks down at me, eyes full of heat. "I've noticed."

I roll my eyes, ignoring the heat that crawls up the back of my neck. He's been up close and personal with my paleness.

"Come on. I'll show you the rest of the shop."

Dare leads me around, showing me the waiting room

that I got a glimpse of on Halloween with the pool table, vending machines, bar, and fireplace, couches…this place has it all. There's a room with tattoo stations and a piercing booth. When we reach the door to the drawing room, we both pause. I bite my lip, and Dare smirks, knowing exactly what I'm thinking.

"You already know what's in there," he says, reaching past me, his arm grazing my waist as he grabs the doorknob. I glance over my shoulder, seeing the desk he almost fucked me on. There's a couch next to it, too, and I childishly wonder if this is where he takes all his hookups.

"Talk to Jake and see if you can work out a schedule. We need the most help on weekends. If you want the extra hours, you can always come in for a while after your shifts, too. I'm pretty flexible…what?" Dare asks when he notices me staring.

"I still don't know why you're doing all this, but regardless, it's really helping me out. So, thank you."

"Stop reading into it and stop thanking me. There are no ulterior motives. No bad intentions—no pun intended."

"Okay." I nod, trying to take what he says at face value. I don't think Dare is a bad guy, but I don't necessarily think he's a *nice* guy, either. I'm just…not used to people helping me. At least not when they don't want something in return. Maybe he really does just need to hire someone and finally caved.

"This place is huge," I say, changing the subject. "It's just the four of you here?"

"I keep my circle small." He shrugs. "I told you. I like my privacy. We have guest artists from time to time, but it's mostly just us."

"I could live here."

"I practically *did* live here at one point," he admits. Another little clue to the mystery that is Dare. I wait for him to elaborate, not prodding for more information, but of course, he doesn't.

Dare's client walks in, all buttoned-up suit and tie, but when he takes his shirt off, his torso is completely blasted with ink. Dare leads him to his chair while I keep busy with cleaning, familiarizing myself with the software and upcoming appointments, and more cleaning. Dare was right. It doesn't seem like it would be a lot, but I haven't run out of things to do yet. It's a good thing, though. When I have downtime, I get anxious. Probably because I've never had the luxury to just…be. I'm always working, cleaning up Crystal's house—which was a full-time job itself—taking care of Jess, fending off Darrell. Having free time is a foreign concept to me.

I constantly find myself looking his way as he works on a back piece. Dare's mostly oblivious to my existence, but every now and then, his eyes find mine with an intense expression before returning his focus back to the task at hand.

"Dare never hires women, you know."

The voice startles me, and I realize it's Matty. He stands, one arm propped on the front desk.

"Don't worry. I'm not really a woman," I say, giving him a bored stare. He laughs.

"I don't mean anything by it," he clarifies. "We were all a little…*surprised* when he told us. I'm just trying to figure out what's different about you."

"Probably the whole *having a penis* thing."

"There's no way you have a dick, but nice try." His smile is contagious, and I crack, unable to keep a straight face.

"I think he feels sorry for me," I admit with a shrug. "I just moved here and needed a job pretty badly."

"But you work next door, too, right?"

"Yeah, but it's not enough. I have to support my little brother, too."

"I feel that," he says, nodding. "Mom's disabled, so it's on me to provide for her and my baby sister."

I decide right now that I like Matty. He's charismatic and real, and who can dislike a guy who takes care of his family? That alone gives him major brownie points. Plus, he's beautiful. All the Bad Intentions guys are good-looking, but Matty is probably breaking some serious hearts with his perfect smile, full lips, and black and gray tattoos covering his golden-brown skin.

"You got any more clients today?" Dare shouts.

"Nah," Matty says, looking at Dare over his shoulder. "I got nothin' till tomorrow."

"Then go home," he grumbles, not even bothering to look up. My eyes widen, but Matty chuckles.

"Think someone's feeling a little territorial," he says for only my ears. I shake my head dismissively.

"It's not like that."

"You're trippin'. Trust me. It's like that." He smirks. "Otherwise, he wouldn't give a shit that I'm over here flirting with you."

"But you're not flirting."

"He doesn't know that."

I laugh, and that earns another grumble from Dare. Matty leaves, and the rest of the night is mostly silent, save for the music coming through the speakers and the quiet whirring of tattoo guns. Eventually, Dare finishes, washing the excess ink off his client's back. He stands, instructing his client to stand in front of the full-length mirror before giving him a handheld one to check out his work.

"Just a few more sessions, I think," Dare muses, one arm across his chest and the other gloved hand under his chin, assessing. "Think you can handle a longer session next time?" This one must have lasted at least four hours. They took a couple of short breaks, but I can't imagine a longer session.

"I'm game if you are. Looks awesome, man. Thanks again." Dare covers his client's tattoo in cellophane and goes over aftercare instructions. I check him out at the front desk, putting him on the books for two weeks from now, and then he's gone.

I help Dare clean up, both of us wordlessly moving around the shop. Earlier in the day, I felt a little lost, but once I figured out where everything was and what was expected of me, I fell into my role pretty effortlessly. Alec and Cordell are still working in their stations, so I ask if their clients need anything. They decline, so I move toward the front of the shop to hold down the front desk.

"Hey, Logan, come here a minute," Dare says from somewhere in the back. I bite my lip, looking over my shoulder, hoping he's not in the drawing room. I don't see him when I get to the waiting area, which means he *is* in the drawing room.

Awesome.

The door is cracked, and I push it open to find him sitting at a desk. He flips his sketchbook shut when he sees me.

"What's up?" I ask, lingering near the doorway. Dare smirks, as if he knows that I'm uncomfortable and exactly why I am.

"I told you I don't bite."

"Unless I want you to," I say, walking toward his desk, repeating what he said to me the night we hooked up. His eyes heat for a minute, and his teeth dig into his bottom lip.

"Right."

I come to a stop next to him and lean my hip against the side of his desk, crossing my arms, aiming for casual and trying not to remember how his head looked between my thighs while I sat on this same desk.

"So, what do you think?" he asks.

"About…?"

"Your job," he deadpans. "How was your first day?"

"I like it. A lot, actually."

"I do, too," he says, which makes me laugh.

"I hope so. It's your business."

"I like having *you* here," he clarifies, and I'm shocked into silence by his admission. There it is again. That tension. That *feeling*. It's impossible to put into words, but it's palpable. He *has to* feel it, too. I swallow hard, looking into those icy eyes. He clears his throat.

"I mean, you were a big help. I've been needing to hire someone for a long time now, but I never pulled the trigger," he says, confirming my thoughts from earlier.

"Oh." Whether I misread his initial comment or he's backpedaling, it stings nonetheless. "Well…*good*." I avert my eyes, focusing on the shelf stocked full of supplies. "I should get back up there in case someone comes in," I say, turning around, but Dare surprises me by sticking his finger through the belt loop of my black skinny jeans, stopping me in my tracks. The back of his hand grazes the inch of exposed skin between my pants and shirt when I turn back toward him, and he jerks it back, like he's surprised by his own actions. That makes two of us.

"Can you come in tomorrow? I want to show you how to open." He seems uncomfortable.

"I don't work at all tomorrow, so I can do that."

Dare nods.

"Ten a.m., then."

"Okay."

The air is charged with a different emotion now. I'm not used to feeling insecure. It's not that I think I'm a beauty queen, but I realized long ago that I have what men want, and I've used that power to my advantage. But with Dare, it's different. Sometimes I think this attraction is mutual, but other times, like right now, it feels one-sided.

"I'm going to close up once these last two clients are gone. Go home and get some sleep. You've had a long day."

I am feeling pretty beat and I should get home to check in with Jess, so I don't argue. "I'll see you tomorrow."

Dare looks like he wants to say something, but he doesn't, so I don't wait around for a response.

I notice the mailbox hanging open, the tin flap rattling in the wind, when I pull into the driveway. I grab the mail out and tuck it under my arm as I walk inside. Jess is sprawled out on the couch in his sweatpants and a dingy wife beater tank reading *The Outsiders*.

"Hey," he says, not looking up from his book.

"How was school?" I toss the mail down onto the kitchen table before taking off my jacket.

He lifts a brow before meeting my eyes. "*How was school*? What is this, *Leave it to Beaver*?"

I roll my eyes. "I'm just making sure you're staying out of trouble. Did you go to detention?"

"I am, and I did," he says, going back to his book. "Don't trip."

Something on the table catches my eye, and I snatch it up, seeing the words *Santa Rita County Jail* on the front. I flip it over, confirming my fear.

"Jess?" I ask, holding it up between my thumb and index finger. "Why?"

Jesse looks equal parts guilty and defensive. We agreed not to tell Mom where we were going, and we agreed on no contact, at least for now. She needs to know it's different this time. Plus, I didn't want to give her the chance to manipulate us into believing her bullshit or feeling sorry for her. Again.

"She has no one," he says, and my heart fucking cracks wide open because his is still so pure and naïve, even after everything we've been through.

"Jess, we agreed…" I try to keep the anger out of my voice. I can't fault a kid for wanting to talk to his mom.

"I know. I *know*." He sits up, running both hands through his disheveled hair. "She seemed…almost *normal*. And we're family. I didn't want to turn my back on her when she's finally making progress."

"I get that, but this is what she does. It won't last. It never does."

"Probably." He shrugs. "But I didn't see any harm in sending her a postcard."

"Have you been talking to her this whole time?"

"No. She tries to call my phone collect every single

day. I ignored it for the first week. Tried to accept it by the second week, just to tell her to fuck off, but it wouldn't let me. Something about our carrier not allowing it. Fuck if I know. When she was supposed to say her name, the last call said, 'Please, Jesse. I'm going crazy in here.'"

I shake my head, furious that Crystal would do this to him, but not the least bit surprised. I'm also pissed that she knows where we are. She's not the brightest crayon in the box, but it doesn't take a genius to figure out who we're staying with in River's Edge.

I flip the postcard back over, reading her chicken scratch handwriting. She explains how she spent the first week in the infirmary—so she could withdrawal safely, no doubt. She asks him to put money on her books for cigarettes, then goes on to ask him to write a character witness letter for the judge. What she doesn't ask is how he's doing. Her underage high school child, whom she knows is staying with his estranged father. Un-fucking-believable. Except it's really not, because this is how Crystal rolls. Selfish and manipulative and always, *always* the victim.

I hand it to Jess, and he shakes his head as he reads it. He leans forward, reaching for his lighter. With a flick of his thumb, he lights the corner of the postcard on fire and watches it burn, turning it this way and that as the flames swallow it whole. Ash litters the table, and when it finally burns out, he drops the remaining piece into the ashtray.

"I'll never tell you what to do," I say, and Jess shoots me a look. "Okay, unless it involves school or your safety or your general wellbeing."

"Mhm," he mumbles.

"And I'll never try to turn you against Mom, or even Henry for that matter. You make your own decisions. You can feel however you want to feel. I just want you to be careful. I hate seeing you hurt."

"I'm not hurt." He scoffs. "I learned not to count on her a long time ago."

"It's still hard. She's still our mom," I say, plopping down on the couch next to him. I kick my feet up onto the coffee table and lie back. "I've dealt with her shit for twenty-one years, and she still manages to let me down sometimes."

"She's trying to get into rehab instead of doing time."

I shrug. "I hope she serves a few months at least, but either way, she'll be sober."

"Is she any better when she's sober? She's never been clean long enough for me to notice."

"Not really. I think she was always fucked up. The drugs just made it worse." I know my mom had a rough childhood. I also know she has a whole slew of mental health issues, but I don't know which came first. Is she a product of her upbringing? Did the drugs cause her issues, or did her issues cause her to turn to drugs?

I don't even want to think about all the shit I saw as a kid and how it might have affected me. Am I broken? Is that why I can't trust? Is that why I always go for the wrong men? Why I gravitate toward older men in positions of power? Teachers. Coaches. *Bosses.* Will I ever have a normal, healthy relationship? Am I destined to repeat the cycle? One of my biggest fears is ending up like my mother—addicted to drugs and love and dysfunction. My biggest fear of all, though, is that Jess will suffer because of her. I've tried so hard to fill that role for him, but the truth is, I'm not his mom. I was just a kid myself.

"I won't talk to her anymore," Jess says.

"That's up to you."

"I know. And I *choose* not to be in contact with her."

"Probably for the best, considering I stopped paying rent…and all the other bills. You don't want to be around when she figures that out."

Jess laughs and plucks a roach from the ashtray and lights it. He inhales and leans back against the couch.

"Does Henry care if you smoke weed in his house?"

"He smokes cigarettes in here," he says, holding out the inch-long blunt in invitation. I shake my head. "That's worse, if you ask me."

"True."

"Plus, he's not home tonight."

He's not around much, though I can't fault him for that since he told us as much in the beginning. I know he sleeps in the room above his shop, but I've wondered if maybe he's got a lady friend he's staying with, too. It would explain why he doesn't seem to be in too much of a hurry to find a new place.

"Any idea where we're going to stay once our time here is up?" Jess asks before he mutters a curse and flicks the roach back into the ashtray. He shakes his hand and then inspects his singed fingertips.

"I'll figure it out."

Somehow.

CHAPTER EIGHT

Dare

"**A**RE YOU HIGH?" CORDELL ASKS ONCE HIS LAST client is out the door. I'm drinking a beer on the couch in the drawing room, waiting to close up shop.

"High on life." I don't know what he's referring to, but I'd bet my left nut it has something to do with Lo.

"You don't hire chicks. Especially ones that look like her." He points a finger toward the front desk, where Lo worked all day.

It's not a secret that she's fucking gorgeous, but the irrational part of me wants to throttle Cord for even noticing. I don't know why or how she pulls this reaction from me, but I need to get this shit in check, so I don't respond. He'll drop it if I pretend not to care.

"*Especially* one that you're into."

It's an accusation—one that I can't ignore. It's not that it's against my rules to hire women. I just haven't in a long time—for two reasons. It's not anything against *them*. On the contrary. Men are territorial sons of bitches for one, and when more than one is interested in a colleague, shit gets ugly fast. I've seen it happen firsthand. The second reason is that there is a shortage of female artists in the area. All the good ones work in the bigger cities.

"Who said I'm into her?" I keep my tone bored, unaffected.

"Uh, anyone with eyes? You didn't take yours off her the entire time she was here. I'm surprised your client didn't end up with her fucking portrait on his back."

"Is there a point to this little chat?" Patience is not something I have a lot of as it is, so it's pretty much nonexistent right now.

"Just making sure you know what you're doing, man."

"I'm not doing anything. We needed help, so I hired help. Isn't that what you've been bitching at me to do for the last six months?"

"Whatever you say. By the way, this came for you earlier. I had to sign for it." He tosses an envelope onto the cushion next to me.

"Thanks."

I tear open the envelope, wondering what's so important that it required a signature. In the upper left corner, it lists a name and address of a business that I don't recognize.

To Whom It May Concern:

I am writing this letter to declare my interest in buying your property in River's Edge, California. I've attached my business plan along with an offer. I'm willing to work with your attorney or handle this personally, whichever you're more comfortable with. Please contact me with any questions you may have.

I crumple the papers up and toss them into the trash

can next to my desk without even looking at his offer. It's not the first time someone has tried to buy Bad Intentions. We're in a prime location, right smack in the middle of what I like to refer to as the tourist trap of River's Edge. It's the first thing everyone sees coming into town, right next to the bars and casinos. Too bad I have exactly zero interest in selling. This place means more to me than anything or anyone ever has. You can't put a price tag on that.

"What was that about?"

"Someone wants to buy the shop."

Cordell snorts out a laugh, knowing I'd sooner chop off my own dick than sell. "I'm going to clean up my station, then grab a beer with Cam. You in?"

"Nah, I'm good." I stand, making my way to my desk to bury myself in a sketch, mostly so I don't have to see the disappointed look I know will be on his face. Cam's usually too busy to go out between his snowboarding career and his new role as a family man, so I should stop being an asshole and just go, but I'm not in the mood.

"All right, then. I'll see you tomorrow."

Alec isn't too far behind Cord, and soon I have the shop to myself. I'm almost back to the drawing room when I hear it. A muffled ringtone coming from the front of the shop.

Someone must've forgotten their phone.

The ringing stops, only to start right back up again. I figure whoever is calling is looking for their phone, so reluctantly I make my way back up front, following the sound. I find it in one of the drawers of the front desk, so it must be Logan's.

"Hello?"

"Who the fuck is this?" It's a man's voice. A very angry

man's voice. Does she have a boyfriend? Seems like that should've come up…ideally, before we hooked up.

"Who's this?" I throw the question back at him.

"Where's Logan?"

"Busy." Some instinct tells me not to tell this guy a damn thing. He's quiet for a minute before responding.

"Be sure to let her know she's only making things worse by avoiding me."

He hangs up, and I'm left wondering who this douche is to Logan. She doesn't seem like the type of person to put up with any shit, so what the fuck is he doing in her life?

"Rise and shine, princess."

I hear her voice, and at first, I think it's a dream. But the kink I feel in my neck tells me I passed out on the couch in the drawing room. Again. Without locking up, apparently. I lift my head off the arm of the couch and rub the back of my neck before peeling my eyes open. I squint up at Logan, who is standing in front of me, amused expression plastered to her pretty face.

"What time is it?" I ask, stretching my neck from side to side. Tattooing people today is going to fucking suck after sleeping in that position all night. I've been known to crash here occasionally, especially since Adrian seems to have taken up permanent residence in my house, but I usually have enough sense to fall asleep in a slightly more comfortable position.

"I don't know. I think I left my phone here last night, but I'm guessing it's right after ten."

I stand, moving past her to my desk, grabbing her phone. "You did."

She looks nervous, worrying that plump bottom lip between her teeth. She snatches the phone out of my hand and stuffs it into her back pocket.

"What?" she asks defensively when she realizes I'm staring.

"You got a call."

Blush crawls up her neck, and her nostrils flare. "You answered my phone?" Her voice is incredulous.

"Calm down, Sally. I didn't know whose phone it was, and it wouldn't shut up. Thought maybe someone was looking for it."

She rolls her eyes at me. "Stop calling me that. Who called?" she asks, scrolling through her phone.

"He didn't say, but he wasn't happy that I answered."

"Goddammit."

"Who was it?" Her reaction tells me I'm right to be wary of this guy. Not that it's my business, but somehow, it feels like it is.

"No one."

"So, you always have random guys calling you, *threatening you*, at all hours of the night?

"Drop it," she says, her voice firm. "You're opening soon. Show me what to do."

Her attempt at diverting the conversation is pitiful, but I let it go. For now. We set the shop up together, and I'm impressed when Logan takes it upon herself to look at the schedule, taking note of who has clients first, and sets up our stations accordingly. With two people opening, it goes by a lot quicker, so I find myself with a few minutes to spare.

I'm hunched over the front desk, making a quick revision to a sketch for a client that's set to arrive in an hour or so. My neck is killing me still and I stretch it side to side, rolling my shoulders. I lean back over my sketch, and then I feel two soft hands on my shoulders. I freeze, not expecting the touch. I've never been a particularly affectionate person. I chalk it up to being starved of it growing up. Hugging, touching, hand-holding, snuggling…it's all foreign to me, and I go out of my way to avoid unnecessary physical contact.

Logan either doesn't notice my discomfort or doesn't care, because she keeps kneading, and eventually, I relax into her touch. She presses her thumbs together, sliding upward toward the base of my skull. I groan at the feeling, my dick pressing against the fabric of my jeans. I drop my head down, letting Logan continue her magic on me. She moves back down to my shoulders, and I feel the tension slowly seeping out of me at her touch.

"Feel better?" she asks. She shifts closer, and I feel her tits on my back as her hair falls forward, brushing the side of my face. She smells like cherry Chapstick and vanilla.

"So fucking good," I mumble. Before I can think better of it, my hand reaches behind me, gripping the back of her thigh. She goes still, her hands pausing on my shoulders, and I let my hand fall. It wasn't even a conscious decision to touch her, but now I've made it weird.

The door chimes, and we both snap into motion, putting some distance between us. Adrian walks in, looking between us with raised brows, but says nothing about our not-so-subtle behavior.

"New employee?" he asks.

"What, stalking me at home wasn't enough, you had to

107

do it here, too?"

"I got bored. You didn't come home last night."

"Maybe I didn't come home because I needed some fucking space."

Logan laughs, bringing both of our attention to her.

"What's so funny?"

"Nothing. You two just sound like an old married couple."

"He's not my type," Adrian says, completely unfazed by her comment. "You, on the other hand…"

"No harassing the employees," I cut in.

"Right. I'll leave that to the boss," Adrian says with a smirk. Logan doesn't seem to be offended by his insinuation. "I just came by to let you know I'm going back to Cactus Heights tonight. Don't look so sad," he says at my relieved expression. "I'll be back soon."

"Can't wait," I say in a flat voice, unenthused. "Get a hotel next time."

"Why, you don't want to cuddle again?" he asks, his face turning down into a fake pout. "I bet your girl will keep this Arizona boy warm at night."

"Only if you put out." Logan grins, playing along, ignoring the fact that he referred to her as *my* girl.

Adrian's eyes widen, and then he throws his head back and howls with laughter. Loudly. "Oh, shit," he says between laughter. "I think I just found my soulmate."

"Don't encourage him."

Once Adrian leaves, we're alone again, but the moment is gone. Cordell and Matty show up shortly after, and soon the shop is busy as fuck. I hear Logan's phone ring a couple of times, only to see her reject the call both times with a distressed expression on her face. I assume she silences her phone, because I don't hear it ring again. I tell myself to mind my own business. She's not my girl—not my responsibility. This girl is obviously complicated. The last thing I need is to involve myself in someone else's mess. Dealing with my own shit is a full-time job.

I spend the whole morning on mindless tattoos—butterflies, hearts, matching BFF tattoos, and bullshit like that. One guy came in and got his daughter's name. I don't have anything against those kinds of tattoos, but they don't exactly get my creative juices flowing. My neck is still fucked, made worse by hunching over clients all day, so it's probably a good thing that I don't have anything too detailed on the schedule. Logan does her job well, making sure everyone is taken care of and everything stays clean. I try to ignore the way her ass looks in her tight jeans and the way everyone's eyes seem to follow her every move.

Around lunchtime, Sutton walks through the door toting a plastic bag of something that smells amazing.

"Hungry?" she asks Logan, holding up the bag.

"Starved."

"I'm stealing the new girl back," Sutton informs me. Logan looks over at me in question.

"Take your break."

"Does anyone need anything?" Everyone declines, and then they head toward the back.

"Maybe you *do* know what you're doing," Cord says, twisting back and forth on his stool. "I like having her around."

"Told you."

"Doesn't mean you don't want her, though."

Yeah, yeah. It also doesn't mean I'm going to act on it.

"Find something to do."

The rest of the day is more of the same. The evening gets even busier, and by the time I have a chance to come up for air, Lo's already gone home for the day. After lunch, she mentioned that she had to work a full day next door tomorrow, so she won't be coming in. I tell myself the disappointment that I feel has everything to do with the fact that she's a big help around here, and nothing to do with how I like seeing her here, in my shop, my space, hanging around *my* friends. Because that would be bad.

Three days passed without seeing Lo, unless you count seeing her go in and out of Blackbear. The third day was Monday, the only day we're closed, so I didn't see her yesterday, either. The guys at the shop have been pouting about her not being here, and I'm not convinced that it's only because she makes things easier. Lo has an addictive personality. With her big smile and sarcastic sense of humor, everyone gravitates toward her.

I've been distracted and moodier than usual. This time of year always gets to me, but this thing with Lo is fucking with my head. I vacillate between fantasizing about fucking her on every surface of my shop and worrying about her. Then, I get pissed at myself for worrying, and in turn, pissed at her for making me worry. Like I said, it's fucking me up.

I was up all night sketching, trying to relax enough to fall asleep to no avail. Eventually, I said *fuck it* and decided to come in early, once again. I managed to catch a glimpse of Lo this morning as she arrived for her shift next door.

Her hair was up high in that messy ponytail, and she was sporting those tight, black leggings that I love so much, a thin flannel over her work shirt, and a pair of tennis shoes. *Doesn't this chick own a jacket?* It's like forty degrees, and only getting colder.

By the time her shift is over next door, it's almost four o'clock. She must've ditched her work shirt, because now her flannel is buttoned up, showing off milky-white tits. Matty gets to her first, greeting her with a bear hug, lifting her off her feet. She squeals and smacks his shoulders to set her down.

"Miss me?" she teases.

"No one makes coffee like you do."

"You guys have a Keurig."

"Still. It tastes different when you bring it to me."

Jesus Christ. I can't contain my eye roll at his obvious flirting. Lo shakes her head at his antics before making her way over to my station. The girl in my chair is getting a script tattoo under her breasts, and I swear I see Lo's eyes flash with…something. She schools her expression before I can decipher it.

"Hey." She smiles, her eyes everywhere except my client, whose tits are completely out with nothing but tape in the shape of Xs over her nipples. "Need anything?"

You. Naked in the drawing room. On my desk.

"I'm good. I'm almost done here."

Lo nods. "What about you? Water?" she reluctantly asks the girl under my needle. I forget what she said her name was. Ashley? Allison? She's a cute girl, but she doesn't shut up.

"I'll take a shot." She laughs, looking uncomfortable. Lo gives her a smile that to some might look polite, but I see the annoyance lurking behind it. I chuckle, turning my attention back to the tattoo. My client rambles on, and I nod and *mhm* at all the appropriate times, not really hearing anything she's saying.

As my client is leaving, the door opens, and I look up to see Lo's little brother. He pops the tail of his skateboard up with his foot and tucks it under his arm as he breaks his neck to check out the girl's ass as she walks out.

"Hang on," Lo says, holding a finger up, then runs toward back of the shop.

"Hey, man," I greet him. He looks at me with his eyebrows pulled together in confusion before placing me.

"Oh shit, you look different without all the…" He trails off, gesturing to his face. *Right.* It was Halloween when we met.

When Lo comes back, she's dangling a set of keys in her hand. "Did you go to detention?" she asks, snatching the keys out of his reach when he goes for them.

"Yes," he says with an eye roll. He reaches for the keys once more, only for her to pull back again.

"Pick me up at eleven. You go buy your equipment, then go straight home until I call."

"This is stupid. I should've just taken the suspension. Do you even know how much this shit costs?"

Lo looks at me from the corner of her eye, and I busy myself with disassembling and sanitizing my machine, pretending not to eavesdrop.

"It's fine," she says, her voice barely loud enough to make out over the music coming from the speakers. "This is a good opportunity. Just get your mouth guard, shoes, and singlet now. We'll worry about the fees and all the other shit later." She reaches into her bra and pulls out a wad

112

of cash before tucking it into his palm. "Here's some extra from my shift today."

Her brother shakes his head, his hand still outstretched as if he doesn't want to take the money, but Lo lifts an eyebrow, and reluctantly he shoves it down into his jeans pocket. I've been in foster care and too many foster families to count, and I've never once seen a brother and sister this dynamic. Lo mothers him, which isn't unheard of for the oldest sibling, but he seems to listen to her as if she's in charge. There's a closeness between them that sends a little jolt of jealousy through me. Not jealous of *him*—I'm not that crazy—but jealous of their relationship. Asher is my brother, but he's not my blood, and he has his own life now.

There was a time when I thought I might have that with one of my foster families, but of course, I managed to fuck that up like everything else. And no one in this town has looked at me the same since. River's Edge is split into three types of people for me: the people who blame me for what happened, the people who don't, and the people who don't know anything about it. For the record, I fall into the first group.

"Straight home," she reiterates. He nods, and this time she gives him the keys when he reaches for them. He pulls her in for a hug, her head not even coming up to his chin. He leaves, and Lo heads toward my station to wipe down my chair.

"I can do it," I tell her. "My client canceled, remember?" She's the one who informed me of the cancellation.

"It's okay. I got it."

"You good?" I can't help myself. I have to ask. She pauses mid-bend as she reaches for the wadded-up paper towels full of ink and the rinse cup, her big hazel eyes locking onto mine. I can see a hint of her black bra peeking from underneath her shirt from this angle, and memories of her perfect fucking tits as she arches into my touch pop into my mind, unbidden.

"Yeah," she says, her voice too chipper for me to believe her. I can't figure it out, but she seems off.

"Have you eaten? I think I'm going to order from next door." I'm starving, and after overhearing Lo's conversation with her brother, I wonder if money's so much a problem that she's not eating enough. She's petite, her waist tiny, but that ass tells me she's getting enough to eat.

"I didn't get a chance to eat earlier," she admits. "Blackbear got busy."

"What do you want?"

"I'm not picky." She shrugs.

"I'll take a burger!" Matty shouts from his station on the other side of the room.

"And some wings," Cordell chimes in.

"Anything else?" I say sarcastically, earning another smile from Lo. This time it's genuine.

Jake drops off the food thirty minutes later, and I motion for Lo to follow me.

"What if someone comes in?" she asks, hooking a thumb toward the door.

"They'll get it," I assure her. I lead her to the bigger waiting area. It's completely empty of clients. I walk over to the table and drop the food down, motioning for her to take a seat on the bench seat. I grab two beers and a water bottle. *Gotta have options.* When I turn back for the table, Lo is sitting there, chin propped on her fist, full lips in a pout, staring at the table.

Don't ask her if she's okay. Don't ask her if she's okay.

114

"You okay?" *Smooth*. She doesn't answer, or even seem to hear me. "Lo." Still nothing. "Logan," I say, louder this time, and her head snaps up. "What's wrong? And don't say 'nothing', because I can tell something is bothering you. Unless you suddenly fell in love with pizza and that's a wistful look on your face and not a troubled one."

She gives a sad smile and shakes her head. "Sorry. I'm just thinking."

"About…?" I hedge. "Is that guy still bothering you?"

"No, I mean, *yes*, he's still calling, but it's not about him." I knew he was, whoever he is, but her confirmation has my hands tightening into fists. I don't have a good feeling about that guy. "I've just got a lot on my plate. I'm worried about Jess, worried about him finishing school, worried that I'm fucking this whole thing up, worried about where we're going to live—"

"No luck on that?" I interrupt. This sad, maybe slightly vulnerable side of her is a stark contrast to the bold, confident one that I'm used to seeing.

"I've looked online, but there's nothing to rent. I found one place, but I haven't heard back."

She's right. In order to find a place to rent in this town, you pretty much have to know someone. Rentals are few and far between, and they go fast.

"Can I ask you a question?" I hate when people ask if they can ask a question, but this one has the potential to piss her off, so I tread carefully. She nods in acquiesce. "Where is your mom?" These aren't things a twenty-one-year-old girl should be worrying about. I get that Henry hasn't been in their lives, but that doesn't explain who's been taking care of them all these years.

"At this very moment? Jail. Drugs," she tacks on as she

reaches into the bag, pulling out a fry. No sadness or shame in this statement. Just cold facts.

"Fuck."

"It's better this way," she says, lifting one shoulder in a shrug. "She was more of a pain in my ass when she wasn't locked up."

"Where's Henry going?" I grab a burger out of one of the bags and hand it to her.

"I assume he'll just stay in the room at the auto shop. The plan was always to get our own place anyway. It just happened a little sooner than we expected."

"Let me know if there's anything I can do to help," I say before clearing my throat awkwardly. I don't know how to do this shit. I don't know how to be a friend. When I took Asher in, it was easy because neither of us was big on talking. He needed a job and a place to sleep, and I gave it to him. He also doesn't get my dick hard, so there's that. With Lo, I have this innate need to make sure she's okay, and I don't know what the fuck to do with that.

"We'll figure it out. We always do. You've helped enough. You know, with the job and all."

After that, there are no words. We dig in, eating in silence. Lo moans when she takes a bite, and the sound goes straight to my cock. Her phone buzzes on the table in between us, and my guard goes up instantly, but I relax when I realize she's talking to her brother.

"Of course, it did," she says, giving a humorless laugh, dragging a hand through her messy brown hair. I can't hear what he's saying, but it's clearly not good news. "Okay. No, don't worry about me. Did you manage to get what you needed?" A pause. "Good. Okay. I'll see you tonight."

"What was that about?"

"The Toyota died. Henry's picking Jesse up and seeing what's wrong. Take me home?" she asks, batting those pretty doe eyes, sticking her bottom lip out in an exaggerated pout.

Like I'd say no to her.

"Yeah, if you don't mind waiting around until I close."

"Nope. I've got nothing else to do anyway."

Once we're finished with our food, we get back to work. Lo calls the next day's clients to confirm their appointments while I set up for my next session. Tuesdays are generally slow, so Cordell and Matty end up taking off around ten, leaving Lo and me alone. She sways her hips, singing along to "Wrong Way" by Sublime as she cleans the windows, and I excuse myself to the drawing room before I do something stupid. Like bend her over the front desk.

I've never been drawn to someone like this. Maybe it's because I'm denying myself the chance to fuck her that I want her so bad. Maybe we just need to give in, just once, to get it out of our system. Because I know she feels it, too. I see it in the way she looks at me, the way she presses her thighs together when we stand a little too close, the way she licks her lips. I'm hyperaware of her presence, and the only thing worse than not seeing her for three days is having her here to torture me. Either way, I can't escape her.

I hear a quiet knock on the door before Lo peeks her head through. "I think I've officially run out of things to do."

I slide my phone out of my hoodie pocket and check the time. Eleven eleven p.m. "You can turn off the sign and flip the lock." Since we don't have any clients and it's too late to take a walk-in, there's no point. If it was the weekend, that would be a different story. Lo bites her lip and nods, like a locked door somehow makes us more *alone* than we are now.

When she comes back, she sits on the couch on the other side of the room, tucking her hands under her thighs.

"Once I finish this sketch, we can go."

"Can I see?" she asks.

I hesitate. I don't like showing people my work, especially before it's done. Even when it's for clients, I still have a hard time handing it over. I always want to make one last change. The problem is, I could work on it for one thousand days straight, and still find something I want to tweak every single time.

"Come on," she drawls. "I can't even draw a respectable stick figure. I won't judge."

"Sure," I relent. She saunters toward me, her too-long flannel sleeves falling to her fingertips, her ponytail crooked and disheveled in a way that somehow still looks hot. She bends over to get a closer look, taking it in. I think her expression is one of awe, but I can't be sure.

"It's gorgeous," she breathes.

"Sure the fuck is," I say, but I'm not talking about the drawing. She looks at it, but I'm looking at her. Her berry-colored lips and soft skin so pale that I can see faint traces of the blue veins that run beneath it.

"What is it?" she asks, tracing the elephant head with a crown of jewels and its trunk that's wrapped around a trinket with her chipped-black fingernail.

"Ganesh. The god of good fortune. One of my regulars wants it on her thigh as a symbol of good luck."

"Maybe I should get one, too," she jokes. "I could use some luck."

"Only if I'm the one to put it on you," I say. She looks

at me to gauge whether I'm joking. I'm not. If anyone gets to put ink on that untouched skin, it's me. The air between us is charged with tension, and when she sucks her bottom lip into her mouth, I press my thumb against her chin until she releases it. Her pulse flutters in her neck, her chest heaving.

Fuck it.

I grip her jaw, and her eyes flutter shut right before I pull her toward me. I lick at her lips, and she instantly parts them for me. My tongue slips inside, sliding against hers. I stand, keeping my mouth fused to hers, and deepen the kiss. The hand around her jaw slides into her hair at the nape of her neck while my other hand snakes around her waist.

I lift her, her legs automatically wrapping around my waist, and she moans when she feels my hardness through my jeans at her center. I prowl over to the wall and roughly pin her to it as our frenzied hands fight to remove the layers of clothing between us, finally giving in to temptation. Lo rips my hoodie off, taking my shirt with it. I shove my hands underneath her flannel, desperate to feel her skin, as she fumbles with the buttons. Flattening my palms, I move them up her stomach and her ribs, pushing her shirt up as I go.

"We're not supposed to be doing this," she breathes, tossing her shirt to the floor.

"Definitely shouldn't be doing this," I agree, pulling down the soft, thin, black fabric of her bra to expose her nipples, pebbled and pink. I brush my thumbs over the peaks, and she arches into my touch, only her shoulders touching the wall now.

"We should stop."

119

My hands pause their exploring, and I lean back to meet her eyes, waiting for her cue. Lo pulls me back in, her hands in my hair, tugging at the short strands, and sucks my bottom lip between her teeth. I groan, gripping her ass, and swing her around. I lay her on the couch, working my thigh in between her legs.

Lo rubs herself against me and reaches for the button of my jeans. I half-consciously register her phone buzzing somewhere in the distance, but we ignore it. The buzzing never stops, causing Lo to mutter a curse beneath her breath. "It could be Jess."

I peel myself away from her body, running a hand through my hair. *Fuck*. Lo sits up, pulling the straps of her bra back over her shoulders before running over to the spot on the supply shelf that she's claimed as her own personal storage space. When she looks at the screen of her phone, she bristles, and I tense up, knowing exactly why. Lo turns her phone off completely, schooling her expression before walking back over to me.

She pushes on my shoulders and straddles my lap, but I stay still, my arms at my sides, hands resting on the leather cushion. Lo grinds on my lap and leans in to kiss my neck. My dick and my conscience are at odds, one wanting answers, the other wanting action. When her teeth sink into where my neck meets my shoulder, my conscience loses the battle and my hands fly to her ass, squeezing and guiding her movements. My hips shift, seeking the warmth between her legs. Lo slides off my lap, sitting in between my legs. She moves down my body, her delicate hands dragging down my chest and her lips follow. Her teeth tug on the small horseshoe-shaped piercing through my nipple as she goes for the button of my jeans once again. Lo gets my pants halfway around my ass before I muster up all my self-control to stop her, my hands covering hers.

"Stop."

Wide eyes fly up to mine, hurt, and maybe a little offended. I groan, because the last thing I want to do is stop where this is going, and putting that look on her face is a close second.

"Who keeps calling you?" I ask point-blank. Her lips turn down, and a crease forms between her eyebrows.

"No one." She's on the defense again. Her default setting, I'm realizing.

"Don't bullshit me, Lo."

"It's none of your business," she says, wrestling her hands from my grip. She stands and picks up her discarded flannel. I know she's going to bolt, so I stand between her and the door, blocking.

"The fact that you just tried to put your mouth on my dick says otherwise." Okay. Not the best delivery, but the point stands.

"Fuck you," she spits, trying to move around me.

"Lo. Stop." I hold her shoulders, trying to get her to meet my eyes. "I'm just...*fuck*, I'm concerned for you, okay?"

"I can take care of myself," she insists, her voice still full of steel.

"I see that. I *know* that," I agree. "But it doesn't mean no one else can give a shit."

Her shoulders sag, and I see some of the fight leave her. I can't fault her for being closed off. I'm the fucking *king* of closed off—to everyone besides her, it seems. I'm a hypocrite. It's like the blind leading the blind, but I'm trying here. Lo sits on the couch, pulling her unbuttoned flannel to cover her chest.

"It's complicated."

I wait for her to continue. She rolls her eyes and exhales harshly when she realizes I'm not going to let it go.

"Eric's someone I used to…date." She says the word *date* like it tastes sour in her mouth as she picks at her black nail polish. "He was my boss. It wasn't healthy. He was manipulative and cruel…and most of all, *a liar*. Everyone thought he was this stand-up guy. He had me fooled for a long time, too…" She trails off. "I didn't like who I was with him, so I left. He thought I'd come back. I didn't. He's not taking it well. The end."

My gut tells me she's oversimplifying things—that there's more to this story. "When he calls you, what does he say?"

"He mostly just asks me to come back. But the less interested I seem, the pushier he gets."

"Has he ever hurt you?" I ask with more bite than intended.

"Not physically. I'm not afraid of him," she says, avoiding a straight answer, and I narrow my eyes. "I just want him to leave me alone." She inhales deeply. "I just want to move on, but I can't if he keeps calling me, reminding me of my mistakes."

I get that more than most people. So many times, I've thought about picking up and leaving and starting over somewhere new where no one knows the gritty details of my past, but something has kept me rooted in River's Edge. It wasn't until I opened my shop—that I had something to stick around for, though I could relocate if I really wanted to.

"Why not just change your number?"

"I have. This number is brand-new. I don't know how he got it. He's very…resourceful."

"Do you want me to talk to him?"

"God, no," she says, horrified. "That would only make it worse. Trust me."

We're both quiet, neither of us knowing how to proceed. This girl. She's beautiful and feral and confusing and messy. And that's exactly why I need to stay away. Neither one of us has room for any more complications in our lives.

I swipe my shirt and hoodie off the floor, balling them up in my hands. "Let's get you home."

Lo

"Let's get you home," Dare says, his voice flat. I knew he'd think differently of me once I told him about Eric—and he doesn't even know the whole story. Imagine what he'd think if he knew that Eric was also married. *Is* married.

I nod, tucking my hair behind my ears as I avert my eyes to hide the hurt. The shame. I've done a lot of fucked-up things in my life—hazard of growing up the way I did, I guess. I was taught to lie, cheat, and steal, to survive by any means necessary. But out of *everything*, Eric is the thing I'm most ashamed of. It's not even the fact that he was married, though that doesn't paint me in the best light. It's the fact that I allowed myself to be one of those stupid fucking girls who falls for everything, as long as it comes from a pretty face.

Eric was larger than life. Successful, smart, charming,

123

gorgeous, and completely intimidating…and he wanted *me*. A ghetto girl from Oakland. I was used to guys like him wanting my body for the night, but Eric…he wanted *me*. Forever. He preyed on my weaknesses. Preyed on the fact that I was poor and that I wanted to make a better life for Jess. Preyed on the fact that I was hungry for a better fucking life. Preyed on my love for his son, Cayden. He wanted me completely dependent on him.

His wife, Olivia, was too busy snorting pills and drinking vodka for me to ever question his lies. But I started to see Eric for who he was, and suddenly, Olivia's behavior started to make sense to me. If I had stayed, that could've been *my* future.

The more Eric tried to control me, the more I pulled away. The money wasn't worth it. None of it was. I stayed longer than I should have because I had this stupid notion that I was one of the only ones in Cayden's life who even *kind of* had their shit together, but who was I kidding? I was the worst possible role model. In the end, I left a town that never loved me and a man who wanted to own me.

The keys on Dare's belt loop jingle, pulling me from my thoughts. He's sliding his T-shirt down over his head, and I can't help but notice the way his tattooed muscles flex with the movement. The same ones I had my hands on two minutes ago, until he rejected me.

"Ready?" he asks, tossing his hoodie onto the back of his chair.

Wordlessly, I stand, following him out. When he stops to lock up, I don't wait for him, heading straight for his truck instead. I hear the truck doors unlock as I approach. I lift one foot onto the bar and reach for the handle to hoist myself inside. I watch Dare as he moves toward me, head down, hands stuffed in his jeans pockets, but when he gets into the driver's seat, I look anywhere but at him.

I hear the truck start, and he hesitates for a minute. I can feel him looking at me, but I don't meet his eyes. He denied me when I was on my *knees* for him. My ego took a blow, and I need a minute to recover from the embarrassment of the situation.

Dare huffs out a breath and starts to drive once he realizes I'm not going to budge. My knee bounces restlessly as I stare out the window. This part of town is decked out for Christmas already, all the buildings and trees glowing with lights. It's such a difference from the city. It's like something out of a storybook. I focus on a huge tree with color-changing lights, when I feel Dare's hand on my knee, stopping my movements. He gives a squeeze, and this time I do meet his eyes. Their blue so bright, even under the night sky. Holding my gaze, his thumb moves back and forth, soothing. I swallow hard, resisting the urge to clamp my thighs shut. He trains his attention back on the road, but his hand stays on my leg. His fingers ghost the inside of my thigh, putting the slightest amount of pressure as he slides them up and down the thin fabric of my leggings. My breath comes out in short pants, and I feel myself clench when he gets closer to where I want him. He teases, getting close to the apex of my thighs, only to glide back down.

"Lo," he says, his voice thick and gravelly.

"Yeah?" I ask, trying to sound normal, as if I'm not all hot and bothered from his touch alone.

"Where does Henry live?"

I do my best to give him directions while he continues his ministrations, but when he grazes my pussy, I freeze. I can't form words. What are words? I don't know anything other than I don't want him to stop this time. I give up trying to act like I'm not affected, my head thrown back against the headrest, gripping the door handle for dear life.

At first, his touch is feather light, but as my breathing grows harsher and my leggings grow damper, he increases pressure until he's rubbing firm circles against my clit. "Oh God," I breathe, unable to keep quiet any longer. I feel my nipples harden against my bralette. Every part of me is hypersensitive, ready to combust.

My eyes are screwed shut, but I sense him slowing down and pulling off to the side of the road, never faltering in his assault between my thighs. Once we're stopped, his hand is gone for half a second before he shifts and replaces it with his left hand.

"You're so fucking wet I can feel it on my fingers," he rasps, like he's somehow as affected as I am. When I open my eyes, Dare's closer than I expected, one arm propped on the center console as he stares at the hand moving between my legs. The sight of him watching what he's doing to me turns me on even more, and a sound somewhere between a whine and a whimper slips free.

I pull his face to mine and lick the seam of his lips. This kiss is all tongues and teeth, rough and clumsy and desperate. I suck his bottom lip into my mouth, and he groans when I tug on it with my teeth. His lips trail down to the corner of my mouth, then my jaw. Dare dips his hand under the waistband of my leggings as he sucks on my earlobe. His warm fingers slip through my lips, and my back bows off the seat. *Oh, holy shit*, why does this feel so good?

"God, I wish this was wrapped around my cock right now," Dare says, pushing a finger inside me. The heel of his hand presses against my clit, and I gasp as he adds a second finger, tangling a fist in his T-shirt. "Are you going to come on my hand?"

I nod repeatedly, unable to find words.

"Come for me."

I'm holding my breath, waiting for my orgasm to wash over me when his teeth dig into my neck, biting hard before sucking away the sting. That's all it takes for me to contract around his fingers, over and over. It's never-ending, completely uncontrollable. Dare continues to lick and nip at my neck, shoulder, and jaw as I come down, still pulsing and completely boneless.

"Holy shit," I breathe when I can finally form words. Slowly, Dare pulls his fingers from me, then rubs me over my leggings—I assume to clean them off—but my hips shift forward, seeking more friction.

"You're fucking killing me, Lo."

I lazily turn my head to look at him when I realize we're parked on Henry's street. It takes a minute for my brain to catch up to the fact that I never ended up telling him where he lived.

"How did you know where to go?" I ask, my voice hoarse.

"Your employee file," he says, without an ounce of shame. I want to ask him why he didn't just say that in the first place, but I decide I don't care enough to press.

Dare cuts the engine and hops out before coming over to open my door. I right my damp pants and tighten my ponytail that has become a tangled mess. Dare helps me down, and when my feet hit the pavement, my still-weak knees almost buckle, but I recover before he notices.

It's so quiet and dark here. The complete opposite of where I'm from. This place doesn't even have streetlights.

The upside is you can actually see the stars out here. The downside is I can't sleep with all this…silence. Ironic, right?

We walk toward the dark-brown battered cabin with the rotted, wooden steps. Henry's truck isn't out front, so he must be staying in the room above his shop. I open the front door as quietly as I can. Jess is sprawled out on the couch, dead to the world. I expect Dare to follow, hoping to finish what we started, but he hesitates in the doorway.

"Coming?" I ask, leaning against the doorframe, my double meaning clear. Dare runs a hand over his mouth, indecision warring on his face.

"Fuck it." He moves past me, and I close the door behind him.

I put a finger to my lips and whisper, "Shh," before taking his hand and wordlessly leading him to my temporary room. I should probably be embarrassed by my setup. Most girls would. But I've never cared much about material things.

I expect Dare to cringe or at the very least look uncomfortable when he sees where I'm staying, but when I flip on the lamp, he doesn't even bat an eye. Eric wouldn't have even made it this far. He would've taken one look at Henry's house and turned up his nose, insisting we get a hotel room.

But I don't want to think about Eric. I want more of the feeling Dare gave me in his truck, and earlier at Bad Intentions. When he's making me feel good, I'm not thinking about Eric or Jess' school, my mom…none of it.

Going for bold, I peel down my leggings, kicking them off along with my shoes. My shirt is next, as I push the buttons through each slit. Dare watches me intently. I lift the bralette over my head, feeling my nipples harden in the cold air. Dare's nostrils flare, and he prowls toward me, curving a hand around my waist.

His thumb comes up to trace the sore spot on my neck as his fingers curl behind my head, his eyes lighting up in a way that tells me he likes that he put his stamp on me. And I like that he likes it.

"What are you doing, Lo?" Dare asks. "I thought this couldn't happen again, but here you are, naked, fucking taunting me. And here I am, about to break your little rule again."

"I don't know," I admit. "I just know that I want you to touch me."

"I have a theory," Dare says, rubbing a thumb over my bottom lip.

"What's that?" I ask, pushing on his chest, making him walk backwards. Once he gets to my bed, I press down on his shoulders until he's sitting, then straddle his lap.

"I think I just need to get you out of my system." His voice is ragged as his eyes move all over my body and his hands come to rest on my waist.

"You think so?" I ask, tugging the bottom of his shirt up, exposing the colorfully inked skin underneath. He lifts his arms, letting me pull it off him.

"Mhm." His warm hands smooth up my ribs to the sides of my breasts. "The only way to get rid of this itch…" He trails off, rolling my nipples between his fingers, "is to scratch it."

"Makes sense," I breathe, rocking against the hardness I feel under his jeans. "So, what you're saying is—"

"We fuck. Just this once. Then we go back to being… friends."

"Just friends."

"Just friends," he agrees, fumbling with the button of his jeans.

There are no more words. Dare shoves his jeans down just low enough to free his cock. I feel the hard, silky head poised at my entrance, and Dare doesn't waste any time thrusting his hips upward, filling me in one swift move. We both groan at the sensation. I'm so incredibly full, and it takes me a minute to adjust to the feeling. Slowly, I start to move my hips. Dare leans back, letting me ride him, his pants still around his thighs. I brace my hands against his chest, increasing speed as he watches me move over him.

Dare sits up and finally touches me. He pulls me flush against him before bringing one arm to band around my waist. The other one comes up to grip the base of my ponytail. He jerks my head back, and the sting of pain only makes it more intense, and I move faster, needing more. I'm so wet I can hear it each time I slide back down his length. *This. This is what I needed.*

Dare flips me over, throwing me to the dingy mattress, not severing our connection. I drag my feet down his ass and thighs, pushing his jeans off. He kicks off his heavy boots and the jeans follow, then he's punching his hips into mine, fucking me with the same urgency I'm feeling inside.

His head dips down, and he pulls a nipple into his mouth, nibbling and sucking.

"Harder," I beg, and he listens, biting hard, causing me to clench around him. He almost growls, pumping faster as he moves to give the other side the same attention.

"I'm going to come if you keep doing that," he warns, but I can't help it. What he made me feel in his truck doesn't even come close to this.

"I don't care. I need it."

Dare sits back on his heels, lifting my hips until I'm flush against him, my back still on the bed. He controls my movements effortlessly, sliding me up and down his cock as if I'm nothing more than a rag doll. Sweat drips down the side of his face, his bottom lip trapped between his teeth.

He leans over me once again, licking up my sternum before clamping down on my nipple, harder than before, and the sensation is more than I can handle. My back bows off the mattress, and Dare's hands slide underneath me to cradle me as I come apart, my body shuddering and jerking before going limp in his arms.

"Fuck." Dare tightens his grip and fucks my boneless body until he tenses up and spills inside me. He loosens his grip and melts into me, his weight crushing me in the best way, as we catch our breath. His damp face rests on my chest, his cock still inside my body. Minutes pass before either one of us speaks.

"Am I out of your system now?" I ask. Dare huffs out a laugh.

"I'm not even out of your *body*." He pulls away, and I feel a gush of wetness that reminds me that he came inside me. Dare must notice it, too, because he's staring right between my legs, his expression intense.

"I'm on the pill," I say defensively, even though he has no right to be upset with me. He was the one who made the final move.

Dare groans, one hand on his length as he guides it back to me, spreading our cum around before slipping back inside me.

"That means I can do this?" he asks, and my eyes roll back.

"God, yes."

Dare makes me come twice more in as many positions before he gets off again. We're both spent and panting by the end of it, and he excuses himself to the bathroom. I mumble some half-intelligible directions on where the bathroom is—not that it would be hard to find, being one out of the three rooms in the place. When he comes back, he looks unsure, probably for the first time since I've known him.

"I, uh…" he says before clearing his throat, scratching at the back of his neck in an uncomfortable gesture. "I should go."

"Oh." I don't know what I expected. It's not like I expected him to sleep over, but I didn't think he'd run out the door before my cum-stained sheets dry. I don't know why I thought this would be different than any other one-night stand, but I can't help feeling rejected by him, for the second time tonight.

"I mean…unless you don't want me to?"

This is the part I hate. Is he saying that because *he* doesn't want to go, or because he thinks *I* want him to stay and he's just trying to be nice? People spend so much time guessing what others are thinking instead of just fucking asking. Myself included.

"This was a mistake." He looks conflicted, his blue eyes swimming with regret. He opens his mouth, then closes it, like he wants to say something but thinks better of it.

"Okay," I say, because what else do you say to that? *So much for having to guess how he feels.*

"Lo!" Jesse's voice breaks through my consciousness, and I stretch my arms above my head tiredly. Soreness between my thighs reminds me of last night's activities.

I usually don't sleep so soundly—another direct effect of growing up in a shitty neighborhood with a shitty mom. I never knew when some drunk asshole friend of hers was going to barge in, thinking it was the bathroom. Even worse was when they knew damn well it wasn't the bathroom and wanted *company*. Of course, we worried about break-ins, too, but I was more afraid of the people we knew than of strangers. Strangers hadn't ever let me down the way Crystal and the people she ran around with did.

Jess throws my door open, looking half-asleep himself. He's wearing a baggy light gray sweatshirt that looks like it hasn't been washed in a hot minute, the hood pulled over his shaggy, still-wet hair. A black duffle bag is thrown over his shoulder.

"Can I take the car today?"

"I'll take you," I say, yawning as I pull the blankets higher. "Just give me a second to get dressed."

"You have to work today. I have to start that wrestling shit after school."

"Can't your coach take you?" It's not like they aren't going to the same place.

"Yeah, let me just ask my teacher for a ride. That won't be weird at all. Come on, Lo. You're the one who got me into this shit."

"Excuse me?" My eyebrows must hit my hairline. "Correction: I got you out of this *shit*," I say, using air quotes. "You got yourself into trouble."

"Whatever. Can I have the car or not?"

"Fine," I say, running a hand through my messy hair. There's still a hair tie in there somewhere, but I know when I look in the mirror, it's going to look like an *actual* bird's nest. "I'll find a ride into work. You still have the keys," I remind him. I never got them back after Henry fixed it last night.

"Thanks. I'm going to have sweaty balls in my face and then have to follow it up with cleaning the whole damn place, so I'll be home late."

"Living the dream, man."

"I hate you," Jess says, but his lips are quirked up in a grin.

When Jess leaves, I grab my phone to text Sutton and see that I have two voicemails from a private number. I delete them without listening. Eric's determination shouldn't surprise me. It's not about *me*. I could be anyone. To him, it's about winning and having the upper hand. Eric probably feels pretty rejected, and there is nothing more dangerous than a man with a bruised ego.

I tap out a text to Sutton, asking if she'll take me to work before her shift. We both go in at noon, but thanks to the new girl, whom I have yet to meet, I'm only working five hours. I'm scheduled to work a shift at Bad Intentions right after. Where I'll see Dare.

I didn't see last night coming. The last thing I wanted was to get myself in another situation like with Eric, but when Dare touched me…he consumed me and excited me and calmed me all at the same time. Dare isn't looking for anything in return. He doesn't want a relationship, and he swore anything that happened between us wouldn't affect my job…what could possibly go wrong? Him regretting it. That's what.

Sutton texts back, letting me know she'll pick me up in a couple of hours, so I throw a load of laundry into the washer and take a shower. I take as long as I can, giving extra attention to my makeup, even blow-drying and flat ironing my hair to pass the time, but I still have over an hour to spare. I decide to clean the house, but even that doesn't take long. I'm *literally* twiddling my thumbs, looking around the small cabin for something to keep me occupied. What do people who have free time do? Watch TV? Twenty minutes before Sutton is supposed to show, Henry arrives, surprising me.

"Hey, kid," he says, sporting black Dickies coveralls and a backwards Raiders hat. He makes his way to the sink before dumping the contents of his thermos inside.

"Lunch break?" I ask.

"Yep. Just thought I'd swing by to get a couple boxes from the garage. I'm slowly moving my shit over to the shop."

I nod, having figured that's where he'd be staying. "Need me to do anything?"

"Nah. I'm pretty much packed besides the living room and kitchen, and I can't fit all this shit anyway. If you and Jess want those couches for your place, have at it."

"Thanks," I say, leaving out the fact that we haven't had any luck finding a place yet.

We're silent for a beat, neither one of us knowing what to say. We've seen each other in passing and we had dinner the other night, but for the most part, we're still strangers.

"Have you, uh, heard from your mother?" he asks, leaning his grease-stained hands against the counter behind him.

"She wrote to Jess. I guess she's been calling him." She hasn't tried to call me once. My guess is she's trying to pit Jesse against me. It's what she does when someone's on her shit list.

"She knows you're here?" he asks, letting out a low whistle. "Guess it's a good thing we'll be out of here soon then."

"Don't worry. Even if she gets off easy, she doesn't like to leave the block, let alone the city."

"If it's in the name of spite, she might."

"Valid point." Sometimes, I forget that he probably knows our mother better than we do. My phone buzzes on the counter and lights up with a text from Sutton, letting me know she's out front.

"Hey, Henry?" I ask, stuffing my phone into my back pocket. "I took a job at Dare's shop. I don't know if Jess mentioned it."

"He didn't. Dare's a good kid."

"He's really helping me out. Anyway, I just thought maybe since I'm not around in the evenings, you could, I don't know. Be more…present?"

Henry swallows uncomfortably, running a hand over his short, wiry beard. "I wasn't sure what I should be doing," he admits. "I wasn't there for you kids. Hell, Jesse barely remembers me. I've been making myself scarce because I'm just really not sure what to do here."

"He just wants to *know you*, Henry. He'll never admit it, though." I clap him on the shoulder before turning to leave. "Take the kid out for a burger or something. I gotta go. My ride's here."

"I'll see what I can do." His arms fold across his chest,

and I can tell that I've planted the seed, at the very least. I'm not expecting Henry to suddenly be father of the year, but I do want Jess to have some sort of relationship with him.

I sling my bag across my shoulder and jog across the fake wood flooring toward the front door. Sutton's black SUV waits in the driveway, and I hop in. She reaches over the middle console to hug me.

"Thanks for picking me up. Jess needs the car," I explain.

"It's all good. I've been dying to get you alone anyway." She wiggles her brows, turning down the radio.

"Not this again." I roll my eyes, throwing my head against the headrest dramatically as she pulls out of the driveway and heads toward Blackbear.

"Come on, Lo. Admit that there's something going on between you two."

"I have no idea what you're talking about," I lie. I've never really had a girl friend. I've never gushed about boys or sex or vented about my problems, for that matter. It's just not something that comes naturally to me. Sutton seems to know everyone, and I haven't heard anyone say one bad thing about her. Even more telling is the fact that she doesn't seem to tolerate bad-mouthing others. Of course, she gossips, like anyone else. But she's also the first one to play devil's advocate or come to someone's defense. Case in point—when Jake had something to say about Dare, she shut that shit down.

"Anyone with eyes can tell." Her head rests against the back of the seat, and she swivels to face me. "I've known Dare for a couple years, and I've never been able to pull more than two words out of him. I was actually sort of scared of him. I mean, turned on, but scared nonetheless."

"Really?" I know he's not the most social person on the planet, but that sounds a little extreme.

"Oh, he's a broody motherfucker. It takes a long time for him to warm up to people. But it's like you just… skipped that stage."

"Hmm." I don't know what to make of that. He's a little rough around the edges, but nothing like what she's describing. "Do you know what happened? Why Jake seems to think he's dangerous?"

"That's his business to tell you. Especially since I've only ever heard rumors. This fucking town is full of 'em," she mutters bitterly. "I truly believe he is *good*. Briar wouldn't love him if he wasn't. I'd warn you if I thought otherwise."

"It doesn't matter anyway." I shrug. He made that clear last night, face full of regret.

"Keep telling yourself that." Sutton laughs, shaking her head. "Speaking of bosses…"

She spends the drive filling me in about work. Apparently, the new girl isn't new. She's the co-owner's niece, and rumor has it, she and Jake spent all summer hooking up when she worked there. Things went south and now, for some reason, she's back. That would explain his saltiness about her being there. Gone is the laid-back, flirty manager who made us pancakes, and in his place is Grumpy Jake.

When we get to Blackbear, I fight the urge to catch a glimpse of Dare in the window, going straight to the back to stash my stuff instead. We're in the middle of the lunch rush, so we don't waste any time. I grab my apron and almost collide with Jake when I turn to leave. He's wearing a white polo with the Blackbear logo, and his usually floppy hair is pushed off his forehead, styled to perfection.

"Hey." I give him a bright smile, and he distractedly mutters a greeting before moving past me. *Okay, then.*

"Told you he's different." She shrugs, tying her apron around her waist as she passes me. "You think he's okay?"

"He'll get over it. My bet is that she'll be gone in a month. She's not the best server. Hey, you want to get a drink after work tomorrow?"

"Sure. Jess has wrestling shit almost every day now, so that works." I'm not exactly feeling social. I'd rather wallow in Dare's rejection and lick my wounds in peace for a day or two. But I've always believed in faking it until you make it.

"Perfect."

The afternoon goes by quickly, and soon my shift is almost over. I'm finishing up with one of my last tables—a family of four on vacation from Sweden—when the door swings open. I look up, mid-smile, only to see *him.* The grin melts off my face and shock has me frozen to this spot.

Tall and tanned with a perpetual five o'clock shadow. Sharp suit, sharp jaw, and an even sharper tongue. Eric. What the hell is he doing here? He spots me, flashing one of his signature smirks my way before taking a seat in the corner booth.

"Enjoy the rest of your vacation," I say quickly before hightailing it to Jake's office. He's at his desk, eyes focused on the laptop in front of him.

"My shift is almost over. Mind if I leave early?" I try to keep my voice even, though my stomach feels anything but. Jake throws me a disbelieving look.

"First, you're mad about not getting enough hours, and

now you're trying to cut out," he checks the time on his phone, "forty-five minutes early?" His tone is biting, and if I wasn't in such a hurry to get out of here, I might take it personally. I'm under no illusion that Eric won't follow me when I leave. In fact, I want him to follow me. I want him as far away from my friends, my coworkers, *my life* that I've made for myself here.

"Please, Jake. I'll explain later. I just really need to leave."

His expression changes as he detects the desperation in my voice, and he stands quickly, coming to my side.

"Are you okay?" He peeks over my shoulder, looking for clues to my sudden shift in demeanor.

"My ex is here." I wave an unconcerned hand, trying to downplay the situation. "I just *really* don't want to see him." I don't tell him that Eric lives four hours away and has probably done some serious stalking to find my whereabouts.

"Grab your stuff. I'll walk you out."

"Jake, it's fine, really. I don't want to bring my drama here."

"Get your stuff, Lo," he insists.

Knowing he's not going to let it go, I do as he says. I wouldn't put it past Eric to come looking for me. Jake puts a hand on the small of my back, ushering me through the restaurant and I walk faster, away from his touch, not wanting to provoke Eric. We're halfway across the floor when Eric rises, along with the dread brewing inside me, and smooths his suit with the palm of his hand.

"Lo." Eric smiles, coming to grab my elbow in a show of ownership. He flicks his eyes at Jake but doesn't acknowledge him otherwise.

"What are you *doing*?" I ask through my teeth, not wanting to make a scene.

"Follow me and we'll talk." His eyes narrow in warning, and I nod my agreement if only to get him outside before I chew his ass out.

"I'll see you tomorrow, okay?" I say to Jake, doing my best to reassure him with my eyes.

"You sure?" Jake's eyes bore into mine.

"Positive." I see Sutton looking at us, a mixture of suspicion and concern written all over her face. I smile at her and mouth *call me later*.

"Let's go," Eric says, losing patience. I lead him outside, intent on steering him away from the building, but he jerks my arm, stopping me.

"What the hell are you doing?" I try to tug my arm out of his grasp, but he tightens it painfully. "Ow, Eric. You're fucking hurting me."

"Still got that mouth, I see," he says disapprovingly.

"Let. Me. Go."

"Why won't you take my calls, baby?" His voice is that menacingly sweet one. The one that barely conceals his rage lurking beneath his calm façade.

"I left, Eric. It's over. What don't you get?"

"It's not fucking over," he grits out, yanking me closer. I shove him, but he never loses his grip.

"You're acting insane!"

Jake pushes the door open, arms folded across his chest. "Is there a problem here?" Sutton is right on his heels, phone in hand as if she's ready to call the police.

God, this is humiliating.

"Why don't you go back to flipping burgers?" Eric spits, condescension coating every word.

Before he can respond, the door to Bad Intentions flies open, and Dare strolls toward us. His fists are clenched, but otherwise, he looks completely calm. Eric doesn't even see it coming when Dare cocks his fist back and smashes it into the side of Eric's jaw.

Cordell, Matty, and Alec walk out of Bad Intentions half a second later, ready to jump in at any moment.

Eric falls to the ground, cupping his jaw before spitting out a mouthful of blood. I gasp, covering my mouth. Matty tucks me into his side, moving me out of the way. Eric laughs, getting onto his feet, but Dare charges him again. He bunches his suit between his fists and throws him against the brick wall. I cringe when Eric's head hits the wall.

"Stop calling her. Stop texting her. Do not fucking touch her. Don't even *look* at her, or we're gonna have problems. You feel me?"

Eric blinks in surprise. "Are you fucking this guy?" he asks sardonically, pointing a finger at Dare. "I thought you were with that tool." He flicks his chin toward Jake. "But clearly, this one knows my business. Or perhaps you're fucking both? I wouldn't put it past you." He shoves Dare away, but Dare head-butts him, effectively knocking that cocky grin off his face.

Eric swipes a hand underneath his bloody nose, and when he looks like he might fight back, Jake steps forward, along with Matty, Cordell, and Alec—their message clear. Despite the fuckupness of it all, something inside me warms at the fact that these boys who barely know me at all have my back. *This is what family feels like*, I think.

"Go home, Eric." I shake my head. "This has gone far enough." Eric's a betting man, and he knows his odds aren't favorable.

"How do you think Cayden is going to feel when he finds out?"

Dare looks at me over his shoulder, questions in his arctic eyes.

"This is on you, Eric. Don't put this shit on me, and don't you dare bring Cayden into it," I say, jabbing a finger in his direction. I don't wait for a response. Ignoring everyone's curious stares, I grab my bag off the ground and dart inside Bad Intentions, all but running to the waiting room in the back.

I drop my bag onto the pool table and pace the floor. How did this escalate so quickly? Why did he have to come here? A minute passes before I hear the door open, hitting the wall. My head snaps up to see Dare prowling toward me, the guys right behind him.

"Let's go."

"Go?" I ask, confused.

"Come on." Dare holds out his hand, his eyes angry and pleading at once. I place my hand in his, and he pulls me toward the drawing room. Cord asks if we're okay, but Dare ignores them, slamming the door behind him before flicking the lock.

"Am I fired?" I don't think he'd fire me for a hookup gone wrong, but for bringing drama to the workplace might be a solid reason.

"What was that?" he asks, ignoring me, pointing to the closed door. "What the *fuck* was that?"

"Why are you so mad? I didn't ask for you to jump in!" His anger seems directed at me, and it throws me off.

"So, was I supposed to stand by and watch while he *hurt* you?"

"I don't need to be saved, Dare. I had it handled!"

"Yeah." Dare gives a humorless laugh. "Sure looked that way."

"Why are you so upset?" His reaction makes no sense to me. I'm humiliated enough, having had almost every person I know here witness my dirty laundry, and his screaming only makes me feel worse. My eyes sting with embarrassment and frustration and I will myself to get it together.

"That's the guy who's been calling you. The ex." He doesn't ask. It's a statement.

"Yes," I say through clenched teeth.

"What else aren't you telling me, Lo? What did you leave out? Because something isn't adding up here."

I shake my head, turning for the door, but Dare's palm slaps against it.

"Who's Cayden?"

I whip around, unable to believe the nerve of him. "And how exactly is *any of this* your business?"

"Cut the shit and just *fill me in*." His voice rises with each word. He's clearly frustrated.

"What do you want me to say, Dare?" I screech back, throwing my arms in the air. "That I fucked the father of the child I nannied? That I'm a whore? That I was too fucking stupid to see how I was being lied to and manipulated the entire time I worked for him?" The tears fall freely now, and I do nothing to stop them. I *hate* crying in front of people. Dare stands there, jaw clenched and speechless, as I walk over and collapse onto the couch, dropping my head into my hands.

Dare sits next to me, putting a palm on my back, but I flinch away from his touch. I don't want his pity.

"Don't."

Dare pulls his palm back and I keep my head down, trying to get my emotions under control. A minute passes before I feel him stand, then he's walking out of the room. I flinch when the door slams behind him before bouncing off the hinges.

I smooth my hair behind my ears, then wipe my face with the palms of my hands as I walk toward the door to shut it gently. I give myself five minutes. Five minutes to calm down. Five minutes to get the fuck over it. Five minutes to put on a happy face and go out there like nothing happened. Just five minutes. It's all I need.

CHAPTER NINE

Dare

CLOSE THE BATHROOM DOOR BEHIND ME BEFORE kicking it once, twice, three times for good measure. I need to reel it in. I have a client coming any minute, and I'm fucking losing it. It's not only about Lo. It's about the fact that I've spent ten fucking years working on my self-control, and I've blown it twice in twenty-four hours. First, when I fucked Lo without a rubber, and then again when I lost my shit in some bullshit attempt to protect her.

My self-preservation instincts war with my desire to keep her safe, and I don't know what to do with it. She's been here for a couple of weeks, and she's bringing shit out of me that I thought had died long ago. Conflicted doesn't even fucking begin to cover it.

I turn the metal knob on the sink and splash some water onto my face. Taking a deep breath, I open the door. I walk straight to my station and focus my attention on putting my tattoo machine together, sliding the needle through the tube before pushing it through the vise into the machine, snapping the rubber band around it, and plugging my clip cord in. I grab a few paper towels, a rinse cup, and some gloves while I wait for my client.

I don't meet anyone's eyes, tapping my foot restlessly.

Everyone here knows me well enough to know that now is not the time. When I'm wound up like this, I need to get inked or fuck to get the anger out of my system. Right now, the closest option is tattooing.

Lo walks out from the back room, surprising me. I figured she'd go home, but here she is, heading to the front desk, looking calm and collected, the only signs of the earlier drama evident by her glassy eyes and red-tipped nose. Cord walks up to her, saying something quietly, and she nods her answer, giving him that bright smile. The fake one, I'm starting to realize. It makes me wonder how often she's had to hide her pain to become a master at faking it.

She's so fucking beautiful and complicated. Feral and distrustful. She's beautiful when she's smiling, when she's crying, when she's fighting, and when she's writhing beneath me. We gave in to temptation last night, and I was being honest when I said it was a mistake. A complete and utter fucking mistake. Because I didn't stop thinking about it once all day. At least, not until Eric showed up.

What kind of piece of shit touches a woman like that? For as long as I can remember, I've battled my anger, but even at my worst, I had my limits. I've never come close to hurting a female. The look on her face when he squeezed her arm flashes through my mind, causing my fist to clench around my machine. I knew something was off the second I saw them. I hung back observing, telling myself to stay the fuck out of it until she pushed him. When he violently jerked her arm, all bets were off. I didn't plan to hit him. I *wanted* to fucking end him, but I've learned my lesson—at least, I thought I had. I let Lo get under my skin, and I lost control.

My next client interrupts my mental self-flagellation

when he ambles through the door. His name is Lopez. One of my regulars. He's inked from his feet to his shaved scalp, including a face tattoo—done by yours truly—that curves along the line of his jaw. The guy is so covered that I'm running out of room for ink.

"Hi." Lo smiles warmly, not seeming even slightly put off by his appearance. I like that about her. She doesn't judge anyone and treats everyone equally. "I think Dare's ready for you," she says without sparing me a glance. Lopez lifts his chin at me in greeting, and I wave him over.

"Who's the dime piece up front?" Lopez asks once he's in my chair. Lo pretends not to hear, but I see her back straighten.

"New girl," I answer shortly. I snap my gloves on my hands and get to work on the piece. He wants "hopeless" in script above his left eyebrow. I will myself to relax—to let shit go—so I don't unintentionally dig my needle too deep. Not that Lopez would mind. He's in it for the pain, but he wouldn't be too thrilled if my heavy hand caused scarring or an infection.

The session is quick, and after Lopez pays Lo, he walks backwards, looking her up and down, doing nothing to hide the fact that he's checking her out before sending a wink in her direction.

This motherfucker.

I toss my gloves and wash my hands, and when I return, Lo's cleaning my station. Her long, brown hair falls into her face as she bends over to wordlessly pick up an empty water bottle Lopez left behind. She puts on a good front, but I can tell she's upset. Withdrawn. And suddenly, my shit takes the back seat. I have the urge to fix her problems. To get the fiery Lo back, that smile back—the *real* one.

Without thinking twice, I reach forward and swipe my thumb under her eye, rubbing away a streak of black. Hazel eyes flash up to mine, her lashes still wet and stuck together from crying.

"I'm sorry," I say, not giving a fuck who hears me, letting my thumb linger on her cheek. Lo averts her eyes, severing the contact.

"Me, too. He shouldn't have shown up like that. I don't even know how he found me." Her tone is deceptively casual, trying to minimize the situation.

"Cord, watch the door and listen for the phone for me?"

"Sure thing."

I offer my palm to Lo, and this time she slips her hand into mine without hesitation. It's small and warm against my skin. I lead her to the drawing room, hoping to convey with my eyes that I'm not going to freak out on her again while simultaneously hoping I can keep the unspoken promise.

Once inside, Lo leans her back against the door, closing it with a quiet snick. I take a seat on the couch, patting the space next to me. Lo angles her body toward me, one leg bent on the couch, one foot on the floor. I scrub both hands through my hair, not knowing where to begin.

"You don't know how he found you?" She mentioned that he had ways of finding things out, and the fact that this guy not only got ahold of her number but her whereabouts doesn't sit well with me.

"I have no idea. I haven't told anyone where we are—" Lo stops short, eyes widening in realization. "My mom," she says, shaking her head. "My *fucking mother*. Jess slipped up. Let her know where we were staying. It's the only thing that makes sense. She's the reason he has my phone number, too, I'm sure."

"Stay with me tonight," I say, surprising us both.

"What?" She's taken aback by the sudden shift in conversation, but it makes perfect sense in my mind. Her ex is a threat. My house is safe. Simple.

"Stay with me," I say more firmly this time. "We don't know if he's going to show up at your house or your job again tomorrow." This guy doesn't seem like he has any intention of giving up.

"I told you, he's not dangerous. Besides, I can't just leave Jess…"

"Goddammit, Lo. The guy manhandled you. Don't tell me he's not dangerous. He stalked *you*. He's not going after your fucking brother."

Lo sucks in a breath, her eyes rolling toward the ceiling, clearly losing patience. She pulls out her phone and taps at the screen for a minute before addressing me.

"Oh," she says, a shocked expression on her face.

"What?"

"Jess is out to dinner…with *Henry*."

"That's good, right?" I ask, unable to read her reaction.

"It's *really* good." She taps out another text. "He also has no idea Eric's in town. He would've been blowing my phone up." She pulls her bottom lip between her teeth, thinking, before continuing, "I'm not going to bother him with this tonight. Jess hates him. He'd just worry if he knew, and he has enough on his plate."

"So, you'll come home with me tonight."

"What did you tell Eric? How did you guys get him to leave?" Lo ignores my statement.

"Nothing." I shrug. "He realized it was a fight he

couldn't win." With a few friendly words and a not-so-friendly send-off from Matty, but I leave that part out.

"I don't have a ride home," Lo admits, as if suddenly remembering. "Jess has the car."

"So it's settled. You're staying at my place. Friends, remember?"

The second half of my shift seemed to drag on longer than the goddamn Cold War. I don't know what I was thinking…insisting she stay over when I can't touch her. *Just friends. Just this once*, we'd said.

Now she's here, on my couch, in my space. It's completely foreign, having her here, yet something about it just *fits*.

"Do you want me to wash your clothes?" I ask, gesturing to her work shirt. She never ended up changing like she usually does after her shift at Blackbear.

"God, yes. I smell like grease."

She doesn't, but I don't argue. Instead, I tell her to wait there while I change into a pair of gray sweatpants and a white T-shirt before grabbing extras for her.

She stands when I approach, holding out the clothes for her to take. "Bathroom's—" I start, but Lo strips off her shirt, letting it fall the floor. Next is her bra. It's simple and white, and I can see the outline of her pink nipples through the thin material.

"What are you doing?" I ask, swallowing hard as she turns her back to me, then reaches behind to unclasp the band.

"Getting dressed," she says simply, holding her hand out in my direction. I toss her the shirt, and she pulls it over her head. She turns back around, my shirt hitting mid-thigh, then pulls down her pants and underwear together in one move. I hand her the sweatpants and she unfolds them, holding them in front of her hips before tossing them at my chest.

"Too big," she explains, and my mind is instantly in the gutter. Lo scoops up her discarded clothes. "Where's your washer?"

"I'll take them." Lo hesitates but hands them over and sits down on my couch cross-legged, her shirt riding up to her thighs but still managing to cover her bare pussy. I clench my teeth together and turn for the laundry room to keep myself from spreading those thighs open and burying my face between them. I look down at the pile of clothes in my hands, a scrap of white material sticking out of her jeans, and I mutter a curse under my breath before tossing them into the washer.

"You don't have a TV?" Lo asks when I return. It's always everyone's first question.

"Nope. You hungry?" I open the fridge, looking for something to offer her, even though I basically only have beer, water, and eggs.

"Not really. I'll take a beer, though, after this day."

Relieved that I don't have to try to throw something together, I grab two and hand her one as I sit next to her.

"Move in recently?" Lo asks after taking a swig, scanning the bare interior.

"Nah. I've lived here for years, actually. I just haven't made it home yet." I used to have a pool table to take up some of the open space, but I took it to the shop for the waiting room. I spent years renovating the place, making it my own…but when it was finished, it still didn't feel like mine. If I bothered to psychoanalyze it, I'm sure it would boil down to constantly jumping from foster family to foster family, never really having a place to call home.

Lo yawns, stretching her arms over her head. Her nipples strain against the fabric of the shirt that inches farther up her thighs with the movement, so close to showing what's between them. She's taunting me, again. She knows exactly what she's doing.

"About last night…" she changes the subject, addressing the elephant in the room. One of them, at least. "You said being with me was a mistake."

"It was," I say truthfully, and she swallows hard, keeping her expression neutral to mask the sting from my words. Always trying to play it cool, this girl. "But not in the way you're thinking." Her eyes meet mine, and I decide to lay it out there. We've already crossed the line. "It was a mistake to hire you because now I have to see you without *having* you every day. It was a mistake to sleep with you because I want to do it again."

"Why can't we?" Lo asks in that seductively sweet voice, her lips settling in a pout. I want to feel that mouth wrapped around me, sucking me, while she looks up at me from her knees.

"We said just friends," I remind her, my voice coming out huskier than I intended. Lo rises to her knees and lifts a knee to straddle me, giving me a flash of pink before seating herself on my lap.

"I'm a shitty friend." She's grinding into me, only my sweatpants between us. "Besides," she whispers, her lips ghosting along the shell of my ear, "sometimes, friends *fuck*."

Lo's hands reach for the band on my sweats before her warm hand circles my cock. I should stop her. She's been harassed and manhandled, and here I am, fighting my desire to throw her down and make her mine.

Mine. What the fuck?

She isn't mine. Not even close.

Lo pulls me out of my pants, and all thoughts of stopping this die as she shifts forward, sliding my dick between her lips. My hands land on the tops of her thighs, gripping hard.

"Fuck, Lo."

Her eyes close and her hands brace against my shoulders as she rocks against me, cradling my cock in the warmest, wettest fucking heaven. It would be so easy to shift my hips and thrust inside her. One little move is all it would take.

"Do friends do this?"

"Absolutely fucking not," I growl, smoothing my hands up to squeeze her ass, pulling her into me.

"What about…*best* friends?" she asks, breathless.

"If they do, I'll be you best fucking friend forever."

Lo giggles, and the sound makes my dick twitch. I push her shirt up, and she lifts her arms for me. Pale tits are decorated with purple marks from last night and the sight shouldn't turn me on, but it does. I flatten my hands against her back, pulling her closer, then softly kissing and licking each mark. Lo sucks in a breath, hands sliding through my hair to keep me close. I suck on her, leaving my mark on her shoulder, collarbone, and underneath her ear while her breathing becomes ragged.

"Don't make me beg." Lo's so wet that my sweats are a darker shade of gray beneath her. I fist her hair in my hands, scraping my teeth along the side of her neck.

"Remember when I said I didn't have bad intentions?"

"Yes," she whines, moving faster, and I feel like I could come from this alone.

"I changed my mind."

"Good."

I lift her at the curve in her hips, her knees landing on either side of my head against the back of the couch, and I latch my mouth to her pussy. Lo screams, fingers locking into my hair to keep her balance, but I don't hold back. I feast on her like she's my last meal as she rubs herself against me.

"Fuck my tongue." I slide it inside her, and she clenches around my tongue. "You like that?" I ask, my hands on her ass, keeping her anchored to my face.

"Fuck yes."

"Then you're going to love this." I slide my hand from her perfect ass to the wetness underneath before circling a finger around her other hole.

"Oh my God, Dare," she whines, slowing her movements at the added sensation. "I can't move. I can't." Her voice is desperate, legs locked tight. Barely breaking our connection, I throw her to the couch, my mouth on her clit, one hand sliding up her stomach, a finger from the other hand pressing against her ass. I don't push inside yet, just rubbing, probing.

Lo presses against my finger, and she moans loudly, her back lifting from the couch, so I do it again before I flatten my palm against her sternum. I slide my hand up to curl my fingers around her throat, testing her reaction.

"Harder," she demands, wrapping a hand around my wrist as her legs start to shake. I apply more pressure as I slip my middle finger inside her tight ring and suck her clit into my mouth.

"I want to fuck this soon."

I only pump my finger once, twice, three times before she cries out, "Fuck!" Her legs lock up, and her mouth parts in a silent scream as she breaks apart.

"You're so fucking beautiful." Still gripping her throat, my thumb glides across her bottom lip before dipping inside her mouth. Her lips automatically close around it, giving it a little suck. I'm so fucking hard. It's a miracle I haven't fucked her yet, but seeing *that* was worth it.

Her body starts to relax, her legs falling limply to the side. I pull my finger from her body, pin her thighs flat to the couch and give her soft licks with the flat of my tongue as she comes down from her orgasm. Her chest heaves as I sit back on my heels, tearing off my shirt and taking my cock out. I take her by surprise when I hook my hands under her knees and jerk her toward me before guiding my dick inside her.

"I'm not done yet." Fucking her spent, boneless body after I've made her come is quickly becoming my favorite pastime.

I fold her legs around my back and scoop her up, staying inside her as I walk up the stairs to my room. She tucks her head between my shoulder and my neck, nipping at my throat while each step has her bouncing on my cock.

Once we're in my room, Lo squeals as I practically throw her off my dick and onto my bed. I shove my sweatpants down my legs, and her eyes are hungry as she takes me in.

"Turn around."

She doesn't ask for clarification. She moves onto her

elbows and knees, sliding her hands forward until only her chest hits the bed, ass in the air. If I had my phone near me, I'd take a picture to remember this ass forever. Burning it into my brain will have to do.

I slap two palms against her cheeks before squeezing hard. I dip my head down to bite one side, then the other. She moans low and desperate as I knead and spread her cheeks. When I lean forward, giving her a long lick from clit to backside, she collapses onto the bed, one side of her face mashed into my black sheets.

"Get back here," I say, grabbing her hips and angling her ass toward the sky while the rest of her body lies flat on the bed. I eat her like this, thighs touching, sliding my tongue between her lips before I pull back and straddle her thighs.

"Hold yourself open for me," I say, and she complies, hair in her face, mouth parted as she spreads herself with both hands. I fist my length, guiding it to her entrance, dragging it through her wetness a few times before finally pushing inside.

"Oh fuck." I thrust forward, keeping my hips flush against her ass. This position is going to kill me. If I could *live* in this pussy, I would. I start to move, and Lo presses back into me, her moans muffled by my mattress. I reach around to rub her clit, and she pulses around me almost instantly.

"Did you just come again?"

Lo looks at me over her shoulder and nods. Clutching her chin between my fingers, I lean forward and kiss her hard and deep. I'm not going to last long. Not when it's like this.

When I pull back, my cock is coated with her cum. My

balls tighten, and the sight of her pussy contracting back to normal, having been temporarily stretched by me, throws me into my orgasm. Lo still holds herself open, and I jerk myself hard, coming all over both her holes.

I slump forward on the bed next to her. There are no words, no movements, nothing besides our harsh breathing. Her hair sticks to her damp, rosy cheeks, and I reach over to tuck it behind her ear.

"Big mistake," I say, tracing my fingers along her ear, jaw, neck, shoulder…she shivers at my touch, eyes at half-mast. I skim down her back, and she arches prettily once I get to the dip in her spine. I slip my fingers between her legs, sliding them through the mess we made. She gives a soft moan.

"Huge."

CHAPTER TEN

Lo

THIS IS BAD. THE THOUGHT PLAYS ON A LOOP IN MY brain. Dare stood up for me. He defended me. He took me home to protect me. Then he fucked me like a god. It's starting to feel like…more.

I step out of Dare's steaming shower and wrap myself in the white towel he hung for me. After fucking me into oblivion, I declared that I needed a shower. I was covered in sex and tears and sweat, and I needed to wash today off me. I spot a pile of clothes that Dare left on the granite sink.

This house is as much of a mystery as the man himself. It's a gorgeous home, but there's nothing personal anywhere, except for a set of three black and white pine trees framed above his simple king-sized bed.

I pull the shirt over my head—this time black—and a pair of boxer briefs over my hips. Combing my fingers through my hair, I look at my reflection. My cheeks are flushed, lips swollen, but my eyes look tired. I open the door and pad across the hardwood floor of Dare's bedroom, not stopping until I reach the edge of the bed where he sits in those gray sweats, no shirt, tattooed torso on display.

Dare slides a hand up the back of my calf to my bent knee and presses his forehead against my thigh. The gesture feels decidedly intimate, and I wonder if maybe something is shifting for him, too. Tentatively, I run my hand through his hair, and he leans into my touch.

"Let's sleep," he mumbles, leaning back to lie down on his pillow, crossing his arms behind his head. I don't argue about sleeping in his bed. That would be weird, considering he now knows parts of my body better than I do. I crawl into his bed, lying on my side to face him. His profile is illuminated by soft light coming from the lamp on his nightstand—sharp jaw, stubble on his cheeks, lips pressed in a hard line.

"What's wrong?" I ask.

"What's the story with you guys?" He doesn't specify what he means, as if he's been fixating on Eric since earlier today. I huff out a breath, rolling onto my back.

"How many times do I have to go over this?" I ask, resigned.

"I just want to understand."

I sigh, staring at the ceiling. As long as I don't have to see the look in his eyes, I can tell him.

"I was nannying for another family. One of the girls had a birthday party, and Eric approached me. He told me he was looking for a nanny and offered me a shit ton of cash." I give a humorless laugh. "We were so broke, it wasn't even funny. It got to the point where we had to decide whether we wanted to live without electricity or food. Mom spent every dime on drugs, and Jess was dealing them to help pay bills. I couldn't pass it up.

"He spun this whole story about how he needed help with his son, Cayden, because his wife was addicted to painkillers and alcohol. Stupidly, I related to that. I wanted to help him."

"That's not stupid," Dare interjects.

"It was," I disagree. "One night when I was about to leave, he sat at his desk—just like he did at the end of every week—to write my check. I remember thinking something was different because he was taking a long time. I sat there, feeling awkward, playing video games with Cayden while I waited. When he finally handed me the check, it was significantly more than he usually paid me, and there was a sticky note attached to it that said he wanted me to meet him in his office in ten minutes."

I inhale deeply.

"That's when we slept together."

Dare grits his teeth, but he doesn't say anything.

"He told me his marriage was over, that she simply stayed there to save face, but they hadn't been together in a long time. I believed him because I rarely ever saw her, and if I did, she was blitzed out of her mind. Part of me felt like I had to be with him, or he'd fire me. Part of me liked that someone of his caliber wanted me." I roll my eyes, knowing how fucking stupid and pathetic that sounds.

"Slowly, he became increasingly possessive. It's like he thought he had the right to control every aspect of my life because he paid me well. I stuck around for way too long because I didn't want to leave Cayden, but I didn't sleep with him again. Eventually, I took other nanny jobs, tried to distance myself. When I wouldn't answer his calls, he started showing up unannounced. I'd be in the shower or sleeping in my bed, and he'd be there. 'Checking in,' he'd say. He accused me of sleeping with the other dads I worked for, called me a whore, a gold digger. He made me feel like shit about myself, and for a while, I thought he was all I deserved. All I cared about—all I still care about—is being able to take care of Jesse. He's the only thing that matters to me."

Dare nods but doesn't interrupt my verbal diarrhea.

"Jess hated him from the start. He knew he was bad news, and they constantly butted heads."

"What made you finally leave?"

This is the part I hate talking about. The part that makes me feel like the worst kind of human. But I decide to purge it all. To get it over with so I don't have to rehash it again. "Right before we left, I went to hang the towels in their upstairs bathroom. Before I could flip the light on, I slipped in something. It was blood. I freaked out. I didn't know who or where it came from, but Cayden was at school, so at least I knew it wasn't him.

"I checked all the rooms before finding his wife, Olivia. She had apparently miscarried and was barely conscious. I didn't know whether it was because she was fucked up on pills or losing too much blood, but both were true." Or at least, I thought she was losing too much blood. I'd never had a miscarriage before—didn't know what was normal—but it seemed excessive to me.

"Fuck," Dare says, reaching over to link his fingers with mine.

"I called an ambulance, called Eric, then waited with her until they got there. She was mumbling incoherently, but I'm fluent in drug-induced ramblings, thanks to my mom. She said she knew I'd slept with Eric. Accused me of being the reason that she was so stressed. Said it caused her to miscarry and that this baby was supposed to fix things."

"You know it doesn't work like that," Dare says quietly.

"I know." I nod. And I do. I know it wasn't my fault. The

only thing I'm guilty of is being too naïve and believing his lies. They were never separated, like he led me to believe. And playing a role in that fucked-up situation doesn't feel good no matter who's at fault.

"Jess got kicked out of school for hacking their system and got caught up in some trouble with the guys he was dealing for. My mom's boyfriend beat the shit out of both Jess and me because we wouldn't give him drug money, and when the cops showed up on our doorstep, I took my opportunity. I ratted my mom and her boyfriend out, and when they took her to jail, I called Henry, packed a couple bags, and left with Jess the next morning."

"That's why you had a black eye when we met?" Dare asks, his voice deadly calm, but his expression murderous. He cups my cheek, and I nod, soaking up his touch, my hands covering his wrist.

"I just wanted a fresh start," I breathe, tears pricking my eyes. "I hate talking about this stuff," I say, covering my eyes with my forearm. "It's embarrassing."

"You were trying to take care of your family. There's no fucking shame in that. I wish I had someone who cared about me half as much as you care about your brother."

"Tell me about you?" I ask, hoping he doesn't deny me after spilling all that stuff about myself.

"Quid pro quo, huh?" He's on his side facing me now. His voice is so nonchalant, but I can tell he feels anything but. "I never knew my parents. I was left in a parking lot when I was four, along with a note with my first name and birthday. No last name. I guess I was found at the store on Adair Street, so that's where my last name comes from."

My eyes widen at his words. He mentioned being in foster care, but I didn't know the details. I feel stupid for being so wrapped up in my own stupid problems that pale in comparison.

"I wasn't where I should've been, developmentally speaking. I was small. Malnourished. I barely spoke. I didn't even know my last name," he says, giving a bitter laugh. "What four-year-old doesn't know their own name? I had behavioral issues, too. No one wanted that. They wanted to adopt adorable bouncing babies with big gummy smiles. When I got older, I was mad at the world, jumping from foster family to foster family, never staying anywhere for more than a few months, and the ones who did keep me were usually abusive pieces of shit who just wanted a paycheck."

"That's awful." My tears are for a completely different reason now. My heart physically hurts thinking of little Stefan, all alone in a parking lot. We might have been dirt-poor, but at least Jess and I always had each other growing up. That was one thing we could always count on.

On the day Dare and I met, he told me he'd wet the bed until he was twelve. I'd laughed, thinking it was just embarrassing kid stuff. Now, I feel like a pile of shit because it was so much more than that. "You never had one family that was good to you?"

A darkness flashes across his features. "I did, for a while…" He trails off, seemingly lost in a memory before clearing his throat. "But it didn't work out."

I reach out to trace the pine tree silhouettes on his forearm. I don't know why, I just feel the need to touch him in this moment. Dare tenses, but he doesn't pull away. I feel something rough and bumpy under the ink, and when I look closer, I see the skin is slightly raised there.

"What happened here?"

"Double compound fracture. Two plates. Ten screws."

"Jesus, what were you doing?" I run my fingers along the line that runs from the top of his forearm down to his wrist.

"Fell on the ice."

"It looks like a centipede," I remark. When I look up, Dare's staring at me intently. I notice the faint freckles on his nose for the first time. They make him look innocent and boyish—two words no one would ever use to describe him, I'm sure.

"What?" I ask, pulling back.

"Can I…try something?"

"If it's anal, the answer is no. I'm too tired," I say, trying to bring some levity to the conversation.

"Not tha—wait, you'd let me if you weren't too tired?" he asks, raising a brow. A half-smile tugs at his lips, and I feel victorious for putting it there.

"I'm joking," I say, slapping his arm. "What were you going to say?"

"This." The brief, playful demeanor is gone, and in its place is something almost vulnerable. I don't know where he's going with this until he nudges me over and settles in behind me, curling his arm around my waist, his nose in my hair.

"Cuddling? You want to try *cuddling*?" I ask, incredulous.

"I've never done it," he admits.

Something shifts in this moment, and I realize Dare and I might be more alike than I thought.

"Me neither," I whisper. He squeezes tighter and cups my breast.

"Just for a little while."

165

A repetitive dripping sound pulls me from consciousness. It's still dark, and Dare is molded to me, arms wrapped around me like a boa constrictor, his knee between both of mine. The rhythmic breathing on my neck tells me he's asleep. Careful not to wake him, I peel myself away from him, following the sound toward the window.

Tiptoeing across the hardwood, I slide open one side of the black curtains and I almost squeal, my hand flying to my mouth to muffle the sound. Everything is covered in a blanket of white, illuminated by the bright moon peeking through the snow-covered trees.

I move silently through Dare's room and down the stairs, shoving my feet into my boots before plucking Dare's hoodie off the back of one of the barstools at his counter. I leave the door cracked behind me and walk out into the field of snow. Dare lives in the middle of nowhere, his closest neighbor probably a mile away, so it's nothing but snow and trees as far as the eye can see. The peacefulness of it all is almost enough to make me emotional, still feeling raw—a lingering effect from our conversation before we fell asleep. I tilt my head back, letting fluffy, oversized snowflakes hit my cheeks.

Arms lock around my waist from behind, and I jump before I hear Dare's sleepy voice in my ear. "What the hell are you doing, Sally?" His taunting nickname now feels almost...endearing. I don't hate it.

"You live in Narnia," I say quietly, leaning into him.

"Why are you whispering?" He nibbles at my earlobe, and for a minute, I forget all about the snow.

"I don't know. It seems like I have to be quiet out here."

Dare chuckles, and I turn around in his arms. He's wearing his sweats, but his torso is bare.

"Aren't you freezing?" I ask, and he pulls his hood over my head, tightening the strings.

"I'm used to the cold," he says, eyes running the length of my body, fingering the hem of his hoodie that falls mid-thigh. "But you look good in my jacket."

I answer him by unzipping said jacket, revealing bare skin underneath. He groans when he realizes I'm wearing nothing else but boots, his hands landing on my ribs. Lifting onto my toes, I use the jacket to cover both of us, our bodies molding together.

Dare brushes his thumbs against my nipples, and I shiver, my lips parting on a sigh. He takes the opportunity to slide his tongue between my lips before sweeping it inside. I circle my arms around his neck, and he lifts me. My legs wrap around him, boots locking behind his back, my already slick center against his lean abs. This kiss is slower. Deeper. Snow falls around us, but our bodies are too busy speaking a language our tongues don't speak to care about the cold.

"Wait here for a second," he says when we finally break apart. I stand, arms wrapped around my middle to keep warm as Dare runs back inside the house. When he comes back out, he has a *Thrasher* hoodie on and two blankets in his arms. He wraps one of them around my shoulders.

"I want to show you something," he says cryptically.

"If you're about to show me a dead body, I'm out." I follow him into the wooded area, my boots crunching against pine needles and leaves coated with a thin layer of snow. We walk for maybe five minutes before we come to a clearing. Dare spreads the blanket out onto the ground, sitting right in the middle. He holds his hand out for me to join him. I move to sit next to him, but he pulls me in between his bent knees.

He takes the other blanket from me and covers my front before resting his chin on my shoulder.

"I've been coming here to be alone for more than ten years. You can probably still find where I carved into that tree over there," he says, pointing off to the left.

"What's it say? *Dare was here*?" I tease.

"Probably more like *fuck off.*"

I laugh, holding out my palm to catch the snowflakes.

"It's beautiful out here. Peaceful."

"That's why I had to live here. My house was nothing more than a shack when it went up for sale. It was a piece of shit and dirt cheap, but I wanted it. I added on and fixed it up. It's taken me years, and it's still not completely done."

We're silent for a while—long enough for the cold ground to start seeping through the blanket. My butt is numb, but I'll sit out here all day long if it means seeing this uncensored side to Dare.

"This is what I wanted to show you," he says, just as the sun starts to peek through the trees, casting a pinkish glow where it hits the fog. This moment feels like magic. Like something out of a fairytale. *Fairytales are for princesses*, I remind myself. Not ghetto girls from Oakland. But right now, in Dare's arms, I can pretend. Even if only for a while.

"I could stay here forever," I say, leaning my head back onto his shoulder. Dare bites the shell of my ear, and I shiver, but it's not from the cold.

"Let's get you warm."

Dare leads me back inside, and I'm confused when he doesn't go back upstairs, but out the back door. Walking over to the hot tub, he lifts the cover, and I all but run over, kicking my boots off on the way. That is *definitely* what I need right now.

"A hot tub, huh? I bet this is where you bring all your dates." I wiggle my brows.

"Actually, I think I'm the only one who hasn't had sex in this thing."

"Well, now it's my turn. It's only fair." I bite my lip, unzipping his jacket before letting it fall to the ground.

"Thank God for chlorine." Dare takes his hoodie off, too, drops his sweatpants, and I gulp at the thin happy trail between his Adonis belt, pointing to his thick cock, already hard. I do nothing to hide the fact that I'm staring. I've never felt this kind of attraction before. I step into the Jacuzzi, lowering my naked self into the water. Goosebumps break out all over my body, and my stomach flips as I watch Dare's tattooed body move toward me. He flips a switch on the side, the jets bubbling to life as he joins me.

He sits on the submerged seat, pulling me onto his lap. His erection bobs between us, and I lean forward to rub myself along his length. Dare fills me with a shift of his hips, groaning once he's fully impaled me. "I think you're my new favorite hobby."

Ditto.

Dare

Seeing Lo in the snow the other night was a sight I'll never forget. Unlaced boots, hoodie to her knees, sleeves hanging past her hands, pretty face tipped toward the sky. She's been hardened by life, and she puts on a tough front, but show the girl some snow, and her eyes fill with childlike wonder. It reminded me that she's still just a twenty-one-year-old girl underneath all that false bravado.

It also reminded me that the girl needs some fucking winter clothes. The snow is officially here, and I saw her head into Blackbear yesterday morning with nothing but that stupid flannel to keep her warm. Which brings me to now. In the tourist trap near The Pines Ski Resort with Briar and Cam's girl, Mollie, on my lunch break. Cam used to teach snowboarding lessons here, and he knows all about brand names and what's best in the snow—shit that I've never cared to learn. When I texted him, recruiting his help, he sent me a text with a bunch of *hahahahahas* followed by *you're next* before sending Mollie and Briar in his place, much to my annoyance. If I wanted Briar's help, I would've asked her myself. She'll never let this go.

"Oh, *this* store," Briar says excitedly, pulling me inside by my sleeve. "What size do you think she is? Small? Medium?"

"Fuck if I know." I could probably guess her bra size, but I don't know shit about women's clothing.

"Let's go with medium to be safe," Mollie says, combing through a rack of coats. "Plus, if it's a little big, she'll have room for layers."

"I don't care what you guys get, just make sure it's

warm. And casual. She doesn't like that fancy shit," I say, earning a quizzical look from Briar. Once Mollie is out of earshot, Briar approaches, and I already know what's coming.

"You really like this girl." It's a statement, one I don't bother denying because I'm starting to think she's right. "Be careful, okay?"

I throw her a confused look. "Be careful about what?"

"Just…everything. I don't want to see you get hurt."

It still takes me by surprise when Briar says something that shows she genuinely cares. I mean, she cares about everyone—that's just who she is—but it's hard to get used to. She's seen a couple of the girls that I've hooked up with, but she's never expressed any feelings about them either way.

"Lo's not like that. She's different."

"And *that's* why I worry." Briar gives me a one-armed hug. "But I'm really happy for you. I like her," she says genuinely.

See? Never letting it go. Girls are so dramatic.

"Okay, so I found this Burton jacket that I'd die for." Mollie appears, holding up a white coat with fur around the hood. "Plus, it's reversible and super warm. And this, too, because puffer vests are so cute right now."

"I'll pick out some boots," Briar says. "I'll grab a seven and a half, but keep the receipts just in case."

The girls raid the shop while I stand in the corner with my hands in my pockets, waiting. They come back, fifteen minutes later, arms full.

"I tried to find sales. I might have gotten a little carried away," Briar says sheepishly, and I laugh. "You can pick through what you want, and I'll put back the rest."

"It's cool. Let's check out." We're at the counter when

a thought occurs to me. I turn to Mollie. "Grab some stuff for her brother, too. Whatever Cam would get." She nods, quickly gathering a beanie, a jacket, some wool socks, and a pair of boots. Briar is looking at me like I've grown three heads.

"What? You don't want them ending up like the Donner Party, do you?"

"Definitely not. Cannibalism is so 1800s." She rolls her eyes. "You have a good heart."

"Yeah, yeah. Don't tell anyone."

"I'd never ruin your rep like that," she says, knocking my arm with her shoulder. I hand her my credit card, opting to wait outside while they hit a couple more stores. I'm not rich, but I make a solid living, and I don't have shit to spend it on.

When Mollie and Briar show up three bags heavier, I thank them both for their help before driving back to Bad Intentions. As I walk up, bags in hand, I see Lo through the window, smiling at an elderly couple as she pulls a pen out of her messy ponytail. I realize I didn't think this thing through. I can't just walk into Blackbear and hand her free shit. Knowing Lo, it would embarrass her. Her pride won't let her accept it.

Saving me from indecision, Sutton walks through the door, a concerned expression on her face. She motions for me to follow her, stopping in front of the brick wall that connects our buildings.

"Do I need to worry about Lo?" she asks, and at first, I think she's referring to me, but then I realize she's talking about Eric showing up the other night.

"I don't know," I say honestly, dragging a hand down my face. "I think he got the message. Matty really drilled it into him." And by 'drilled it into him', I mean beat the shit out of him.

"Good," she says, unfazed by the implication. "She tries to act like he's harmless, but I get bad vibes."

"Yeah, she does that," I say bitterly. "Speaking of Lo, you mind giving these to her?" I hold out the bags. Sutton lifts a dark eyebrow, peeking inside.

"What's all this?"

"Figured she'd need some warmer stuff. She's too stubborn to buy anything for herself." I know she's gotten paid from Blackbear, not to mention the fact that she gets tips daily. I also know things are tight. Most of her money goes to Jesse, between food, lunch money, wrestling equipment, and fees. In her mind, there will always be something more important to spend her money on. I get it. I'm the same way. Even though my circumstances have changed, some things are just too deeply ingrained to change at a certain point.

Sutton gives me the same look Briar did. The one that tells me she just saw me in a different light, and for some reason, it irritates me. People used to look at me like I was a rabid dog. I didn't mind it because it meant they left me alone. But now, I'm being looked at like a baby golden retriever. "Just make sure she gets them, okay?" I snap.

"Fine," Sutton relents, shrugging her shoulders.

"And, uh…" I scratch at the stubble on my cheek. "Don't let her know they're from me."

She hesitates, then finally gives me a nod before heading back inside. I don't wait around to see Lo's reaction. When I open the door to my shop, Cam is sitting in his brother's chair, getting a touch-up on his leg. Cordell lets out a low whistle when he sees me, while Cam smirks, clearly amused. Apparently, he told him about my phone call.

"You can both fuck off." I walk straight back to the drawing room while I wait for my next client. Not five minutes goes by before I hear the door ding, and Lo's voice echoes through the shop.

"Where's Dare?" she almost yells. *Shit.* She's angry.

"He's definitely not back in the drawing room!" Cam yells loudly for my benefit. I'm mentally gearing up for a fight, listing all the reasons she needs to just shut up and accept it when she barges through the door.

"Did you do this?" she demands, thrusting the bag she's holding in my direction.

"I…no?"

"Don't lie to me. I can tolerate a lot of things, but liars aren't one of them." Her eyes fill with tears, and her bottom lip trembles. Jesus, I knew she'd fight it, but I didn't know she'd be this upset about it.

"Fine. I bought it, but it doesn't mean—"

Lo cuts me off, throwing herself at me. Her lips land on mine, and her tongue slips inside, kissing me fiercely. I don't question the sudden shift. Instead, I lift her onto my desk and kiss her back just as enthusiastically. I dip both hands down the back of her leggings, soaking up her warmth. Feeding off it. She pulls back, eyes still glassy.

"You thought of Jesse," she says, sniffing.

"He's important to you," is all I can think to say. I kiss the single tear that runs down her cheek, and as if a bell sounds, announcing round two, we go at each other again. Lo grips me through my jeans, and I half-chuckle, half-groan.

"I'd have bought you clothes a long time ago if I knew

it got you so hot," I tease.

"Shut up," she says against my lips. We kiss some more, never taking it further—just kissing and touching and rubbing—before she pulls away, breathless. "I have to get back to work."

"Have you heard from him?" I ask, cupping the back of her neck, not bothering to specify whom I'm referring to.

"Not a peep. It's weird. Whatever you guys said to him seems to have worked."

I nod, pulling her in for another kiss as I squeeze her ass and then give it a slap. "Can I see you later?"

Lo bites her lip and nods. "I'm having a couple drinks with Sutton after my shift, but I'll stop by after." She hops off the desk, straightening her ponytail and adjusting her shirt before meeting my eyes again. "Thank you," she says, gesturing toward the bag on the floor. "I'm going to pay you back for all of it. I promise."

"Don't make it a big deal."

"It is to me."

CHAPTER ELEVEN

Lo

"**Y**OU WERE GONE A WHILE," SUTTON REMARKS with a knowing look when I come walking back through the door at Blackbear noticeably less upset.

"We talked," I say, unable to hide my smile.

"Mhm." She doesn't believe me for a second.

We're a girl short today, so Jake asks me to man the bar as well as my tables. We've been swamped with tourists since the first snow a couple of days ago, and from what I hear, this is nothing. We're one of the closest bars that's not on the mountain, so we're the first place people see when they're done. Two guys approach, putting their boards on the rack outside before taking their seats at the bar.

"What can I get you fine gentlemen?" I ask, placing a napkin in front of each one.

"Besides your number?" one asks, earning a punch in the shoulder from the other one.

"Don't mind him. He busted his ass along with his ego on the mountain, then proceeded to get white girl wasted."

I laugh, not offended in the least. "So, water for you then," I joke. "How about some appetizers?" I suggest, thinking it might be a good idea to get something in homeboy's stomach.

"What do you suggest?" the sober one asks while the drunk one fumbles with his phone.

"Our potato skins are pretty life-changing."

"Potato skins and a Rebel IPA it is."

"On it." I reach for a glass as Jake rounds the corner. He greets the customers with a nod, but when his eyes land on me, he frowns. His eyes are locked on my neck, and I pull my hair out of its tie to cover the love bites Dare left me with.

He doesn't comment, though, thankfully. I spend the rest of my shift on autopilot. I can't seem to get Dare out of my mind. At first, I couldn't believe that he thought it was a good idea to buy me expensive things, knowing everything he does about Eric. I can't be bought, and I thought I made that clear. But when I saw what it was, I realized the difference. Dare bought those things for me because he knew I'd need them. Because he *cared*. Eric used to buy me material things—jewelry, electronics, fancy dresses. All frivolous shit that served his own selfish wants and needs.

Dare made Sutton agree not to tell me who it was from. She didn't, but I knew right away it had to be him. Who else would it be? Once I saw the men's clothing, I was done for. The fact that he considered Jess in this whole thing had me swallowing a lump in my throat and fighting back tears. Dare is selfless and kind and caring, but he'd rather slam his hand in a door than let anyone know.

"Ready to drink, bitch?" Sutton asks as we ditch our aprons and freshen up in front of the mirror in the break room.

"Actually, yes." Jess is at wrestling again, and Henry's house is practically vacant.

"You wanna go somewhere else or just drink here?"

"Here," I say, wanting to stay close for reasons I don't want to decipher. Plus, free drinks. Can't beat free.

"I thought you might say that." She rolls her eyes. "But that works because I want to get a tattoo afterward. If I work up enough liquid courage, that is."

"What are you going to get?"

"I want the phases of the moon right here," she says, gesturing to the inside of her upper arm. "Here, let me show you." She pulls out her phone, scrolling before showing me the screen as we walk toward the barstools. It's a vertical row of eight moons in various phases.

"I dig it. And I bet they'd take you as a walk-in. That probably wouldn't take too long."

"Then booze me up, baby!"

"Oh, this should be good." Jake laughs, amused, once we take our seats at the barstools. He doesn't ask what we want. Instead, he slides two lemon drops our way before handing me a beer and Sutton her Jack and Coke. I look down to see two missed calls from a private number, but I don't want to think about Eric right now, so I turn my phone off and stuff it into my bag.

"Thank you, kind sir," Sutton says and then raises her shot glass to mine. "To liquid courage," she declares, and we clink our glasses together.

Liquid courage. I could use some of that. Because this thing with Dare…I think it's starting to get real. And that scares me more than I want to admit. I'm about four beers in when the conversation turns to him. Honestly, I'm surprised it took this long.

"Guys who want casual don't usually buy clothes for you and your little brother, do they?" I ask, maybe a little too loudly.

"Nope," Sutton says, popping the word from her lips. "Especially when they're already getting that ass for free."

"That's what I was afraid of." I prop my chin in the palm of my hand. Somewhere in the recesses of my brain, I register that I essentially just admitted to sleeping with Dare. "I think I like him."

"I think you're an idiot if you're just now realizing it."

"You're a real peach." I laugh, taking another swig of beer. "Are you liquored up enough to get your tattoo yet?"

"As ready as I'll ever be." Sutton downs the rest of her drink and slams it on the bar top. I hop off my stool, and I suddenly feel a little drunker than I thought I was. I feel happy and buzzed and excited at the thought of seeing Dare.

"Be careful," Jake calls after us as we're walking toward the door.

Sutton slings an arm around my shoulder and yells back, "Never," causing Jake to roll his eyes.

"Have you guys ever hooked up?"

"Ew, Jake?"

"Yes! He's kind of protective of you."

Sutton shakes her head. A strand of her sleek black hair gets stuck to my lips with the movement, and I spit it out, making us both laugh.

"No, you dumbass. He's protective of *you*," she says right as we enter Bad Intentions. My face screws up in confusion. Jake barely knows me. *Why would he feel protective of me?*

"What up, girl?" Matty greets me, pulling me in for a hug.

"I brought you a present," I say, gesturing to Sutton.

"Got time for a walk-in?"

"Hell yeah. What do you have in mind?"

Sutton nods, and she pulls out her phone. The two of them start discussing placement and coloring, but I check out of the conversation when I see Dare. His head is down as he ambles in from the back. A pencil in his mouth, sketchbook in hand. A piece of dark hair hangs in front of one eye, and he jerks his head to flip it out of the way. Once he notices me, he falters for half a second.

"Hi," I say, walking toward him.

"Hey, Sally," he says with a smirk. He sits at his stool, and I follow, plopping down on his tattoo chair thingy.

"What is this thing called, anyway?" I ask, swinging my legs onto the chair, then leaning back into a reclining position. "I should probably know these things. I'm like the worst tattoo shop girl ever."

Dare chuckles. "A...tattoo chair?" he says like it's the most obvious thing in the world. "Client chair, if you're fancy."

"Pft. Fancy is my middle name."

Dare squints one eye, assessing. "Something is different."

"What?"

"You're drunk."

"I mean...I'm not *not* drunk," I admit, earning another laugh from him. I love the sound. "I like it when you're happy." As soon as the words are out of my mouth, my cheeks burn hot. I didn't mean to say it out loud. Not much embarrasses me, but revealing too much about how I feel is the exception.

"I like it when you're unfiltered," he counters.

"I'm *always* unfiltered."

"I like it when you're forthcoming then. How's that?"

The only one I've been lying to is myself about how I feel for him. I don't say that, though.

Matty and Sutton come from the direction of the drawing room, and she sits in his chair, next to Dare's station. I didn't even notice that they had gone back there. Matty coats the inside of Sutton's arm with a mixture of soap and water before applying the stencil to her skin.

"Check it out," he says, handing her a handheld mirror.

"Perfect," she beams. "Let's do this."

"I want a tattoo," I declare suddenly.

"As much as I'd love that—and I would fucking love it *a lot*—no can do."

"I'll do it!" Cordell calls from somewhere in the back. I whip my head in his direction, but I still don't see him. I didn't even know he was here.

"The fuck you will!" Dare yells over his shoulder before turning his attention back to me. "You're drunk. I can't tattoo you tonight."

"But Sutton's drunk, too." Resorting to tattling to get my way. It's a new low for me.

"Am not! I had *one* drink! You had like five. Proceed," she says to Matty with a wave of her hand. Come to think of it, besides the lemon drop, she did nurse the same drink the whole time.

"Come on, Dare Bear." I stick out my bottom lip, and he lifts an eyebrow, clearly amused. *I need to up my game.* "I think I want it *riiiiight* here," I say, folding the band of my leggings down dangerously low. Dare's eyes narrow, and I bite my bottom lip at the look in them. He groans before slipping a finger underneath, slowly pulling them back into place. My skin breaks out in goosebumps, and he gives me a knowing look. "You're always so cold."

Something dark passes over Dare's features as his eyes lock onto mine, but he shakes it away. "If you're serious about it and you still want one tomorrow, we'll talk. Besides the fact that you could change your mind when your buzz wears off, you'll probably bleed more and delay your healing process. I'm not doing that to you." The hand that adjusted my pants has curved around my hip, and even that slight touch has my insides feeling floaty, like a balloon full of helium.

"Fine."

"Do you know what you want?"

I haven't thought that far ahead. Instead of admitting that, I say, "I want you to choose."

"What?" His forehead scrunches up, confusion written all over that pretty face.

"You heard me. I want something that represents me. Something beautiful. I trust you." As I'm saying it, I realize how true it is. Dare is *covered* in beautiful. I trust his taste. He's also insanely talented.

"You sure about that?" Dare asks, his voice a little raspier than before. I nod, looking deep into his eyes to convey my sincerity.

The door dings, effectively breaking the moment. Dare excuses himself to greet the customer, who's a walk-in, and I opt to hang out with Cordell to pass the time.

"Wanna shoot some pool?" Cord asks, handing me a bottle of beer from the fridge.

"Depends on if you can handle being beat by a girl."

"I'll try my best," Cord says, laughing. I might be exaggerating my skills, but I'm decent. I practically grew up in the shithole bars that Crystal dragged us to while she was on the hunt for men, money, drugs, or a combination of the three. Jess was too young to realize what was going on, so I made it fun for him by letting him pick the songs on the free jukebox and playing pool.

Jess actually got so good that he was hustling grown ass men by the age of seven. They were very *drunk* men who were shit at pool in the first place, but it was impressive nonetheless. Naturally, Crystal saw an opportunity and tried to use him to her advantage. That's when I started insisting we stay home. We could scheme and hustle all day long, but I wasn't going to let her benefit. I never understood why we had to go with her in the first place. I was eleven, but I'd been babysitting Jess since the ripe old age of seven. It didn't occur to me until later that maybe we were unknowingly part of her scheming. People always felt bad for kids and animals. If only she'd had a dog…

I lean forward and break, making my shot. "I call solids."

Cord's eyes widen just a little. "Lucky shot."

"Totally." I laugh.

I'm rusty and intoxicated, but I end up winning the first game, which prompts Cordell to declare, "Best two out of three." He wins the second, and then the third, but it was a close game.

"BOOM!" he yells, throwing his hands in the air. Dare must be finished, because he shows up, looking between the two of us. "I won," he explains to Dare. I roll my eyes.

"Only because I scratched on the eight ball."

"Aw, don't be a sore loser." He throws an arm around my shoulders, turning his attention to Dare. "Your girl here has mad skills."

"You have no idea."

His insinuation, along with the fact that he didn't deny me being "his girl," has my stomach flipping with anticipation. As if reading the look in my eyes, Dare reaches for my hand and pulls me toward him.

"You have your keys?" he asks Cordell.

"Yeah, yeah. Get out of here."

Dare drags me through the shop, and I practically have to run to keep up. I stop to admire Sutton's tattoo for half a second before she waves me off, telling me she'll show me tomorrow. We're almost to the truck when Dare asks me where my coat is.

"Shit. I left my stuff at Blackbear." How was that only earlier today? It's been the longest day ever.

"Wait in the truck."

A minute later, he's back, bags in hand. He tosses me my jacket, shoving the rest into the back seat. I put it on and zip it up to my chin.

"Good?"

"It's perfect."

Dare gives a brusque nod before starting the truck.

"Thank you."

"You don't have to keep thanking me," he says, scratching at the hair at the back of his neck, his signature move when he feels uncomfortable.

"I want to." And I plan to thank him in other ways tonight.

The rest of the ride is filled with sexual tension so thick you could cut it with a knife. I know exactly what's going to happen when we get to his house. Hell, the whole shop knows exactly what's going to happen.

When we pull up, Dare retrieves my bags from the back and carries them inside. He drops them at the door before turning to me. Sliding a cold hand around the back of my neck, he leans his forehead down to rest against mine.

"You're always so warm," he says, slipping his other hand up the back of my shirt. I shiver, but I lean into his touch anyway, gladly giving away all my warmth. Letting my purse fall to the floor, I push up on my toes, bringing my lips to his stubbled cheek. Dare clenches his eyes shut, as if in physical pain. I leave another kiss next to the first, then another, and another. I cup his cheek with one hand, pressing my lips to his sharp jaw, making my way to his mouth. I kiss his top lip first, and his mouth parts, letting me explore. When I suck the bottom one into my mouth, he groans, lifting me by my ass, and finally kisses me back.

He surprises me when he walks me over to the counter, sitting me on top of one of the barstools. He moves to the fridge, grabbing himself a bottled water, then stands on the opposite side of the counter.

"Don't tell me you're not going to fuck me, either," I say, disappointment lacing my tone.

"You may be too drunk for a tattoo, but I never said anything about being too drunk to fuck."

Thank God. Dare opens the lid before tipping the bottle to his lips. God, even the way his throat moves when he swallows is sexy. As soon as the bottle hits the counter, I slide it toward me and take a drink. Dare rounds the counter, coming to a stop behind me. His arms circle my middle, and he reaches for the zipper of my jacket, pulling down. He peels it off me, letting it fall to the floor, nudging it aside with his foot.

His hand flattens against my chest, and I wonder if he can feel my heartbeat kicking furiously at his touch.

He smooths his palm up my neck, then his fingers wrap around my throat.

"I want you," he says, his lips against my ear.

"Have me." I roll my head to the side, giving him access to my neck as my eyelids fall shut.

"I want you every day. And I don't want anyone else to have you." His nose grazes up and down the length of my neck.

"I think that's called a relationship," I breathe. He freezes, halting his movements.

"Then that's what I want."

I don't trust my ears. Eyes flying open, I twist my head to look into his eyes. *He's serious.* There are a million and one reasons we shouldn't be together. The timing is all wrong. But something inside me tells me this is different. Something in the air tells me things are shifting. Something in his eyes tells me he feels it, too.

I tilt my head back to answer him with a kiss. His thumb strokes my cheek before the hand at my neck glides down to grip my breast over my shirt as he deepens the kiss.

I arch my back, pressing into Dare's hand, and he pinches my nipple through the thin fabric, causing a moan to slip free. Suddenly, his hands are gone as he kneels behind me. I don't get a chance to ask what he's doing before a palm between my shoulder blades forces me to lean forward.

I'm bent over the counter, feet on the bar of the stool, ass lifted from the seat. I jump when he smacks two hands against both cheeks, then squeezes hard. I feel his breath through my leggings—which aren't much thicker than a pair of tights—and then he's biting me through the

186

material. My breathing grows harsh as he continues grazing his teeth up and down my thighs, my ass. Sometimes soft nibbles, sometimes hard enough to make me squirm.

I feel his face move between my legs. He uses his teeth to bite a hole before ripping them wide. I gasp when I hear the *rip*, feeling the cold air hit me a second before his tongue does.

Holy shit.

My elbows are firmly planted on the counter, and I drop my head down as he licks me. My thighs burn from holding this position and my arms are already shaking, but I don't dare do anything that will stop what he's doing to me. Dare clutches my hips, arching my butt higher. He eats at me, devouring me from front to back and everything in between.

"Oh my God," I cry, my own voice sounding foreign to my ears. Dare nudges me high enough to get underneath me—the back of his head resting on the leather-cushioned stool—before pulling me back down to straddle his face, spreading my legs open wide. His hands that lead to tattooed wrists hook around the tops of my shaky thighs.

"Fuck my face, Lo."

I start to move above him, rocking my hips, but Dare pulls me down, flush against his mouth. I brace my hands on the edge of the counter as he grips my hips. I watch his face move between my legs, shamelessly grinding against his mouth. He licks me from ass to clit, and I shudder at the foreign sensation.

"You like that?" he asks, his voice taunting, but I'm too wrapped up in lust to be embarrassed. I nod enthusiastically, unable to focus on words. Suddenly, he slides out from underneath me, and I could cry at the loss. He drags a hand down his mouth, wiping my wetness from his stubble.

"Turn around." His tone has shifted, along with the look in his eyes. The sweet words and gentle touches were Stefan, but this is Dare, and my stomach swirls with excitement.

I sit back down on the stool, facing the opposite way. Dare walks around the counter and reaches into a high cabinet, his icy eyes heavy-lidded, before coming to stand behind me again. I hear him fiddling with something, unscrewing a cap, maybe, before he sets the white glass jar labeled *coconut oil* onto the counter next to me, the lid falling to the floor with a loud clang.

Dare's hands on my hips slide me backwards so my ass is hanging off the stool. I don't have time to question it before his hands are there, between my legs, coating everything. I hear him undressing behind me as I hold my breath, waiting for his next move. I'm shaking for him, for whatever he's about to give me.

I don't have to wait long, because two seconds later, I feel his tip notching against my entrance, hot and hard. He slides into my pussy effortlessly, thanks to my arousal and the coconut oil. Knees locked together, I push back against him, but after a few thrusts, he pulls out with a curse.

"I don't want to come in your pussy this time," he explains, dragging the head of his cock through my lips and back toward my other hole. He nudges against my ass, rubbing and circling but never fully penetrating. I should be nervous at what I know is about to happen. I've never done this. But Dare has a way of making everything feel good, even when it's outside my comfort zone.

Dare leans over, covering my back with his front. He

bites my shoulder hard enough that I know I'll have a mark tomorrow before asking, "Has anyone fucked your ass before?" His voice is strained in my ear.

"No," I breathe.

"Tell me I can take it. Tell me I can be the first."

"Take it," I all but beg, pushing onto him again.

Dare's weight is gone as he stands behind me once more, haphazardly digging four fingers into the jar before lubing me up some more. I look behind me to see him using the excess to coat his cock before he's pushing against the tight ring. I lock up, not expecting the sharp sting, but Dare soothes me, rubbing my back and thighs, coaxing me to loosen up.

"Relax, baby," he says before nibbling on my shoulder, softer this time. He snakes a hand in between my legs, playing with my clit as he starts to move again. I melt into his touch, his pretty words. Slowly, so slowly, he nudges inside. I feel the moment he pushes past the tight muscle, and I slump forward on the counter in relief.

"I feel so full."

Dare groans at my admission, pumping his hips a little faster after giving me a minute to adjust. I half-moan, half-whine at the feeling. "Play with your pussy," he instructs as his hands move back to spread my ass. I look over my shoulder once more, watching him as he watches himself move inside me. His lean abs flex with each thrust and I do as he says, rubbing my clit. The heady mixture of pain and pleasure is like nothing I've ever felt before.

Soon, he's fucking me just as hard as he would my pussy, and my whole body is vibrating, shaking with the sensations running through me. I feel drugged, completely out of my mind. My body is on sensory overload.

Over-stimulated to the point that tears stream down my cheeks.

Dare pulls my back to his front, arms wrapping around me as he ruts into me, his hips slapping against my ass that's still half-covered by my ripped leggings. One arm dips down to cup me between the legs while his other arm wraps around my neck.

"Fuck my hand while I fuck your ass," Dare rasps into my ear. "Come for me, Lo."

His words send me over the edge as I grind against his hand while he fucks up into me without remorse.

"I'm coming," I cry, holding his hand in place while I ride it. He curls two fingers inside me, hitting a spot that makes my eyes roll back as I spasm around him.

"Fuck," Dare grinds out. "Your ass is squeezing me so hard."

I slump forward with my cheek pressed onto the cold granite countertop, my palms flat against the smooth surface. Dare's hands come over the tops of mine, folding his fingers between my own as he gives two more powerful strokes. I feel the moment he spills inside me, and then he's sinking against me, kissing the notches in my spine before he slowly pulls out of my spent body.

We're depleted and sweaty, lying on top of Dare's couch as he traces his fingertips up and down my side. He's on his side behind me, head propped on his hand, my ripped leggings and the rest of our clothes strewn all over the floor.

"I love tickles," I say sleepily, as goosebumps pepper my skin.

"Did I hurt you?" he asks. I'm raw and sore, but I'm still in a state of euphoria, I think.

"A little," I say, downplaying it. "But I liked it."

That same dark look flashes in his eyes again. "I didn't mean to lose control."

I roll toward him, my eyebrows cinched together in confusion. Our noses are almost touching with how close we are. "What are you talking about? You didn't. I literally asked for it."

He looks away, clenching his jaw, but I flatten my palm against his cheek, forcing him to look at me. His stubbled jaw scratches against my skin, and it dawns on me that I get to touch him like this, when no one else does. It's a thrilling thought, as weird as that may seem.

"Talk to me. You know all my shit." Dare opened up about his past, but I suspect there's still more.

"I *told* you my shit," he bites back, and I flinch, taken aback by his tone. His eyes soften at my reaction, and he grabs the back of my head, pulling me under his chin. My cheek is pressed against his chest, and I inhale deeply. I could drown in his piney scent.

"I was an angry kid, and an even angrier teenager," he starts. I wonder if it's easier for him to talk this way—with me tucked into his chest rather than looking me in the eye. "I had anger management issues. Abandonment issues. Authority issues," he ticks off. "Basically, every *issue*. Self-control was always my weak point. I fucked shit up, and I fought. A lot." He takes a deep breath, and I hear the steady beat of his heart against my ear. I don't respond. I'm not the best at this whole feeling-sharing thing either, so I stay silent, waiting for him to continue.

"When I was sixteen, I almost went to prison. I've spent the last ten years making sure I'm not that kid anymore."

"That's it?" I say, tilting my head back far enough to meet those eyes that are bluer than water that this town is so well-known for. "You *almost* went to prison?"

Dare looks at me questioningly. "I was a fucking monster. Is that not enough for you?" There's no heat behind his words. He states them as a fact. As if he were merely commenting on the weather.

"You didn't *actually* go, though? Did you at least get to wear handcuffs? Or sit in the back of a cop car?"

"*That*, I have done," he says, the corners of his lip tugging into an almost smile.

"Meh," I tease, unimpressed. "You're still behind most of the people I grew up with." So, he has a temper. Big deal. Show me a kid who's been through half the shit he's gone through who *doesn't* have anger issues.

"I never know what's going to come out of your mouth," Dare muses.

"I don't care about your past," I say truthfully, because, you know, *glass houses* and all that. I'm not exactly in a position to judge.

I'm blissfully drifting to sleep when I hear my phone buzzing from the inside of my purse. I groan and start to sit up, but Dare stops me with a hand on my shoulder.

"Where is it?" he asks. I point toward the door.

"In my purse."

Dare squats to pick it up. "Got enough shit in here?" he asks, rummaging through my bag. "Found it." He pulls my phone out triumphantly, walking back toward me. It stops buzzing but starts again by the time it's in my hands. Jess' name flashes across the screen.

"Hey," I say. "How was practice?"

"Fine. Listen, don't come home."

"What?" I sit up so quickly, I almost crack heads with Dare. My heart threatens to pound out of my chest because I know, *I just know,* something isn't right. "What's wrong?"

"I'm fine. But I'm looking out the blinds right now, and either I'm super fucking baked or Eric is parked across the street. I think it's both."

Fuck. I didn't even give him a heads-up because I thought for sure Eric would've given it up by now.

"I'm gonna go outside and have a little chat with him. I just wanted to make sure you weren't on your way home."

"I'm at Dare's, but Jesse, *do not* go out there. I don't know what the fuck Eric's thinking."

Upon hearing Eric's name, Dare stands and practically runs up the stairs.

"I've been waiting a minute to fuck this fool up," Jess says, sounding almost excited. I shake my head, knowing that Stubborn Jesse does whatever the hell he wants. Always has, always will.

Dare flies back downstairs in black sweats and a long-sleeved black shirt. He swipes his keys out of the pile of shit we left at the door in our haste, then throws his boots on.

"Where are you going?"

"Tell him to stay inside till I get there."

"Goddammit, Dare! I don't need you to fight my battles."

"The fuck you don't. Stay here," he says, and then he's gone, the door slamming behind him. I drop the phone, scrambling to find my clothes, but my leggings are ripped and full of cum. By the time I throw Dare's T-shirt on, he's already peeling out of his driveway.

"Fuck!" I kick the side of his couch.

"Lo!"

Shit. Jesse. I pick the phone back up, bringing it to my ear.

"Dare's coming."

"Oh, goodie. Two against one. This should be fun."

"Please don't do anything stupid."

"Who, me? Never."

I can hear the smirk in his voice, and it does nothing to calm my nerves. He hangs up without another word. I try to call Dare, for the first time ever, but it goes straight to voicemail. I clasp my phone between both hands, bringing them to rest under my chin as I pace the living room floor.

This night is never-ending.

CHAPTER TWELVE
Dare

T HIS MOTHERFUCKER. I THOUGHT ERIC WOULD HAVE taken the hint, but clearly, he needs a little more convincing. I try to calm myself on the way to Henry's, taking deep breaths, not wanting to lose control like I did last time.

But is it really so bad to protect the people I care about? Because I do. Care about Lo, that is. She's wormed her way through the frozen cracks, and she's been slowly melting the ice inside me ever since.

I flip on my brights when I pull onto their street. I see Jess on one side of the road, a cigarette dangling from his lips, casually holding a baseball bat in his right hand. Eric is outside of his Range Rover with his arms folded across his suit-covered chest. *Douche.*

I swing into the driveway and jump out, leaving the truck running. This won't take long. I walk up to stand next to Jess. "What is this, the fucking Wild Wild West? Are we about to have a shootout?"

"I'm just waiting for this pussy to step foot on Henry's property," he says, flicking his chin in Eric's direction. He looks over to me, lowering his voice. "I promised Lo I'd be good." He shrugs. "But if he steps to me, it's fair game."

Cutting the bullshit, I walk over to Eric.

"Well, if it isn't Logan's knight in shitty tattoos, here to save the day." His face is still busted up from the other day, and I get more satisfaction than I should from the sight of him.

"Did you come here for a reason, or were you just planning to stand outside her house like a fucking creep?"

"I came to talk to Logan. I'm simply waiting until she gets home."

I suck my teeth before saying, "Well, you'll be waiting a while. She won't be coming home tonight."

Eric huffs out a laugh. "Let me guess. She's staying at your trailer tonight."

"Yeah. Something like that."

Eric's eyes narrow, probably pissed that he missed the mark in his attempt to insult me. I don't give a flying fuck what anyone thinks about me, especially this asshole. He leans in closely, but I don't back away. This guy is used to intimidating people. He's not getting that from me.

"She tastes sweet, doesn't she?" He inhales deeply, closing his eyes like he's reliving a fond memory.

My fists clench at my sides, but, still, I don't react. Don't even respond.

"You should have her do that thing with her tong—"

I bob my head in a nod as if to say, *okay, we're gonna do this?* striding away before he's even finished his sentence. He laughs, thinking he won. Jess knows my plan, though, because he casually hands me the bat once I'm within arm's reach. The look on his face tells me that if I didn't do something, he would. I turn back for Eric, and I see the moment the fear finally sets in.

"What, regular old assault isn't enough? You're going

to add *aggravated* assault to the list?"

I don't answer him. I'm completely calm on the outside, even though I'm raging inside, fucking dying to bust his head open. Once he realizes I'm not bluffing, he jumps out of the way. But I'm not going for him. I'm aiming for that shiny Range Rover behind him.

I hit one headlight first, then my bat cracks against the other.

"What the fuck!"

I go for the hood next, gripping the bat with both hands, swinging it straight down.

"Okay. Okay! I get it. You're a tough guy. You've made your point," he yells, holding both hands out in front of him.

"See, I don't think I have. I'm just getting started," I say between hits, and I hear Jess laughing behind me.

"You're psychotic."

"That's what they tell me." Heard a lot over the years.

I bash his side mirror off next, and it falls to the pavement with a satisfying crunch. Once I go for the windshield, Eric rushes to the driver's side. It takes a good two or three hits before I'm able to bust through the tempered glass, but it finally gives right as he starts the engine, sending glass all over him and the seats. He hits the gas and speeds off down the street, sans headlights.

I walk back over to Jess and hand him the bat. "That was fun."

"And I didn't even have to get my hands dirty. Now Lo won't chew my ass out."

"I might not be so lucky."

Jess laughs.

"Can I use your phone?" I ask, knowing Lo is probably

out of her mind at this point, worrying about Jesse. My phone is dead and forgotten in a pocket somewhere at home.

Jess looks at me, assessing, before flicking his cigarette to the ground. "Sure. It's inside."

I follow him inside. The first thing I notice is that it's pitch-black, the only light coming from the flickering of a candle that sits on top of the coffee table. The second thing I notice is the fact that somehow, it feels even colder inside than it does outside.

Jesse retrieves his phone from the couch and hands it to me before sprawling out, folding his arms behind his head like this is his normal. And fuck, I can't help but see myself in him. How many times was I without heat or electricity...or food for that matter? How long have they been living like this?

I walk into the kitchen, checking the top of the fridge and the junk drawer, until I find what I'm looking for, stuffing it into the back of my sweats.

"Let's go," I say, dropping his phone back on his lap.

"Where?"

"My house."

"Nah, man. It's late and this wrestling shit has me beat."

"Does your sister know the power's out?"

Jess shrugs. "No idea."

He isn't like most high school kids—that much is clear—but he's still just that. A *kid*. He wants a warm bed and a hot meal, but he won't say that shit. I know this because I *was* this kid. Too stubborn to ask. Too proud to take a handout. And that's exactly why I won't leave him here. I just need to present it in a way that doesn't resemble pity.

"Your sister's pretty freaked out. I'm sure she wants to see that you're okay."

He's not dumb. He knows my angle. But he nods anyway, taking the out I offered, grabbing his backpack from the floor before stuffing a sweatshirt inside.

"I've gotta stop and get some gas."

"Ride with me. I'll drop you off at school tomorrow. I have to come back this way anyway."

Wordlessly, Jess walks over to the door and picks up his board, sticking it underneath his arm.

Once we're in the truck, we don't speak. Both too fucking tired to force conversation just for the sake of it. Jess stuffs his earbuds in his ears, leaning his head against the window for the duration of the drive.

As soon as my headlights shine on my house, Lo throws open the door, standing there in my T-shirt and socks up to her knees that I recognize from my little shopping spree with Briar and Mollie, arms folded across her chest.

"Annnnd, she's pissed," Jesse says with a chuckle, wrapping the cord of his earbuds up before stashing them in his backpack.

We both approach her like a couple of dogs that just shit all over the carpet, but once Jess is within reach, she pulls him in for a hug. "You good?" she asks, holding his cheeks in her hands. He nods, and she ruffles his hair before jerking her chin, telling him without words to wait inside.

"I didn't touch him," I say before she gets a chance to speak up. "I exhibited excellent self-control." It's technically the truth. I took my anger out on his Range Rover instead of his face.

Lo stares at me intently, and I don't know whether she's going to punch me or hug me. She does neither.

"Don't leave me like that again," she says, pointing a stern finger at me. "You made me feel like he did. Like I'm a child, incapable of making my own decisions. Like I'm something you…own. I don't like it. I've been taking care of Jess and me all by myself for a long time now."

The fact that she can even compare me to that piece of shit pisses me off. I get that she's still raw from that asshole, but she has to see the difference.

"That's the thing. You don't have to fucking do it alone." I reach for her hand, and she lets me pull her into me. Lo wraps her arms around my waist, and I bask in the warmth that seeps into me.

"I don't know how to do that," she admits, propping her chin against the center of my chest as she looks up at me.

"I'll be Jack and you'll be Sally," I joke, and she huffs out a reluctant laugh.

"Thank you for bringing him here. I'm sorry I snapped at you. I hate feeling helpless. It makes me ragey."

"I know. I'm sorry." I lean down to kiss her on her forehead, and her eyelids flutter shut. "Did you know there's no heat or power at Henry's?"

"What?" She pulls back. I figured she wouldn't just leave him there like that. I nod, running my hands up her arms to keep her warm.

"Let's talk inside. It's cold as fuck."

"Wait," she says, stopping me. "Are you sure?"

"Yeah. It was dark inside. Figured maybe he was just going to sleep. But it was freezing in there. I had to talk him into coming with me."

She shakes her head. "I didn't know. I mean, it's not the first time this has happened. But we've never lived in the arctic fucking tundra before."

I pull her inside and shut the door behind us. Jess sits on the couch, looking half-asleep.

"Help yourself to whatever food you can find if you're hungry. There's a bed for you upstairs. First door on the right," I tell him.

"Thanks, man."

"I'll be up soon," Lo says as I walk up the stairs to give them some time to talk.

"How…domestic," Jess remarks, and I hear Lo tell him to shut up right before I close my door.

I take off my clothes, leaving my boxer briefs on since Jesse's staying over. I fall onto my bed, thinking about how much chaos has fallen into my lap since Lo entered my life, but even more troubling is the fact that I don't mind the mess. It's a nice reprieve from my own.

When I wake up, it's still insanely early. Too early. My own personal furnace is lying halfway on top of me, one of her legs between mine, cheek smashed against my chest. I brush the hair out of her face with my fingers, noticing how young and innocent she looks in her sleep. Sometimes I forget she's only twenty-one.

Slipping out from underneath her, I walk quietly to my bathroom, making sure not to wake her. She had a long night. Shit, this girl has had a long *life*. I take a piss and brush my teeth before throwing my black jeans and hoodie on. My cabinets are pathetically bare, so I decide to stop by Sissy's and Belle's for some coffee and breakfast to bring back.

Jess is still asleep, if the colossal fucking snores coming from his room are anything to go by. Once I'm downstairs, I glance at the time on the stove. Six thirty. I don't remember what the fuck time high school starts, but I'm guessing around eight, so I have time.

Sissy and Bella are elderly sisters, and two of the small group of people who never treated me any differently. Sissy runs the coffee shop while Belle runs the diner. You'd think they hated each other with how much they bicker, but that's just how they've always been. Ever since I've known them anyway. I grab a couple of orders of waffles before heading over to get coffee from Sissy. You can't go to one without the other.

Sissy hands me a drink carrier full of coffees, then walks out from behind the counter with a bag of extra pastries, like always, as she gives me shit about seeing "that old hag" next door before coming to see her. When I remind her that she's the older sibling, she flips me off.

"Nice to see you, too, Sissy."

CHAPTER THIRTEEN

Lo

WHEN I WOKE UP THIS MORNING, DARE WASN'T here. A sense of panic rose inside of me. Then I panicked even more *because* I was panicking. Panicking equals falling for someone. *Depending* on someone. And as soon as that happens, they leave. Everybody leaves.

So much for not getting attached.

As I wash my hair—helping myself to Dare's shower—the rational side of my brain starts to wake up. He probably had an errand to run, or something. Last night, he implied that he wanted a relationship. Nothing happened to change that in the middle of the night, and he did go out of his way to make sure Jess and I had clothes to survive the winter that we severely underestimated, fucked me like he worshipped me, then bailed my little brother out of a potentially dangerous situation.

Those aren't the actions of a man who plans to leave.

Once I'm finished, I step out, my wet hair dripping onto the cold floor. I wrap myself in a towel, then brush my teeth with my finger, which is about as effective as it sounds, but it's better than nothing. Remembering the clothes downstairs, I run to grab the bags and dump the contents out onto Dare's bed.

Jesus. He really went all out. Beanies, leggings, thermals, boots, long-sleeved T-shirts, a pair of gloves, more of the socks that I plucked off the top of the bag last night. Something lacy catches my eye, and I fish it out from underneath one of those puffy vests. I hold it up in front of me. It's strappy, black lingerie, and I can't help but laugh. So maybe his motives weren't *purely* selfless.

I decide on a light gray fitted hoodie with the black puffy vest and leggings. I'm surprised to find that not only does it fit, but it still feels like…*me*. I pull on the pair of tan boots with a black toe. They're fur-lined and probably the most comfortable thing my foot has ever been inside. They're maybe half a size too big, but with the right socks, they'll be perfect.

I hear the alarm on Jess' phone go off, so I scoop his stuff up and make my way to the room he stayed in. He's sitting on the edge of bed, shirtless, hands in his hair, appearing to still be half-asleep.

"Hey. Got some things for you," I say, lifting the bag. He eyes it suspiciously.

"What's all that?"

"Just some warm clothes. Boots."

"Where'd it come from?"

I drop my shoulders, sitting next to him on the bed. "Dare."

"Ah." He nods. "Eric two point oh?"

"It's not like that with Dare. I really like him."

"And it has nothing to do with the fact that he has money and you have…assets?"

"Fuck you, Jess," I say, standing. "That was a low blow."

Sure, at first, that was part of the appeal with Eric. But

Jess knows it was more complicated than that.

"My bad," he says. "For what it's worth, I actually like this guy. It just looks a lot like how things started with Eric."

It's not the same. Not even a little. But Jesse wouldn't know that. He wouldn't know that I've felt more for Dare in the first week of knowing him than I ever felt for Eric, or that Dare fought this thing between us just as much as I did.

"I think he's broken, Jess. He's broken, but he still tries to save me every single day. The job, the clothes, the defending of my questionable honor," I say, huffing out a laugh that lacks humor. "He brought you here when I was too wrapped up in my own shit to realize my little brother was without fucking heat or lights." I'm still beating myself up for that one. Jess has always been my first priority, and I slipped up this time.

"Oh, come on, Lo." Jess rolls his eyes. "We've probably lived half our lives without that shit."

"It's not the same. You were alone."

"Quit being dramatic. Look, if this guy makes you happy, fuck the rest. I don't think you've ever done a goddamn thing for yourself. I'm not eight anymore, Lo. You don't have to take care of me."

"That's not true. We take care of *each other*. Always." I need Jess to know that I'm not going anywhere. Ever. "Like, it's going to be you, your future wife, and then me hanging out in one of the eighteen spare rooms in your mansion when you become a legitimate hacker for the government or some shit. You aren't getting rid of me."

Jess cracks a smile, picking at a piece of fuzz on his pants.

"How were things with Henry the other night?" I've been meaning to ask him.

"Good," he says, and I wait for the *but* that never comes. "He offered to take me to my first meet. I guess he did wrestling in high school, too."

"Wow," I say, shocked and impressed…and maybe a little hurt that I didn't even know about his meet. "When is it? I'll see if I can request the day off."

"It's like an hour and a half away. Henry said he'd get us a hotel room and we'd make a weekend trip out of it."

"I still want to go," I insist, and he nods. I'm proud of Henry for stepping up. I'm wary, but optimistic. Jess needs this. I just hope it doesn't backfire.

"I'll send you the information. It's in my locker."

I lean over to give him a one-armed hug, then pull away, wrinkling my nose. "You smell like a foot. Why don't you go take a shower and get ready for school?"

"Blame your stalker. He was the one who cockblocked my shower."

"What did Eric say to you, anyway?"

Jess shrugs a shoulder. "Not shit. He just said he wanted to talk to you."

"That's it?"

"That was it. Well, until your new boyfriend came and smashed your old boyfriend's car to pieces."

"What?" I screech, right as I hear Dare's truck pull up.

"Sorry, I'd say more, but my shower calls."

"Asshole."

Jess walks away, chuckling, and I make my way down the stairs to meet Dare at the bottom. I stand on the last step, arms crossed, waiting for him. He walks in, hands full of coffees and two white paper bags.

"Morning, Sally." He extends the drink carrier toward me in offering, but I don't take one.

"What happened last night? Did you lie to me?"

"Your brother's got a big mouth." Dare sighs, setting the drinks and bags onto the floor, before walking up to me. He still towers over me, even with the extra inches from the step. His arms circle my waist. I arch an eyebrow, waiting for an answer.

"I didn't lie—not technically. I didn't touch *him*. He ran his mouth, so instead of killing him, like I wanted to, I beat up his car instead."

I shake my head, hating that he's involved in this at all. "You shouldn't have done that."

"Why are you worrying about him?" he asks, his voice slightly more accusatory than I'm okay with.

"I'm not worried about him, you idiot. I'm worried about *you*. This isn't your mess." Eric isn't used to rejection. The man probably never heard the word *no* before I came along. It's not about me. It's about winning. He's like a child throwing a tantrum, and everyone knows the fastest way to make it go away is to ignore it.

"I'm a big boy, Lo," he says, his hands smoothing down the dip in my lower back before palming my ass. Ducking his head down, his nose burrows into my still-wet hair, and I feel his breath on my neck. "I can make my own decisions."

"I have to admit…you getting all protective does get me kind of hot."

"Oh, yeah?"

"Mhm." I nod, bottom lip between my teeth. "But you're still an idiot."

"Yeah, well, this idiot brought you the best cherry

danish you'll ever have. Where's Jesse?"

"Shower," I answer simply, as if I'm not swooning on the inside. Dare nods.

"These the new clothes?" he asks, backing up to look me up and down.

"What do you think? Do I look like a real local now?"

"Hotter," he says. "But I can't take all the credit. I had some help from Briar and Mollie."

"Ah, that would explain the lingerie." I laugh.

"Say what now?" Dare asks, hooking a finger into the neck of my shirt and peeking inside. I slap his hand away, earning a groan.

"Later." Besides, I'm not wearing the pretty stuff right now.

Jess barrels down the stairs, louder than a herd of elephants, and helps himself to a cup of coffee. "What's in the bag?" he says, eyeing it like he's about to score something illegal.

"Pastries," Dare says flatly. He bends over and fishes something out before handing the bag to Jess. "Go to town."

Jess doesn't need to be told twice, taking it over to the counter to inspect the goods. Dare hands me a danish with cherries and cream cheese in the middle. The sweet, tart smell alone has my mouth watering, but the taste is what has my eyes rolling back into my head.

"This is amazing," I say around a mouthful. Dare's eyes land on my lips. He swipes his thumb across the bottom one before sucking the excess off.

"Ready to go?" Jess asks. Dare clears his throat and schools his features before turning around.

"Ready when you are."

Jess shrugs his backpack over one shoulder while I grab my purse, making sure to bring my danish and coffee, then we're on our way.

"What are you up to today?" Dare asks as we near Henry's house.

"Well, it just happens to be my first full day off. I thought I'd grab some groceries and other necessities. Look around for a place to rent." Buying warm clothes is one less worry, thanks to him.

"Still want to get your tattoo?" He surprises me by asking. I smile, sheepish, having forgotten about that with everything else that went down.

"Clearly, the alcohol clouded my ability to think rationally. I can't afford that right now."

"Oh, you didn't know about the employee discount? Free-ninety-nine."

"I am not taking a free tattoo," I say, bringing the warm cup of coffee to my lips.

"It's only fair, since I get to pick what I put on you. It's basically free advertisement. Really, I should be paying *you*."

I laugh, shaking my head.

"I have some time around six. I wanted to talk to you about something anyway."

Oh, come on.

"You can't just say that and expect me not to freak out all day."

Dare smirks. "Just come see me. Now, get out before you make your brother late for school."

"Fine," I say, opening the door, but he surprises me by grabbing my chin and pulling me in for a kiss. It's slow, but chaste. He smooths his thumb across my chin as his eyes

209

search mine, and there it is again. That shift. It leaves me breathless and hopeful and terrified all at once.

"Don't mind me," Jess says from the back seat, effectively ruining the moment.

"See you tonight," Dare says, his voice husky. I nod before jumping out.

"Call me after school. And don't forget to send me the details for your meet," I say to Jess.

"I won't."

"Love you."

"Love you, too."

I shut the door and watch them drive away, thinking how strange it is that someone else is taking my brother to school. Things like that probably seem so trivial to most people, but it's almost unfathomable to me that someone wants to share my load, to do something nice for nothing in return. It's freeing, but it also makes me anxious and guilty. Like I shouldn't be letting this happen. Like I should take care of my shit on my own. Like it somehow makes me *less than* for accepting help.

I stop inside to grab the keys to the 4Runner and a hair tie to throw my damp hair on top of my head. The temperature inside serves as a reminder that we need to find somewhere to go. Fast. I've been so busy with work and Dare—admittedly—that I haven't had a chance to do much else.

I hit the local grocery store. Stocking up on food for the week that doesn't require a microwave or refrigerating is harder than I thought. I grab some candles, wood for the fireplace, and splurge on some pricey protein bars, thinking Jess could use something to get him through these long wrestling days.

Afterward, I follow up with the only lead on a house I had, only to learn that they've already rented to someone else. I sit in my car, searching for rental listings on my phone. I can't find anything even close to our budget. Not one thing. I drive through neighborhoods for hours—searching out *For Rent* signs—my frustration building with each failed block. I'm all but convinced that we're going to have to move back to The Bay.

"Shit!" I take my anger out on my steering wheel, pounding my fists against the old cracked leather until my hands hurt. I know exactly what will happen if we move back. No school will take Jess back, so he'll drop out. He'll go back to selling drugs and hanging out with the wrong people. Mom will weasel her way back into our lives, and all of this, every single minute of it, will have been for nothing. I'll have to leave this place and these people who have slowly started to feel like home. And *Dare*. I don't even want to think about what that would mean for us.

Dropping my forehead to the steering wheel, I breathe deeply, willing my tears not to fall. I don't know how many times I can fail before I just…give up. If it were just me, I would've thrown in the towel long ago. But Jess? Jess is smart. He can actually go somewhere in life. He deserves the opportunity, and I thought I could give it to him.

My phone buzzes from the seat beside me, and I reach for it.

Jesse: Home. Power's back on.

Huh. I wonder if it wasn't shut off for non-payment. Must have been an outage. I never bothered to mention it to Henry because I figured he'd simply quit paying it since he was moving out.

Me: Nice. Upside-Down Day?

Jess: Hell yeah.

I smile, despite my current state of sadness, loving that he still gets excited about things like that.

I notice the time on my phone and realize it's almost time to meet Dare. Angling the rearview mirror down, I fix my smudged eyeliner, tighten my ponytail, and give myself a mental pep talk.

Suck it up, Lo. You've been in worse situations. You'll figure this out, too.

I decide to run back inside the store to grab what I need for Upside-Down Day since I can use the stove now, then I drop off the groceries at Henry's. The kitchen table is gone. With each load he moves to his shop, my anxiety about finding a place intensifies.

The whole drive to Bad Intentions, I'm racking my brain for a solution that never comes. I don't even know if we have a home to go back to in Oakland. We are, quite literally, out of options.

I park behind the shop, running toward the back door to escape the freezing wind. No one notices my arrival. Matty and Cordell each have clients, but I don't see Alec. Dare sits at his station, his back to me, head down. His foot taps against the floor as he focuses intently on whatever he's working on—a habit I'm not even sure he's aware of.

I walk up behind him, covering his eyes with my hands and kiss his neck.

"Dammit, Cord. How many times do I have to tell you? Not in front of the customers."

"Shut up." I laugh. He tosses his sketchbook to the floor and pulls me onto his lap, my arms automatically circling his neck. I already feel lighter being around him, but heavier at the same time, knowing our time here has an expiration date.

"Hey, Sally. Thought you might chicken out."

"Pft. Do I look like a pussy?"

"Mmm, you are what I eat," he says, wiggling his brows.

"I don't think that's how that saying goes." I bite my lip, suddenly feeling a little apprehensive.

"So, are we doing this?"

"We're doing this," I confirm.

"Do you want to see what I've been working on?" He flicks his chin toward the drawing pad on the floor.

"Nuh-uh. I want it to be a surprise."

Dare pins me with a skeptical look. "You don't want to see something that's going to go on your body forever?"

"Nope," I say resolutely. "Surprise me. I trust you."

Trust. A foreign concept in my life. But, somehow, I do trust him, and not just with the tattoo.

"Okay, then. You're not allowed to be pissed if you hate it."

"Just do it." I roll my eyes, hopping onto the black leather chair.

"I designed it for the top of your thigh, up to about here," he says, pressing a finger into my hip, "but I could tweak it to make it fit between your breasts if you'd rather that. It would look good there, too."

I almost make fun of him for saying *breasts*. He slipped into professional mode so quickly.

"Thigh sounds good. How do you want me?" The question is unintentionally suggestive. Dare shakes his head, pinching the bridge of his nose.

"Lie back on the table. Let's do your right side."

I do as he says, taking off my vest first. I kick my boots off as Dare takes my vest from me and throws it over another chair. Might as well be comfortable as possible as a needle digs into my flesh.

"I'm going to have to pull your pants down. Do you want to go to the private room?"

"I'm good."

Dare nods, slipping his fingers into my waistband. He tugs them down to mid-thigh, then pushes my hoodie up to sit above my waist. The leather chair is cold against my bare skin.

"This okay?"

"Mhm."

Dare pulls the band of my plain white thong down to sit where my pants do before turning around to put on some gloves. When he turns back around, he has a wet paper towel in his hand.

"This is just for the stencil," he explains as he applies a generous amount of the soap and water mix. There's something so sexy about seeing Dare in his element.

"I'm going to put the stencil on now, so try to stay still."

"Okay."

I look at the ceiling, feeling him place the wax paper onto the side of my thigh where the band of my underwear sits, ending right above my hipbone. He peels it back slowly.

"This is the part where I'd ask if you were happy with the placement, but…"

"Just do it," I say before I cave. I'm dying to know what it is. For all I know, he decided to put a giant penis on my hip.

"I'm going to do a small line first, just so you know how it feels."

I hear the buzz of the tattoo gun, and when it touches

my skin, I'm surprised that it doesn't hurt. Not much worse than getting a scratch.

"You good?"

"Yep."

"Okay," he says, giving my knee a squeeze. Such a simple, yet endearing gesture. "This will probably take about two hours if you want to do it all in one go."

"I can do it," I insist.

"Let me know when you need a break."

I nod, and he takes that as his cue to begin. It's not bad at first, but like picking an open wound, over and over, it starts to hurt after a while. There's also something exhilarating about it—cathartic, even. I wonder if that's how it started for Dare—as a way to purge his pain.

As I stare at the beams in the ceiling, I wonder what he wants to talk to me about. I'm dying to ask, but I'm also trying to let him be the one to bring it up. Now doesn't feel like the time to push.

I'm not sure how long passes before Matty's face comes into my line of sight.

"Look who's sober," he says, hovering over me, and I flip him off. Turning to Dare, he says, "That's sick," jerking his chin toward my thigh.

"Thanks. Now stop distracting my client," Dare replies, but there's no bite in his tone. Matty holds up his hands in surrender as he walks away.

"Can you turn onto your side?" Dare asks, pulling the machine away from my leg. I do as he says, rolling onto my right. When he doesn't say anything or make a move to continue, I look behind me, careful not to look at my tattoo, only to find him staring at my very exposed, very *bare* ass.

"This was a bad idea," he says, seemingly to himself, blue eyes full of heat.

"Get back to work."

"Yes, ma'am." He smirks, shaking his head before rolling his chair toward me. The tattoo machine whirs back to life. He leans over me, one gloved hand on my hip, wiping away the excess ink every once in a while with a napkin, while the other one controls the needle that digs into my skin incessantly.

After a while, my right side starts to go numb from lying in the same position, and Dare must notice my squirming, because he stops.

"Let's take a break. We're halfway done." Dare puts his tattoo machine down and snaps his gloves off, tossing them into the trash, before pulling me to a sitting position. The tattoo stings a little, but it's nothing I can't handle. I stand to stretch my legs, pants still below my ass, and pull my hoodie off over my head. I'm only wearing a thin camisole, but I feel hot and sweaty. Maybe it has something to do with the adrenaline coursing through me.

"Should've taken you to the private room," Dare grumbles. I look behind me to find three sets of eyes on me— Matty, Cordell, and Cordell's client. All three snap their heads down as if they weren't looking.

Dare takes my discarded hoodie and ties it around my waist, effectively covering my butt, but not touching the tattooed area. I wonder what I'm supposed to wear when we're done, but I decide to cross that bridge when we come to it.

Dare grabs a water bottle, taking a swig before handing it to me. I guzzle it down.

"How you feeling?" he asks, rotating back and forth on

his rolling chair.

"Fine." I shrug. "Just wondering how I'm going to wear pants after this."

"Ah, yeah. That. You'll just have to skip those for a few days."

"Oh, is that all?" I laugh.

A smile pulls at the corners of Dare's lips. "You ready to go back in?"

"Let's do this." I untie the sweatshirt around my waist and lie back on my side. Dare slaps a palm against my ass cheek before leaning down to bite it.

I squeal, pushing his head away.

"Sorry. Had to get that out of my system."

Out of his system. We both know how well that worked last time. The needle hits my skin, and I close my eyes, trying to think about anything other than the pain. It's hurting more than before now. Almost like scratching a raw sunburn.

"Tell me what you wanted to talk to me about earlier?" I ask, abandoning my plan to let him bring it up.

"What, now?"

"Yes, now. I need a distraction."

Dare clears his throat. "Did you find a place to stay yet?"

A wave of sadness crashes down on me. I didn't want to have this conversation right now. "No. The place I wanted fell through."

"You and Jess should move in with me."

Well. Ask for a distraction and you shall receive.

"What?" I say, turning my head to face him.

"Easy," he says. "Try not to move."

I lie back down, waiting for him to continue as my

pulse kicks into high gear.

"It doesn't have to be like what you're thinking. You can even have your own room, if you wanted to," Dare explains.

"As tempting as your offer is, I can't do that." My voice is quiet as I focus on the glowing pink light of the Bad Intentions sign in the window.

"Why the fuck not? You need a place to stay. I have the space."

"Because if things between us ever get...*messy*, what does that mean for Jess and me?"

"I would never—" Dare starts.

"I *know*," I cut him off. "I know. But Jess needs to be able to depend on me. To have stability and consistency and to always know that he has a place to stay."

"And I can give you guys that. Or you can just stay with me until you find a place."

"Why are you pushing this?" He's done enough. The job. The clothes. It feels like all I ever do is *take take take* from him.

"Aside from the obvious?"

"What's obvious?" I ask, clueless. The tattoo machine ceases in its buzzing, but I don't turn to face him.

"The obvious being that you're my fucking girlfriend and you need a place to live. I don't want you to run, Lo. Do you think I can't see it in your eyes? That you're three seconds from bolting? Because it's written all over your face."

The word *girlfriend* echoes in my head. Is that what I am? His girlfriend? He said he wanted a relationship before, but everyone knows declarations made during sex should be taken with a grain of salt. What he's saying makes sense, but I still feel like I'm doing something wrong by taking him up on his offer.

"What if I paid rent? Like, with a real written agreement and everything."

Dare blows out a harsh breath, and I feel it on my exposed skin. "If that's what you need."

"I'll talk to Jess."

Dare nods his head, wiping down my thigh. Before he starts back up, I roll onto my back and tug him toward me by his sleeve.

"Thank you," I say, looking into those sad ocean eyes. I reach up and pull him into me, pressing my lips to his. His right hand comes down beside my head to brace himself as he kisses me—slow and deep—uncaring that we most likely have an audience. I feel the kiss right between my legs, and I clamp them together.

Dare pulls back, adjusting the crotch of his pants before sitting back in his chair. He goes back to work on my thigh, and there aren't any more words. It takes another twenty minutes or so before he announces that he's finished.

Nerves twist in my stomach as he cleans me up. He helps me sit up before handing me a handheld mirror. I stand, ass facing him instead of flashing the rest of the shop, as I take in the reflection.

"It's beautiful," I breathe. It's a flower with strings of delicate beading hanging below like a chandelier. It's feminine but somehow badass at the same time. The shading and detail are incredible.

"You said to choose something that represented you," he says, his voice unsure. Maybe even vulnerable.

"You think I'm a delicate flower?" I laugh.

"It's a lotus. They grow from mud."

Sounds about right, I think. But he continues.

"They're born from darkness. But they bloom anyway—rising above the mud, still remaining beautiful and pure. *That* is you."

Tears instantly prick the backs of my eyes, my nose stings, and I feel a lump in my throat. I can't speak, can't do anything to stop the tears. Instead, I throw my arms around him, burying my face in the crook of his neck. He lets me cry, his hands rubbing my back, and his gentle touch only makes me cry harder.

"Let's get you wrapped up back here," Dare says, leading me to the drawing room. I know it's his way of giving us some privacy.

"I'm sorry," I say, smoothing my palms across my wet cheeks. "I don't know why I'm crying." I lean against his drawing desk, and Dare kneels, applying some ointment to the fresh ink before covering it in plastic wrap, securing it with tape on each end. Once he's done, he kisses the inside of my knee, then stands, walking behind his desk to grab something. He rounds the desk, kneeling in front of me again, as he peels my leggings down, taking my underwear with them.

How stupid must I look? Crying over a tattoo with my pants down. I laugh then sniffle at the ridiculousness of it all. He holds up a pair of black basketball shorts for me to step into.

"You thought ahead."

"Wishful thinking."

When I lift my left leg, he surprises me by leaning in, face flush against my center as he gives me a long, flat lick. My eyes roll back, and my ass hits the edge of his desk. My leg is still half-bent, suspended awkwardly, and Dare grabs my knee, lifting it higher to have better access. I bury my hands in his messy black hair as he eats me, alternating between sucking and nibbling and fucking me with his tongue.

I have the sudden urge to please him. He's always making me feel so good. I want to do the same for him. Clenching the collar of Dare's hoodie, I pull him up before dropping to my knees in front of him.

"Careful," he says huskily, probably referring to the tattoo, but I can't feel anything other than him. I have his belt buckle undone and his pants unzipped in seconds, then I'm jerking his jeans down below his ass. I grip his hips over his white boxer briefs, seeing his thickness straining against the fabric. My tongue darts out to lick the outline of it.

"Fuck," he mutters, dropping his head back. "Pull my cock out." I love this side of Dare. Dirty and bossy with a side of needy. I do as he says, sliding his boxers down until his hard length bobs free. I lick the underside of his shaft from bottom to sensitive tip, and Dare groans, hand landing on my ponytail, gripping it tightly. He tugs, pulling me away, while his other hand circles his cock.

"Open."

I feel myself clench at his command. I open my mouth, and he slaps the head against my tongue twice before he slides inside my mouth. I close my lips around him, and Dare jerks forward with a harsh breath. He controls my movements with the hand wrapped around my hair, pulling me back, then forward. He moves slowly at first, but he picks up the pace, and I steady myself by holding on to the front of his thighs.

Without leaving my mouth, he spins us both around, so my back is facing the desk. Letting go of my ponytail, he brings his hands to rest on the edge of his desk as he pumps his hips into me, fucking my mouth. His lean, tattooed torso is stretched above me, his muscles flexing with each thrust. His lips are parted, head dipped down between his shoulders, eyes clenched shut.

I slip a hand between my own thighs, unable to resist, causing me to moan around him. His eyes fly open and flare with lust. "I want to touch you."

I release him with a pop, holding the base of him, and shake my head. "This is for you." I work my hand up and down his length, holding his gaze as I close my mouth around his head.

"Fuck yes," he groans. I dig my fingernails into his ass, pulling him deeper, wanting to take all of him, to make him lose control, to make him feel a fraction of the kind of crazy he makes me feel. The hard floor hurts my knees, but I ignore the pain, working him with my hand and my mouth.

Dare tenses up, hips stilling. "I'm gonna come."

I suck him harder in response. He mutters another curse and pulls back to jerk himself while the tip is still between my lips.

"You're gonna swallow my cum, Lo?"

I nod, holding my tongue out.

"Touch your pussy while you do."

I clench at his words, bringing my fingers between my legs once more. It only takes a few seconds before my orgasm hits, right as Dare's does, the salty liquid hitting my tongue. When he's done, I swallow before wrapping my lips around him, giving one last light suck.

Dare shudders, pulling me up. I'm surprised when he presses his lips to mine. Most guys are weird about that kind of thing, but Dare is unconcerned, his tongue sliding along mine.

He reaches between my thighs, two fingers swirling around in my wetness.

"Does that mean you like your tattoo? Because that was one hell of a thank you."

I laugh, sagging against him. "I love it," I say honestly, ignoring that pang in my chest that tells me it might not be the only thing I feel that way for.

"Are you coming over tonight?" Dare asks, nuzzling into me, his stubble scratching against the thin skin of my neck and shoulder. I want to feel it between my thighs.

"I can't," I breathe, feeling raw and vulnerable from the crying, the tattoo, the closeness, the orgasm—all of it. "I need to be with Jess tonight." We need to figure out our next move. I honestly don't know which way he'll lean, but I know he deserves to be included in the decision.

Dare nods, kissing my forehead. He bends over, retrieving the forgotten basketball shorts and slides them up my jelly legs, careful not to touch the fresh ink. We walk back into the main room, and I pull my hoodie back over my head, hearing my keys jingle in the front pocket.

Dare gives me instructions about caring for my tattoo. He tells me to take off the wrap in a couple of hours, then wash it with a mild soap and water. I thank him again, promising to call him later tonight. I have a lot to think about.

CHAPTER FOURTEEN

Lo

WHEN I GET BACK TO HENRY'S, JESS IS FRESHLY showered, his hair a mop of damp curls. He's sitting on the couch with his eyes glued to the phone.

"What's up?" I ask, kicking the door shut behind me.

"Watching *Mad Men* on Netflix," he says, dropping his phone to the couch.

"We have Netflix?" I ask, doubtful.

"Nope. I just keep creating different email accounts to get the free trial."

"Seems legit."

"What the fuck are you wearing?" Jess asks, looking me up and down.

"Oh, I got this today," I say, pulling the loose fabric up to expose the tattoo. "I'm part of the no pants club for the next few days."

"Hell yeah," Jess says, examining the ink through the plastic wrap. "Think he'll do me next?"

"When you're eighteen," I say, raising an eyebrow.

I head into the kitchen and make all his favorites— eggs, sunny-side up, pancakes, and bacon, mentally weighing the pros and cons of moving in with Dare.

"Do you like it here?" I ask as we eat our breakfast-for-dinner on the couch, since there is no kitchen table to speak of.

"Yeah." Jess shrugs, crunching on a piece of bacon. "Coach wants me to play lacrosse in the spring. I think I might."

"So, you wouldn't be okay with going back home?"

"Like, *home* home? Like *Oakland* home?"

I nod.

"Fuck no. Why would we do that?" he asks, seemingly offended that I even brought it up. "We're both finally doing good. I have friends. Ones who've never even been to jail," he deadpans. "I have a shot at college."

I almost start crying again, knowing how much he really has going for him here, and how much it would kill me to have that taken away. College wasn't even on his radar before. Just knowing that he's considering it is huge.

"What is this about? The money? Because I can pick up an after-school job. Coach might even let me work for the club."

"No—well, yes and no. There just aren't any homes or apartments available to rent. I thought I had something, but it fell through. We're shit out of luck unless we can swing twenty-five hundred a month on rent." I was hoping to find something for half the price.

"So, what? We go back to Mom's? Pretend we didn't send her ass to jail and go back to living life in the fucking hood?"

"No."

"No? What the fuck else can we do, Lo?"

"There is one other option," I hesitate, not knowing how he'll feel about it. "Dare wants us to move in. We'd pay him rent and have a written agreement with him. And it would only be temporary."

Jess sits back in his chair, folding his arms across his chest.

"I'm for whatever the fuck keeps us here."

"Yeah?" I ask, still not sold. "You sure?"

"I'm not going back, Lo. This guy…you say he's legit. If your fairy fucking godmother wants to help, then why the fuck not?"

"I'll think about it."

CHAPTER FIFTEEN

Dare

IT'S BEEN FOUR DAYS SINCE I THREW OUT THE OFFER, AND I haven't heard a word about it since. The first two days, I figured she was just thinking it over, but now, I'm wondering if she's just trying to figure out a way to tell me she's leaving.

At least I know she's not staying in a house with no heat. I pocketed the past-due invoices from Henry's the night I busted Eric's car up and paid them the other day. Lo told me the power was back on, but she never asked if I had anything to do with it, and I never told her.

I haven't had a chance to fuckin' breathe this week. My books are jam-packed with appointments. Tourist season is in full swing now. Between that and Lo working over at Blackbear, we haven't seen each other in the past few days, except in passing. Even when she comes in, we're both so busy that we don't get anything other than stolen glances.

My phone vibrates from my pocket. I pull it out to see a picture of Lo waiting for me. A picture of Lo's tattoo, more specifically. She's on that pathetic excuse for a bed at Henry's, legs bent, showing off the curve of her perfect ass. She's wearing those knee-high socks she likes. No pants. *No underwear.* Her shirt has ridden up, exposing fingertip-shaped bruises in various stages of healing that go with the scratches down my back and teeth marks on my shoulders. My dick is instantly hard, which is unfortunate, seeing as how I have a girl in my chair who's eyeing my lap like it's hard for her.

"You ready?" I ask dryly. This chick has taken approximately eighteen cigarette breaks, two phone calls, and one pee break for a tattoo of a dreamcatcher that should've taken thirty minutes, tops.

Once I'm finished with my client, I excuse myself to the drawing room. I'm still fucking hard, and I'm half-tempted to rub one out right here and now to the memory permanently seared into my spank bank of the last time we were in here together. I was helping Lo get dressed, but I ended up eating her pussy. I hadn't even meant to do it. It was instinct. Completely involuntary. Then I was surprised, yet again, when Lo dropped to her knees and gave me the best head of my life.

I sit at my desk, dick threatening to bust through my jeans, and tap out my reply to Lo.

Me: Are you teasing me, Sally? I want to see that in person.

Me: You know, to make sure it's healing properly.

Lo: Day after tomorrow, unless seeing a bunch of sweaty, half-naked men is your idea of a good time. 😏

Me: Come again?

Lo: Jess has a wrestling match. Going to Sac.

I debate on taking her up on her non-invitation. Crowds, family outings, and events, stuck with people in a confined space for an hour and a half drive…all things I avoid like the plague. But for some reason, I find myself willing to do just about any-fucking-thing to get my fix.

Me: Count me in.

CHAPTER SIXTEEN

Lo

"**F**UCK," JESS SAYS UNDER HIS BREATH, ROUSING me from sleep. I lift my head from his shoulder and rub at the kink in my neck. I didn't mean to sleep almost the entire way home. I was exhausted after a long day of driving and watching Jess wrestle. That shit was an all-day event. Then Dare and I did a little wrestling of our own in the back of his truck late last night.

Dare drove separately so he didn't miss work. I was surprised he wanted to come at all, but he did. It was fun to see Jess out there, doing his thing. I don't know the first thing about wrestling, but I do know he won all three matches and looked happy doing it.

We went out to some Mexican restaurant afterwards, and I sat back while Dare, Henry, and Jess shot the shit, thinking how crazy it was that this is my life now. Two months ago, if you would've told me I'd be enjoying a meal with my brother, my dad, and my new boyfriend, I'd have thought you were as high as my mother.

"What is it?" I ask groggily, before my eyes land on the ball of purple curled up on the porch. I'd recognize that jacket anywhere. "Shit."

"Crystal's back."

"Son of a bitch. This isn't gonna be pretty," Henry says, throwing his Jeep into park.

"How long has it been since you've seen her?" I ask. I always wondered if Crystal ever tracked him down. He left me his phone number, but I tucked it away, never once showing it to Crystal.

"The day I left."

"You okay, Jess?"

"Fine," he says, shrugging, feigning indifference.

We all hop out, stopping in front of Crystal's slumped over body.

"Think she's dead?"

"Nah. I'm not that lucky," Jess says, nudging her with his foot. Crystal stirs, lifting her head. Mascara is smudged down her face, and her wrinkles look even more pronounced than before. She looks around, probably trying to figure out where she is. She rubs her eyes, and I see when the confusion clears.

"My babies!" she yells, and her pack-a-day voice grates on my nerves already. She stands, stumbling, and moves to hug us. Jess catches her arm before she makes contact, and we both take a step back. Hurt flashes in her eyes briefly, but she conceals it just as fast.

"Henry," she breathes, looking up at him like he hung the moon. "It's been a long time."

"There's a reason for that, Crystal."

"Come on, guys. Don't be like that."

We step around her, and Henry unlocks the door.

"Got room for one more?" Crystal asks, not waiting for an answer. She follows us inside, looking around the place. Not one of us speaks. We know her game by now. But Crystal is an expert at avoiding social cues.

"I can't believe my family is back together again," she says, bringing a hand to her mouth as the crocodile tears start. My mom was beautiful once. But then drugs and life happened.

"Go home, Crystal," I say, shaking my head, quickly losing patience.

"Oh, I see how it is. You guys find someone else to take care of you, to give you a place to stay, and all of a sudden I'm chopped liver?"

"And there it is," I say flatly. Jesse exhales, throwing himself down onto the couch. Henry grabs himself a beer from the fridge, probably wishing he had something stronger right about now.

"I know I fucked up, but what mother doesn't?" Her speech is slurred, and I know she's high on something. "I'll be better, Logan."

I don't respond. I don't even look at her.

"Jesse?" she pleads, looking to him for acceptance, but she doesn't find it there, either.

"I can forgive you for sending me to *jail*, but you can't forgive me? Un-fucking-real. I did everything for you two!"

This is it. This cycle right here. Cry, beg for forgiveness, lash out when she doesn't get her way, and repeat. My anger bubbles inside me, threatening to boil over.

"You *forgive* me?" I ask, my voice deathly calm and quiet. "What exactly should I forgive you for? For letting your boyfriend beat on us? For being a fucking junkie? For abandoning your children with no money or food for months at a time? Or maybe it's for fucking my boyfriend after you sent me to the store to buy you smokes. Oh, or maybe I should forgive you for stealing Jesse's brand-new bike just to pawn it?" My voice rises with each question, my face inches from hers. "Should I forgive you for chasing away our father? The only fucking halfway normal person in our lives?" I shout, pointing toward Henry.

Crystal surprises me when she cackles, her eyes lighting up with glee. I don't trust it. She looks at Henry. "You didn't tell them *why* you left?"

"Crystal. Don't," Henry warns.

My stomach twists with nerves, and I just know whatever comes next isn't going to be good.

"They deserve to know."

"Get out. *Now*," I say between clenched teeth. Jesse stands, suddenly interested in the conversation.

"Deserve to know what?"

"Don't pay any attention to her. This is what she does. She's jealous of our relationship with Henry and she'll do anything to sabotage it. Isn't that right?"

"I am your mother!" she screeches. "He isn't even your dad!"

What? I hear the words, but it takes a minute for my brain to catch up. Jess staggers back, as if he took a physical hit to the gut. My eyes dart to Henry's in question, and the guilt tells me all I need to know.

It's true.

Henry isn't my father.

Before I realize what's happening, Jess snatches the keys off the coffee table and shoves his way past Crystal. I hear the 4Runner start, and I run outside after him, but he's already gone.

"Jess!" I scream after the taillights glowing red in the night sky.

I run back inside. "Give me your keys," I demand,

holding my palm out. "I need to find him." Henry hesitates for a second before dropping them into my hand.

"Kid—" he starts, but I cut him off.

"Don't. Just don't. Make sure she's gone before we get back," I say, tossing a look at Crystal who is now crying with her matted, blonde head in her hands.

I can't think about what this means right now. I can't think about how I feel. My only focus is finding Jess. I run out into the cold night air. It's snowing now, which only adds to my worry. I jump into Henry's truck, leaving him and Crystal to hash it out inside.

I don't even know where to start. I try his school first. Don't ask me why that makes any sense in my brain. The parking lot is completely empty. Next, I try the two restaurants that are still open—still nothing. I drive by a few bars. Jess might just be dumb enough to try his luck. Nothing.

My panic grows by the minute, fingers tapping restlessly against the steering wheel. When he stormed off in Oakland, I didn't worry. I knew where to find him. But this…this feels different.

This is what I was afraid of. And it's my fault. I dragged him out of the city, threw him into Henry's life, they bonded, and now…this. Poor kid is never going to trust again.

I call Dare, hoping he'll answer. He said he was stopping by Bad Intentions before going home, but he left before us, so I don't know if he's still there. It rings three torturously long times before he picks up.

"Lo?" Confusion paints his tone. I don't usually call him.

"I can't find Jesse." My voice sounds shaky and panicky to my own ears.

"What do you mean? What happened?"

"Fucking Crystal," I answer, as if that explains everything. "He has the 4Runner. Are you at work? Do you see his car outside anywhere?"

There are a few bars, including Blackbear, in that area.

"I'm here. I don't see it out front, but I'll drive around." I hear him moving around, and then a second later, the sound of his engine starting.

"He doesn't know how to drive in this weather. The windshield wipers don't work for shit, and the tires... they're not good in the snow—"

"Calm down. It's just a little snow. Jess will be fine. We'll find him. Do you want me to come pick you up?"

"No, I think it's better to split up."

"Okay," he says after a long pause. "Are you okay?"

"Henry's not my dad," I say softly, and Dare curses under his breath.

"I'm sorry, baby." And it's not sympathy. It's empathy. Because if anyone knows how it feels, it's Dare. But on a much larger scale.

"I'm sorry," I say, regret lacing my tone. "I know this doesn't even come close to what happened to yo—"

"Hey, don't compare tragedies. It's okay to be upset, Lo."

I wouldn't call it a tragedy, but I appreciate him in this moment more than he'll ever know.

"I'll let you know if I find him," Dare says. I thank him and hang up the phone, racking my brain for places to search. I drive around for another hour without luck. I wish I knew his coach's number, or even where he lived. Maybe he went there.

My phone lights up with a text from Dare.

Dare: No luck. Anything?

Me: No. I'm going to go home and see if he went back. Get some sleep.

One of us should.

Dare: I'm going to go home to pick up my phone charger, then grab a cup of coffee. I'll come to you.

There he goes again, making me feel all supported and shit. My chest physically aches when I think about all he's done for me. For us. Everyone in town seems to be intimidated by him. Even he thinks he's some kind of monster. But he's never been anything other than an angel to me. My broken boy. Doesn't he know he's not really broken at all? It's everyone else who's flawed.

When I get back to Henry's, Jess isn't there. But fucking Crystal is. And she's wearing a bath towel. I throw my hand up in her direction, looking to Henry for answers.

"Don't look at me. She won't leave."

"So call the cops. I'm getting real good at that," I say, fishing my phone out of my jacket pocket. "You're on probation, right?" It's an educated guess, but her reaction tells me I'm right.

"Logan, sweetie—"

"I know you told Eric where we were, too. I've always known you were selfish, but damn, Crystal. Do you have to make sure everyone else's lives are as pathetic as yours? You couldn't just let us have this?"

"I was helping you!" she screeches. "That man loves you, and he has money. He could take care of you for *life*. You're an idiot to pass that up."

Fucking typical.

"This may come as a shock to you, but to *most* people, there are more important things in life than money for your next fix."

She opens her mouth to respond, but I hold my hand up to stop her as my phone, still in my other hand, vibrates with a text from Dare. I see the two words that have me sagging in relief: **He's here**.

He went to Dare's.

He went to Dare.

CHAPTER SEVENTEEN
Dare

KNOW SOMEONE IS IN MY HOUSE THE MINUTE I OPEN the door, even though I don't see anyone. I walk into the kitchen, noticing an open cabinet, then wet footprints leading to the back door. I open the sliding glass door to see a shirtless Jess, nursing a near-empty bottle of Jack in my hot tub.

This is going to be a long night.

He stares ahead, unmoving. I shoot a text to Lo, letting her know that I've found him before pocketing my phone. I brace myself for the angry, drunken mess Jess is sure to be. I know because looking at Jess is like looking at myself ten years ago.

"Up we go," I say, leaning over the stairs, lifting him underneath his armpits. Kid is solid and drunk, which equals dead weight. I finally hoist him up out of the water, only to realize he's butt ass naked.

"Ah, what the fuck, man," I say, averting my eyes.

I lead him down the steps, keeping a healthy distance. He drops the bottle of Jack, glass shattering at our feet. I try to lead Jess away from the glass, but he walks across it, unfeeling. Uncaring. Once inside, he sits his naked ass down on my couch, and I run upstairs to grab him a towel and some clean clothes.

"Put these on." I toss the clothes next to him. He doesn't move, head bent, cradled in his hands.

"Come on, man. Get dressed."

He finally listens, moving slowly. Facing away from him, I call Lo.

"Is he okay?" are the first words out of her mouth. I scratch at the back of my neck, putting some more space between us.

"He's fine. Drunk, but fine."

"Thank God," Lo says, letting out a relieved breath.

"There is one problem, though."

"What?" Lo asks, like she's afraid of the answer.

"*Jess* is here…but the car isn't."

"Of course, it isn't. That would be too easy."

"Do you want me to bring him to you?"

"I'm coming to you now. Henry's dropping me off. I don't think Jess should be around either of our parents right now. And I use the word *parents* loosely," she adds, probably for Henry's benefit.

"Okay. We'll look for the car in the morning." It must be around two a.m. by now.

We hang up, and when I turn back, Jess is dressed—thankfully. I hand him the coffee I bought on the way over and sit down next to him, unsure of what to say. I think about how I'd feel if the situation were reversed. I wouldn't want anyone to say a damn thing to me, especially in his state. So, I don't speak at all, content to sit in silence unless he breaks it first.

That's what we do for maybe ten minutes as he drinks his coffee, before he looks over at me, eyes bloodshot and glassy. "Don't hurt her."

"Not planning to."

"Everyone lets her down. Even me."

"I'm not everyone," I say bluntly.

"Good."

Another pause.

"What's your issue?"

"Come again?"

"Your drama. You know mine. What's your story?"

"I was left in a parking lot when I was a kid. Bounced around from foster family to foster family until I aged out." I leave out a lot, but those are the Cliffs Notes.

"Life sucks," Jess mutters, running a hand down his face.

"Sometimes," I agree.

Jess looks over at me, annoyed. "Thanks for the sage advice."

"Would you take my advice if I offered it to you?" I ask, lifting a brow.

"Probably not."

"That's what I thought."

"But if I were to…" he hedges, "what would you say?"

"I guess I'd tell you to take a day or a week to be pissed off, but after that? Don't waste so much time worrying about the people who've wronged you that you don't see the ones who've been there all along. You have Lo to take care of you, but who's been taking care of her?"

I hear a car door slam outside about two-point-five seconds before my front door flies open. Lo hesitates in the doorway, taking in the scene before her. Jesse, drunk and wet, streaks of blood decorating the floor from the back door to his feet from the broken bottle.

Jesse stands, lumbering over to where she stands

before throwing his arms around her. His shoulders start to shake, and Lo's face crumples as she hugs him, soothing him with soft words of comfort. I hear Jess mumble about being sorry, and she shushes him. He pulls away and wipes at his eyes with his forearm.

"I, uh…" Jesse starts, clearing his throat. "I think I just need to go to bed."

"Get some sleep." Lo nods. "We'll talk tomorrow."

Jesse ambles up the stairs, and I make my way over to Lo. I cup her face with my right hand, and she holds on to my wrist, leaning into my touch. She looks tired, but beautiful.

"He came to you," she whispers. She grabs the back of my head, lifting onto her tiptoes, and presses her lips to mine. I anchor her to me with an arm around her waist as I slip my tongue through her lips. This kiss is different somehow. Like we're finally shedding all the bullshit and allowing ourselves to *just be*. Lo pulls back and whispers a *thank you* against my mouth.

"He trusts you. He came *here*. That means something."

I don't deserve the way she's looking at me right now—like I'm Mother Teresa instead of a monster.

"You okay, Sally?" She gives a small, sad smile at my use of my nickname for her, but a smile nonetheless. "He's not the only one who found out his father isn't really his father."

"I'm too tired to be upset. I'll figure out how I feel in the morning." Lo circles her arms around my neck, chin resting on my chest. She never ceases to impress me with the way she adapts to life's curveballs. "Take me to bed," she says before sticking her bottom lip out in a pout.

Wordlessly, I carry her up the stairs, her warm body

wrapped around me. I don't stop until we're at the foot of my bed. Setting her to her feet, I peel her jacket off, followed by her shirt and bra, revealing her pale pink nipples. I press a kiss to one before I pull down her pants, and she holds on to my shoulders as she lifts one foot, then the other.

Lo lies down on my bed, flat on her back, the tip of her thumb between her teeth as she watches me reach behind my neck to pull my shirt over my head. I stare at her, thinking how fucking perfect she looks in my bed. Her porcelain skin against my black sheets, my ink on her thigh, signature messy ponytail spread across my pillow, face stripped of makeup. This is when she's the most beautiful.

I kick off my pants, dropping my knee to the mattress and crawl up Lo's body, settling in between her legs. I lift her left thigh and slowly push into her warmth. She gasps at the feeling, her back arching off the bed. Fuck, I love this girl.

Love.

The words are on repeat in my head, over and over, as I try to bury myself so deep inside her that she'll feel me forever.

"I didn't mean to fall in love with you," I admit. "But I did. I love you," I say, feeling her clench around me, her legs starting to shake. Her telltale sign that she's close to the edge already.

"Stefan," she breathes, and another piece of ice falls away from my heart upon hearing her say my name.

"Say it again," I all but beg, rutting into her. Black fingernails dig into my chest. I welcome the sting.

"Stefan," she repeats. I roll onto my side, pulling her with me. Lo's leg goes over my hip, and I grip her perfect ass as I slowly tunnel in and out of the warmest, wettest heaven.

"Again," I command, wrapping one arm around the small of her back and cradling her head with the other one.

"I love you, Stefan. I love you, I love you..." She trails off, clenching and contracting around me as she comes. Another piece of ice melts away, and I'm no longer frozen, but liquid inside as I spill inside her.

I roll onto my back and pull her on top of me. Her legs bend, thighs cradling me, torso flat against mine as I lazily thrust into her while we both come down. She tucks her head into the space between my neck and shoulders, kissing and sucking on my collarbone softly. I slide my palms all over her body—her arms, her back, her thighs—before finally coming to rest on her ass.

Lo's breathing starts to even out, her warm breath rhythmically ghosting across my neck. She falls asleep while I'm still inside her, and in this moment, I decide that even though I don't deserve her, I'm too fucking self-serving not to take the only thing that offers me peace. The only thing that allows me to feel warmth when I've been cold all my life. Add it to my list of sins, right next to *murderer.*

CHAPTER EIGHTEEN

Lo

"**A**NYONE WANT TO TELL ME WHY MY HOUSE IS condemned?" Crystal asks before taking a drag of her cigarette. I pluck it out of her wrinkled lips and put it out in the ashtray.

After Dare drove us to where Jess remembered leaving the 4Runner, we got a call from Henry asking us to come over, so we could hash everything out. Dare offered to come with us, but he has to work, and this isn't his mess. Besides, I don't necessarily love the idea of him meeting Crystal. Ever.

"Should I have paid your bills while you were locked up?" I ask.

"Well, it would've been the decent thing to do," she says.

Jess snorts out a bitter laugh, and I try to smother my own with the back of my hand. "Tell me more about how to be decent like you," Jess says, sarcasm dripping from every word. "The only reason you're here is because your boyfriend is still behind bars and you have no one else."

"All right, all right," Henry says, standing next to the fireplace. Crystal sits on one end of the couch, and Jesse and I are huddled together on the other end.

I was afraid of what I'd find when I went to wake Jess earlier, but to my surprise, he'd already been awake and showered. And when I asked him how he was feeling, he acted like nothing happened at all. I have a feeling it will all come out sooner or later, though.

"Someone better start talking," I say, cutting to the chase. No one speaks. "Okay, I'll make it easy on you. Henry, I'm going to go ahead and assume that you're not, in fact, our dad?"

Henry adjusts his ball cap, clearing his throat before answering. "No."

Jess grits his jaw next to me but doesn't react otherwise. He's sitting slightly behind me, his back all the way up against the cushion while I'm leaning forward with my elbows on top of my knees. I reach my open palm behind my back, and Jess puts his hand in mine. I give it a squeeze of reassurance.

"How long have you known?"

"I always knew you weren't mine," he says to me, and despite myself, I feel a jolt of disappointment at the fact. "I didn't meet your mother until you were two. I thought maybe Jesse was, for a while, but the dates didn't add up. She always insisted that he was mine, so eventually, I figured, what the hell do I know about pregnancy?"

I never questioned why Jess and I didn't have Henry's last name. I always assumed it was because they were never married.

"It's not exactly rocket science," Jess deadpans.

"Yeah, well, you'd be surprised at what you can convince yourself of if you really want it," Henry says, looking at the steel toe of his boots.

"So, why'd you leave? If you wanted it so badly?"

Jess asks.

"Because he's a selfish shit," Crystal spits.

Henry's face reddens and contorts with anger like I've never seen coming from him. "I *was* selfish," he agrees. "I was selfish when I stayed with you for years because I loved those fucking kids even though you'd use them as leverage or threaten to take them away every time something didn't go your way. It was selfish of me to pretend they were mine. *And yes*, it was selfish of me to leave them to finally get the fuck away from your crazy ass."

Crystal jumps off the couch, getting in Henry's face. They argue for a minute, but I don't hear it. Years of practice have made me a professional at blocking her voice out once it reaches a certain decibel.

"How did Eric contact you?" I ask, interrupting their yelling.

Crystal turns to face me, her expression full of resentment. "He came to visit me in jail, unlike my children. He put money on my books for smokes. He told me he was worried about you and couldn't find you, so I gave him your new number. Told him I thought you were staying with Henry. What's the big deal?"

I roll my eyes, letting out a hollow laugh. "I'm done here," I say, standing. "Henry, thanks for letting us crash here, but I think our time is up."

The look in Henry's eyes almost makes me feel bad, but he's not the victim here. Jess is. "Crystal, you can fuck off. For good."

Jess follows me out, without a word to either one of them. We get into the trusty old Toyota, and I start the engine.

"Lo?" Jess asks, eyes focused on something outside his window.

"Yeah?"

"I don't want to go back to The Bay."

"This doesn't change anything," I assure him as I drive us home. To Dare's.

CHAPTER NINETEEN

Three weeks later

Dare

"**O**KAY. I'VE GOT YOU DOWN FOR NEXT Thursday at noon. See you then," Lo says before hanging up the phone. I walk up behind her, gathering her hair into my fist before scooping it out of the neck of the hoodie she commandeered from me. She tilts her head back, flashing me one of her real smiles, and I kiss her forehead. Funny how I went from not being comfortable with affection to constantly needing to touch her in just a few weeks.

"How could you ever think you're a monster?" she muses, looking up into my eyes. I give her hair a tug before letting go. I still haven't come clean about everything. I know I should, but things have been good for once, and I didn't want to do anything to throw a wrench in it.

Crystal reluctantly went back to Oakland. Jesse's doing well in school. We haven't heard anything from Eric. They've even talked to Henry a few times. Lo won't admit it, but she was more hurt than she led on. I know she wants Henry to stay in their lives in some capacity, even if he isn't their biological father. I think we all know that blood doesn't mean shit.

It's been three weeks of fucking and laughing and eating and drinking and falling in love with Lo. Watching my friends fall in love with her *and* Jess. So, why dig up the past? That would be self-sabotaging behavior.

"Ready to go?" I ask Lo a couple of hours later after everyone has gone home for the night.

"Yep," she says, bending over to pick up her bag from underneath the front desk. I lock up, then we trudge through the snow to my truck.

Once we're home, we head straight upstairs. Lo talked me into buying a TV for my room, so we've gotten in the habit of falling asleep to a movie almost every night.

She drops her bag onto my bed—*our* bed, I should say, because even though I said she could have her own room, we both knew that shit wasn't happening—and fishes out a Redbox DVD with a goofy smile on her face.

"What is it? If you make me watch *Grandma's Boy* one more time…" I say, wary of her selection. She has the same taste in movies as a college frat boy.

"First of all, that movie is a national *treasure*," she says, rolling her eyes. "Second of all, no. It's even better." She tosses me the red plastic container, and I open it up to find *The Nightmare Before Christmas*.

"Good one," I say, a smirk tugging at my lips.

"'Tis the season. I just need a shower first," she says, stripping out of her clothes as she walks toward the bathroom.

"Weird, so do I." I follow her, staring at her perky, round ass as I pull my shirt over my head and kick off my jeans and boots. One of the best parts about living with Lo is getting to shower with her.

She opens the glass door and steps inside. I'm right

behind her. She pulls the faucet up, and we stand back, waiting for the water to get warm. I take the opportunity to kiss her, long and hard, and I feel her nipples pebbling against my torso.

The shower fills with steam and I wash her body, loving the feel of her slippery, soapy skin underneath my hand. Lo moans when I rub between her legs.

"Don't stop," she insists, grabbing my wrist. I don't listen, pulling back my hand, earning a glare and a growl from Lo. But that doesn't last long, because I back her up against the wall and lift her thigh as I push inside her. She gasps, her head hitting the wall.

I fuck her slowly, getting as deep as I possibly can, applying pressure to her clit with my pelvis with each thrust. She comes quietly, her body shaking as she clenches around me, pulling my release from me.

Still inside her, I lean my forehead against the wall behind her, panting, and Lo absently toys with my nipple ring as she peppers kisses against my shoulder.

What happens when fire meets ice? *Fire wins*. Every time.

"Meet you at the shop?" I ask Lo as she heads for the door to drop Jess off at school.

"Yep. My shift at Blackbear doesn't start until three, so I'll get a few hours in first."

I decide to stop at Sissy's and Belle's for some coffee and Lo's favorite cherry danishes. Sissy hooks me up with a bag of extra pastries, per usual.

I turn for the door, bag of pastries between my teeth, hands full of food and coffee, when I see her walking through the door. Sarah. She looks exactly the same. Long, wavy blond hair. Bright, blue eyes. But there's a sadness behind those eyes that wasn't always there. And I'm the one who's responsible for that.

Sarah gasps, and we both stop short, not knowing what to do. She hates me. Her parents hate me. *I* hate me. I haven't seen her in almost ten years. Haven't spoken to her since they took me away in handcuffs. Her family moved away a long time ago. She's the last person I expected to see here.

Sarah's wide eyes fill with tears and she glances behind her, as if she's looking for someone. A second later, Mark appears. Sarah's father. My old foster dad. These are the people who I thought might actually become my permanent family. But all of that changed in an instant, reminding me that I didn't have a real family, and nothing could ever change that.

Mark's eyes burn with a mixture of rage and pain when he recognizes me, and the same emotions consume me, as if it just happened yesterday. I feel my throat closing up. I feel the break in my arm and the stabbing cold of ice puncturing my skin as I jump in. I feel my oxygen running out, and I see the blood spilled along the ice above me.

The bag of pastries falls from my mouth, tumbling out of the bag on the way to the floor. The cherry danish splatters across the white floor. Dread slams into my gut like a thousand-pound weight as all three of us stand before each other, reliving the worst day of our lives in the span of three seconds.

"You're still here," Mark spits, voice full of disdain. If he could kill me where I stand and get away with it, I have no doubt in my mind that he would. He wanted me in prison. And he almost got his wish. But I can't fault him.

Guilt, my only friend, is ever-present. It took the back burner when Lo came into my life, but right now, it threatens to swallow me whole. I don't speak. I couldn't find words even if I wanted to. I move around them, accidentally smashing another pastry underneath my boot. Somehow, I manage to hold on to everything else as I bolt the fuck away from there.

I was stupid for thinking I could have something real with Lo. These past few weeks, I thought something had shifted. I could almost feel the ice thawing inside me. But, nothing has changed. I'm still a fucking murderer. The guilt, the anxiety, the self-loathing…it's all still there. Lo was just a Band-Aid. A distraction. And maybe that's all she's doing with me. Maybe we're just using each other to escape reality. To feel good for once.

The only difference is, I deserve this life. Lo doesn't.

CHAPTER TWENTY

Lo

"**S**TILL NO WORD FROM DARE?" I ASK CORDELL and Matty. After dropping Jess off, I went straight to the shop, thinking Dare would be there early, like usual. I waited around for a while, but he never showed, so I went back home to see if he was there. No luck.

I didn't think much of it. I told myself he'd show up when the shop opened, because I knew he had a twelve o'clock appointment. He never misses an appointment. But it's now almost dark. His clients have come and gone, and still, no sign of Dare.

"Not since last night," Matty answers, looking perplexed.

A knowing look passes over Cord's face.

"What do you know?" I ask as unease pricks the back of my neck.

"I don't know where he is," he hedges.

"But…?"

"But this time of year, he always goes a little…quiet." He's being intentionally cryptic, and what started out as mild concern is quickly morphing into full-blown panic.

"What does that even mean?"

"It means you should talk to him," he says curtly, but his tone also has a hint of softness. I get the feeling that he wants to tell me, but his loyalty to Dare won't allow it.

Just when I'm about to go check his spot in the pine trees, I hear the back door open. Three sets of eyes snap to the back room in time to see Dare staggering inside, leaving the door open behind him.

"Fuck," Cord mutters under his breath.

"Is he...drunk?" I wonder out loud, as my heart starts hammering in my chest.

My phone rings, and I'm about to throw the damn thing against the wall when I see *Private Caller*. Again. I quickly answer, too angry to keep letting this go on. "Don't fucking call me again or I'm filing a restraining order on you like I should've done months ago." I hang up the phone, in a hurry to get to Dare, but it buzzes in my hand with a text a second later.

Eric: *A piece of paper isn't going to keep me away from you.*

I shove my phone into my back pocket, too worried about Dare to wonder if Eric's threats are empty. Cordell seems to be on the phone, whispering quietly to someone. Matty gives me a nod of encouragement before he follows me to the back of the shop. He stops in the doorway, letting me know he's there if I need him, but I'm not worried about me.

I find Dare in the drawing room, sitting at his desk, disheveled black hair has fallen in front of his eyes. "Is my client here?" His voice sounds like he's swallowed glass, and he smells like whiskey.

"You missed all your appointments," I say softly, and some instinct has me walking toward him as if I'm approaching a wild animal. "Where were you?"

He finally looks up at me, his icy eyes bloodshot and broken as he gives me a cold, dead stare. "You should leave."

My throat feels thick and my stomach rolls at his words.

"What are you talking about?" I ask, afraid to hear his answer.

I move closer, but I pause when he yells, "Just go home, Logan!"

I stand, frozen in a mixture of shock and sadness, but something in the back of my mind whispers that I knew this would happen. I knew it was too good to be true. I just don't know *why*.

"We both knew this wasn't going to last," he says, echoing my thoughts, his voice lower but no less detached.

"Yeah." I nod. "I guess we did. But you're clearly fucked up, and I'm not going anywhere until I know you're okay." Dare has employed me, protected me, *sheltered* me, and loved me even when I fought it. Even if this is the end for *us*, I'm not walking away from *him*.

I grab the first aid kit off the supply shelf behind me before walking over to where Dare sits, dropping to my knees in front of him. His knuckles are bloody and appear to have pieces of bark protruding from the torn skin. He doesn't object when I take his hand in mine.

"So you *were* in the woods," I say, more to myself, as I pull the splinters of bark out and clean the cuts with an antiseptic wipe. His elbows rest on his knees, hands hanging down as I work. He doesn't stop me. Doesn't even look at me.

Once I finish, I sit with my palms on top of my thighs,

waiting for him to say something—anything. I can't see his eyes with the way his hair falls in front of them, and I have the urge to brush the inky black strands away. Using one finger, I do just that, and his scowl deepens, eyes clenching shut, almost as if my touch causes him physical pain.

"What happened to you?" I try once more. Yesterday, I had a boyfriend who would move mountains for me. Who couldn't keep his hands off me. Today, he doesn't even want me near him.

Dare stands abruptly, his chair rolling into the wall behind him, then storms out of the drawing room without a word. I stand and walk back into the main room. Cord has Dare by the shoulders, trying to get him to focus on what he's saying, and I'm surprised to see Asher and Camden, Cordell's brother, coming toward me.

"Give me a few. I'm going to take him next door. Get some coffee into his drunk ass and see if I can figure out what the fuck is going on," Asher says, his tone brusque.

I nod, sliding my hands into my front pockets. Camden gives my shoulder a squeeze with his tattooed hand.

"He'll be all right," he says knowingly. "We all have our shit. Believe me, this has been a long time coming."

Asher seems to be about as confused as I am, throwing a questioning look at Camden.

"I'll be here," I say, biting the tip of my thumbnail.

Cord, Camden, Asher, and Dare all head out, leaving me with Matty. Dare looks over his shoulder at me, and the tormented look in his eyes crushes me. How do you fix someone when they won't tell you what's broken? As soon as they're out the door, I cover my face with my hands, and Matty pulls me into his arms. I let him hug me for a minute before stepping away. I don't want to cry right now.

I pace back and forth by the cork board on the wall, full of flyers and pictures—including the ones of Dare and I from Halloween—for what seems like hours. In reality, only twenty minutes have passed. Done with waiting, I decide to go check on Dare.

"I'll be right back," I say to Matty as I push open the door. I'm halfway between Bad Intentions and Blackbear when I hear my name called from somewhere to the right. I look over to find Eric prowling toward me.

"Not now." I sigh, unable to deal with any more drama.

"Hear me out," he says, pulling out a manila folder. I'm skeptical, but for some reason, I don't walk away like I know I should. Somehow, I know that whatever is in his hands is about to change everything.

"I told you to stay away from me."

"I just thought you should know the kind of scum you're shacking up with."

"I don't care what you think you know," I seethe, getting into his space. I'm so sick of Eric fucking with my life. "Dare is a good person, which is more than I can say of you."

"Highly doubt that, considering he's a murderer." Eric chuckles darkly, opening the folder. He holds it out in front of me, and I snatch it from his hands. There are several articles in here, but on the first page, I see a headline in bold letters with a picture of a young Dare below.

Teen suspected of killing foster brother.

I slowly turn my head toward Blackbear, my eyes finding Dare almost instantly. As if he senses me, he looks up and we lock eyes. The folder slips out of my grasp, papers fluttering to the sidewalk around me. Dare's eyes widen, and when they land on Eric, they narrow into slits.

I don't believe it. Not for a second. Not even with the murderous expression on his face right now.

"It's amazing what you can find on the internet," Eric says smugly. I'm still looking at Dare as he stands when something inside me snaps. I curl my fingers into a fist and launch it into the side of Eric's face. Shock replaces his cocky smile.

"Fuck you, Eric."

Eric's hand darts out, wrapping around my throat, and then I'm slammed against the wall behind me, only my tip-toes touching the ground.

"Your boyfriends aren't here to help you this time, Logan," he taunts, and I swing my foot forward to kick him in the balls. He jumps away, but not fast enough.

"Fuck!" he screams, and then his fist is coming straight for my face. My head cracks against the wall behind me, and I feel dazed for a few seconds before the pain sets in, causing me to cry out.

"Look what you made me do!" he yells back, and from the corner of my eye I see the door to Blackbear open, then Eric is gone. I sink down the wall, but Dare scoops me up, holding me in his arms as Cordell, Camden, and Asher pin Eric to the pavement.

"Lo, are you okay?" Dare asks, tipping my chin up. My face feels wet, and I bring my hand to my nose only to realize it's blood. *That son of a bitch.*

"I'm fine. I'm fine," I say again, this time firmer. It hurts, but I'm more angry than anything.

"Cord!" Dare yells and Cordell, not needing further instruction, walks away from Eric and over to me, wrapping an arm around my shoulders. Dare moves toward Eric and sends a boot into his side. Eric jerks and moans, bringing

257

his knees to his chest.

"Dare!" I yell. It's not worth it. *Eric* is not worth it.

"Take her inside," Dare orders, pointing a finger at me.

"Come on, Lo. Let's get you cleaned up," Cord says, guiding me inside.

"Cord, no," I say, digging in my heels.

"It's okay," he assures me. "Asher won't let him go too far."

Reluctantly, I let him guide me away. Once inside, Matty walks out of the bathroom, his eyes bulging.

"The fuck!" he yells, jaw hardening as he marches toward me.

"The suit is back," Cordell informs him.

"I should've gone with you." Matty says, guilt painting his features.

"It's a bloody nose, Matty. I'm not dying." I try to laugh to make him feel better, but it sounds fake to my own ears.

I make my way over to the clean myself up in bathroom, ignoring the pain in my throat and face, but the door dings, and I whip around. Only it's not Dare. It's Jake. And he has one of the crumpled articles in his hands.

"Cops are here," he says, and I rush toward the front, but Jake blocks my way.

"Jake, *move*," I say through gritted teeth.

"I just need to say something." His eyes are pleading with me.

I don't respond, and he takes it as permission to continue.

"I'm not Dare's biggest fan. In fact, I've spent a lot of years hating him."

"Yeah, I'd say that was pretty clear," I deadpan, trying to move past him, but he blocks me again.

"But this?" He holds up the article covered in shoe-prints. "This isn't how it went down. His foster brother was my best friend, and while I blame him, it *was* an accident."

I give him a terse nod. He's telling me what I already know to be true.

"Anyway, I told the cops that he was defending you."

"Thanks," I say, and when I go for the door again, he moves out of the way.

I walk out just in time to see Dare being led toward the flashing blue and red lights down the street in handcuffs and Eric being shoved into the back of a separate car.

I run up to the one handling Dare. "Excuse me, officer?"

"Yes, ma'am?" he asks, turning to face me, his expression morphing from mildly irritated to concerned when he sees the state of me.

"I'd like to press charges."

CHAPTER TWENTY-ONE

Dare

"**S**TEFAN ADAIR," AN OFFICER CALLS, AND I stand, my body feeling like lead as I make my way to the opening of the holding cell I've been in for God knows how long.

"You're being released."

"About fucking time," I grunt. My body hurts. I'm hungover. Weak. Tired. But mostly, I need to see Lo. What the fuck must she think of me now? I was close to bailing. Thought about selling the shop to the most recent prospective buyer. Leaving Lo would be easier than losing her. But then Asher got through to me, reminding me of how he almost threw it all away, and when I saw that asshole Eric with her outside Blackbear, I knew I could never turn it off. This girl is a part of me. The one part of me I love.

I sign paperwork, and then I'm handed my belongings. My phone is dead—no surprise there. I decide to walk the mile and a half home, in the snow, hoping like fuck Lo's there.

When I walk into my house, Jess is awake on the couch, as if he's waiting for me.

"You said you wouldn't hurt her," he accuses, not bothering to look at me.

"Where is she?"

"She just fell asleep."

"I need to talk to her," I say, hoping Jess doesn't make this an issue, because I'm really not in the mood right now.

"Fucking fix it," he says, and I don't waste another second, running up the steps to our room.

Lo is curled up in a ball on top of the blankets at the foot of our bed. Her cheeks are streaked with tears and faint traces of blood, like she tried to wash it off but lacked the energy to do so.

Not even bothering to kick my boots off, I climb in behind her, tugging her into me. I need to feel her warmth right now. To feel her skin against mine.

"Lo," I say, my voice a hoarse whisper.

She jolts awake, sitting up in bed.

"It's okay. It's just me," I say.

The confusion in her eyes clears, but it's replaced with sadness. "Are you okay?" She asks, and I nod. "I don't know how to help you. To be what you need."

"You *are* what I need," I insist, sitting up and swinging my legs over the side of the bed. "I'm sorry. I'm so fucking sorry."

"I don't even know what you're sorry *for*," she says, exasperated. "Because you don't tell me anything."

"Come here, Lo," I say, laying back and holding out my arms. She hesitates before letting me wrap them around her. "I'm ready to tell you everything."

Hazel eyes look up at me, tired yet full of hope. I take a

fortifying breath, steeling myself for her reaction.

"When I was sixteen years old, I killed my foster brother."

Lo doesn't blink. She stays quiet, her face blank, and I slip into the memory of that day.

"Come on, Dare." Sarah pouted, outstretched arms covered in her puffy, bright yellow winter coat from her place on the frozen lake. "Dance with me."

"Get off the ice. It's not safe," I warned her. This winter wasn't as cold as it usually was.

"It's frozen. We do this all the time," she argued, spinning around as if she were ice-skating. "Ugh, fine," she huffed when she realized I wasn't budging. She trudged through the snow to take her place on the bench next to me.

"I just wanted to see you smile for once," she admitted, tucking her gloved-hand into mine. I gave her hand a slight squeeze, softening my rejection before pulling it away, causing those blue eyes to dull with sadness. She knew I wasn't one for physical affection.

I knew she had a crush on me. I also knew this thing between us was a bad idea. She was my foster sister. Her parents were the closest thing I had to family. Her brother, Luke, was one of my good friends, too. He was two years older than me. Soccer superstar. Homecoming king. I was just a fucked-up kid who liked to drink and draw, and sometimes, when the opportunity presented itself, I'd get my dick wet. We had nothing in common, but somehow, we got along.

"You should be in class," I said, and it was so cold I could see my breath. Typical for the time of year.

"So should you." She laughed. She insisted on skipping with me today. Sarah never missed a day. I doubt she even had a tardy before today. She packed a thermos of hot

chocolate and drove us out to a secluded part of the frozen lake.

"Why are we here?" I asked, trying not to sound too harsh. I cared for Sarah like a sister, or at least I thought I did. I never had anything to compare it to. Sometimes when we made out, I thought I might like her in that way, too. When you grow up without any type of love or affection, it's hard to differentiate these things. I was starting to realize that there were many types of love, and whatever I had for Sarah, it wasn't of the romantic variety. Of course, my dick felt differently, but that was just…biology.

"I wanted to ask you something," she said, her cheeks turning pink either from the cold or embarrassment or both.

"What is it?"

"I want to lose my virginity," she blurted out, and my eyebrows shot up to my hairline. "God, this sounds so stupid out loud," she groaned, shaking her head, burying her face in her glove-covered hands.

"I don't even know what to do with that information," I said honestly, pinching the bridge of my nose. Was she saying she wanted to lose her virginity right now? With me? Or was she looking for advice?

"I just figured…I don't know. I don't want to lose it to some guy at a party or something. I want it to be with some-one I trust. Someone like you."

"Sarah…" I shake my head. "That's not a good idea." Part of me was flattered. Part of me was pissed that she'd do anything to jeopardize things with her family. It's not like she's the one with anything to lose, I thought bitterly. No matter what happened, she'd still have parents, a home, a bed…things I'd never had.

I was tempted. If she were any girl other than my foster

sister, I'd have already bent her over this bench. Sex is sex. It's not about love or even like. But it was for Sarah. Plus, I had two more years until I was eighteen. I didn't want to have to move again if shit went south.

Sarah leaned over, pressing her lips to mine. I let her kiss me, but when she lost her gloves and went for my pants, I swatted her away. She backed down, seemingly content to make out instead. When she reached for my dick again, it was harder to push her away. No pun intended.

"This doesn't make me your boyfriend," I said right as she palmed me through my jeans.

"Who asked you to be my boyfriend? It's practice."

I had mixed feelings. On one hand, it felt different with Sarah. Wrong. "Sarah, no," I said, trying to let her down easily, knowing how sensitive she could be.

"You've got to be fucking kidding me," the voice I knew to be Luke's growled from a few feet behind us.

"What are you doing here?" Sarah squealed, her hand jerking from my lap, looking like she wanted to disappear.

"What am I doing here?" he asked, incredulous. "I'm looking for you. The school called Mom. She and dad are both out looking for you right now. Saw your car and thought something happened to you. What the hell were you thinking?"

"She skipped school. She didn't rob a bank. Give the girl a break," I said as I stood to face him. His eyes zeroed in on my crotch and I looked down, noticing for the first time that Sarah had managed to get my fly down.

Shit.

I pulled my zipper up, and Luke's face turned bright red right before he charged me. Before I could react, my back was hitting the frozen lake. My head hit the ice a second

264

before his meaty fist connected with my face, and Sarah screamed for him to stop.

"What the fuck!" I yelled as Luke straddled my torso, gripping the front of my jacket.

"Are you fucking my sister?" he bellowed, landing another punch. Pain radiated through my face.

"Luke! Stop!"

He ignored his sister's pleas, and we scuffled, rolling around, each of us fighting for the upper hand. I pinned him down, giving him one good hit before I stood to walk away. Luke swung his arm out and grabbed my foot. Reflexively, my arms flew out behind me to catch my fall. I heard rather than felt the snap. I knew before I looked that it was bad, and I was right. My forearm was bent in the opposite direction.

The sight of my arm bent at an unnatural angle, combined with the blinding pain that followed, had me gagging, but I don't think Luke noticed any of it, because he was on his feet, coming back for more.

"I didn't fucking touch her!" I shouted through the pain, using my good arm to scramble away, choking back the vomit in my throat. "My fucking arm!" I tried to tell him, but Luke wasn't listening. He bent down, reaching for me again, but this time I pulled my knees back and kicked both feet into his stomach, sending him flying backward.

That's when I first felt it. The ice wasn't thick enough, and it splintered beneath us. It felt like it happened in slow motion, but in reality, we'd only been fighting for seconds. I tried to drag myself toward the edge, but my arm was fucking useless.

Luke yelled as the ice finally gave, and he gripped the edge. His eyes were wild as they locked onto mine. He started to hyperventilate, frantically trying to pull himself over the edge.

Sarah was sobbing now, running toward us, screaming her brother's name.

"Sarah! Do not walk onto the ice. Call nine-one-one," I instructed, and she halted where the snow-covered shore met ice, fumbling for her phone. "Luke, try to stay calm." I kept my voice steady in spite of the excruciating pain that radiated through my entire arm. I remembered hearing somewhere that more often than not, it's the cold shock that causes sudden death. Not drowning.

I knew I didn't have long to act. I flipped onto my stomach, one-armed army crawling toward a thrashing Luke. Each time he tried to pull himself up, the ice broke off, submerging him even more. Once I was finally within reach, I extended my good arm—the right one—and told him to grab it.

His hand gripped mine, just like we did when we arm wrestled many times before, and I gritted my teeth, eyes squeezing shut as I mustered all my strength to pull him out.

"Get me out, get me out, get me out!" Luke chanted, completely panicked as I got his top half above water. He lifted a knee onto the ice, and before I could so much as blink, it cracked, giving way under his weight, sending us both under.

The cold was something I never could've prepared myself for. It took my breath away, and my heart sped up so fast I thought it would burst out of my chest. I paddled my way toward the surface, using the top half of my broken arm like a wing, as I kicked my feet. As soon as I broke through, I gasped for air, looking around for Luke.

"Where is he?!" I didn't get an answer. Sarah was wailing, so full of fear and despair that I knew I'd never forget the sound if I lived to see another day. I tried to calm my erratic breathing, knowing that staying calm was crucial, while also knowing it was futile.

Sarah dropped to her knees, digging around in the snow-covered ground, looking for something. I could feel time slipping away, and I did the worst thing I could've done in that situation. Taking a deep breath, I dove back in. I opened my eyes underneath the water, searching for any sign of Luke. I moved under the ice, hardly seeing a thing, but finally, I made out a large blurry form.

I went back up for one more deep breath before going back under, moving to Luke as fast as I could. My body felt heavy, but my adrenaline kept me going. Before I could reach him, he started to sink.

No. No, no, no.

Summoning the strength and speed I didn't know I had, I jetted toward him, managing to clench the hood of his jacket with my fist before he slipped out of reach. I was slow, so fucking slow, pulling him to the surface. His weight threatened to pull us both down and my lungs felt like they were going to burst, but somehow, I managed to get back to the hole we fell through.

"Dare!"

I heard Sarah's muffled screams as I got closer to the surface, and when I finally broke through, she was lying flat on her stomach with a long branch extended toward us.

I heard the sirens, and I knew I just had to hold on a little bit longer. I tried to push Luke's limp body onto the ice, but I only succeeded in tiring myself out. I felt like I was fading. Shutting down. Like my life was slipping away. In a last-ditch effort, I clutched Luke's head to my chest and hooked my broken arm over the branch. I struggled to keep us both *above water, my eyes closing, my muscles giving out.*

"Just a few more seconds," I told Luke.

And those were the last words I'd ever say to him, though he never heard them.

Lo's sniffling brings me back to the present. I can't meet her eyes, afraid of what I'll find. "What happened after?" she asks, her voice a broken whisper.

"I don't remember," I say truthfully. "I passed out right as we were being rescued. They tried to revive Luke, but…" I clench my eyes shut, shaking the images of his lifeless body out of my mind. "They took me to the hospital, fixed my arm, and treated me for hypothermia for a few days."

"Dare, you have to know—"

"Here's what I know, Logan," I interrupt, the harshness in my tone causing her to flinch. "I know that I delivered the kick that sent my brother, for all intents and purposes, into that water. I killed him. It's a fact. There is no gray area here, so stop looking for one." There's no other way around it. I killed him. I took another life. *I stopped a heart from beating.*

"You tried to save him," she argues, and I finally look at her face, hating the mixture of pain and pity I see looking back at me.

"But I didn't. I couldn't. And it's my fault."

"It was an accident," she presses.

We're quiet for a beat. Both of us trying to navigate what this means before she asks, "What set you off?"

"I saw Sarah and her dad at Sissy's. This time of year always fucks me up, but I hadn't seen them since that day, and it all came flooding back."

Lo nods, understanding. "I didn't believe it, you know. Even when I saw the article, right there in black and white."

"And why's that?" I ask, genuinely curious.

"Because, since I've met you, you've been nothing but good to me. You became mine and Jess's family when our lives were falling apart. You're *good*, even if you can't see it."

"So, what does this mean for us?" I ask the only question that matters, brushing a thumb across her slightly swollen lip.

"It means we get to be together without any secrets between us."

My eyes close, reveling in the relief I feel from her words. "Sometimes, it's hard for me to come out of the darkness. But I'm trying."

"I'll sit with you in the dark. I'm not a fan of the sun anyway," she says, yawning.

"You *are* the sun."

EPILOGUE

Dare

CRUNCH THROUGH THE TWIGS AND PINECONES THAT litter the soft ground. June in River's Edge means the snow has finally melted, giving way to lush greenery. Lo sent me a text telling me to meet her at my spot. Don't ask me what the fuck she's doing in the middle of the woods at dusk.

It's been seven months since Lo came to River's Edge and fucked my world up, in the best possible way. Five since the night all my sins came to light. Eric went to jail for a whole five seconds, much to my dismay, but when he returned home, the police were waiting for him. Surprisingly, his wife actually did get help like he told Lo, but his wife had also concocted a plan. Turns out, Eric had a history of hurting women, his wife being his primary victim. She set up a video camera, documented a couple of months' worth of abuse, and filed for emergency custody. Rumor has it, she and Cayden moved away to start somewhere fresh. Meanwhile, Eric won't be getting out of prison any time soon.

It isn't always easy. There are still days when I'm convinced I'm going to hell for what I did, but that's okay, because Lo brings heaven to me when I get to come home to her, to sink inside her, every single night.

When I finally get to the clearing between the pine trees, I see her standing there, looking nervous as hell. Cut-off jeans so short that they show off a hint of the ink I gave her, her favorite shirt—a baggy D.A.R.E. shirt she found at Goodwill—dirty white tennis shoes, and wild hair in a high ponytail. She twists her hands together, teeth caught between her bottom lip.

"What's all this, Sally?"

There's a large wooden crate on top of a blanket and a bunch of throw pillows tossed around. Lanterns hang overhead from a line between two trees, and she has a spread of food and candles on top of the crate.

"Happy birthday," she says, sounding unsure, her big eyes waiting for my reaction.

"Why do you look so nervous?" I ask, walking toward her. Her shoulders sag, and she rolls her eyes at me.

"Because you hate surprises."

As a rule, I do hate surprises, but this one I can make an exception for. I chuckle, wrapping an arm around her. She jumps up, her legs circling my waist, both hands on either side of my face. "I love you," she says before she slips her tongue between my lips. I groan, turning to prop her up against a tree as my hands find her ass. I'll never get tired of hearing her say those words. I kiss her back, already hard for her. I grind into her heat, and she moans, fingers clutching the back of my neck. I slide a hand to the front of her shorts before slipping a finger inside. She lets me play with her pussy for a minute before pulling away, breathless.

"The food is getting cold," she breathes, face flushed.

"Fuck the food. I'm craving this," I say, flexing my hips

into her.

"Later," she insists, straightening her legs and breaking out of my hold. "I worked hard on this."

"It's perfect." And it is. The two things that bring me peace—my spot and my girl.

Lo takes my hand, tugging me toward the piles of pillows and blankets. She brought takeout from my favorite Italian place and cherry danishes for dessert. Lo is tense and quiet through our meal, still appearing nervous. I don't know what the fuck to make of it, so I ask.

"What else is going on, Lo?"

"I have one more surprise for you," she admits, seeming almost scared of my reaction.

"What is it?" The way she's acting has my gut twisting with dread. Lo doesn't get shy or nervous. What could possibly have her all twisted up? She pulls out her phone, tapping at her screen for a minute before putting it away.

"Five more minutes," she says cryptically, before crawling across the pillows, coming to sit on my lap, linking her ankles behind my back. "Just remember I love you," she says. I dip my head, pressing my nose into her neck, unable to resist inhaling her scent and her warmth.

"Dare," Lo whispers right as I hear footsteps behind me. I tense up, and Lo rubs my back, as if taming a scared animal—which I guess would accurately describe me at this moment. Lo unlatches her legs and stands. I follow her lead and turn around to face whoever it is. Lo tucks her small hand into mine as I look at him, trying to place his familiar face.

"Stefan," says the deep voice belonging to the man standing across from me in a police uniform. The corners of his eyes crinkle when he smiles at me. "You probably don't remember me. I'm Officer Davies. The officer who found you."

As soon as the words are out of his mouth, I'm flooded by memories I didn't even know I had. Drawing on a notepad in the front seat of his police car, him taking off his jacket and wrapping it around me. Then later, sitting on his lap at the police station as I ate his trail mix, not wanting to separate from the first person to show me kindness in my whole life.

So many emotions slam into me at once, and for a minute, I'm that dirty, neglected four-year-old again. I remember sitting on the cement parking block, feeling cold and hungry and confused. I was trying to stay warm in my Ninja Turtles jacket when a bright light blinded me. Seconds later, Officer Davies came into view, bending over to pick me up.

"I've got you, buddy," he said over and over as he held me, probably more scared than I was.

Letting go of Lo's hand, I pinch the bridge of my nose, ducking my head, not wanting to give in to the urge to do something stupid like shed a tear. I hear Officer Davies move closer, and then he's wrapping his arms around me for the second time in twenty-three years. He gives me the man-clap on my back, and when I look up, his eyes are shining with unshed tears.

"I never got to thank you," I say, my voice thick with emotion before I clear my throat.

"No thanks needed. I'm just glad your girl tracked me down. Throughout my entire career, I've wondered where you ended up."

"You did this?" I ask Lo, who has tears streaming freely down her cheeks. She nods.

"I looked you up. Of course, it didn't say *your* name, but I had enough details to find an old article about you. I thought you might like to meet him."

I hear what she's not saying. She knows I have no desire to find my mother, so she did the one other thing that could bring me a piece of my past without involving the person who abandoned me. I have so much fucking love for this girl. I hook an arm around the back of her neck, pulling her close and pressing my lips to her forehead. She smiles up at me, and I know she feels the gratitude I can't put into words.

"I brought these for you," Officer Davies says, holding out an envelope. I hesitate, not sure I can handle any more of the past. When I take it, I find drawings of stick figures scribbled in pencil. They look as if a kid much younger than four drew them.

"You saved these?" I ask, and he nods. "I think you were the first person to put a pencil in my hand."

"He's an artist," Lo supplies.

"A tattoo artist," I correct. She gives me too much credit.

"I'll go ahead and take credit for that then," Davies says with a chuckle. "I have one you drew for me at home, too."

I notice a couple of photos behind the drawings, and I look at the pictures of my younger self with detached eyes. There's one of him holding me in the parking lot, my head on his shoulder and his radio to his mouth. Another of me in a hospital bed—I assume getting checked out after Davies rescued me from freezing temperatures. Another one of me sitting at his desk, a dazed look in my eyes. In every photo, he's next to me, or in the background. He didn't leave me once.

I pluck out a picture of me, after a bath by the looks of it. My hair was lighter. It's strange to see this kid and know it's me. I've never known what I looked like as a child—never thought it was something that mattered, though I did wonder occasionally. It seems like something so…unimportant, but I finally feel like I have some sort of closure. A part of me that I didn't realize I had been missing. Kind of like how I feel about Lo.

"I'll let you get back to your birthday," he says before turning to Lo. "Thanks for making contact, Logan. You've made a two-decade-long wish come true."

Logan peels herself away from me, hugging him around the neck. I hear her thank him softly, but I can't make out the exact words. He gives her a solemn nod, then turns to leave.

"Have I told you how much I love you, crazy girl?" I say, tugging her back toward me by her belt loop.

"I wouldn't mind hearing it again." She smiles, linking her fingers behind my head before kissing the column of my neck. We're interrupted when we hear Davies approaching again.

"I almost forgot. I don't know where your other stuff ended up, but I was able to save this."

He tosses me a dark, wadded-up ball of fabric. I untwist the t-shirt, revealing the last thing I thought I'd see. Lo's eyes shoot up to mine, equal parts amusement and awe swirling in them before she tips her head back, letting out a laugh.

"Jack Skellington."

THE END

ACKNOWLEDGMENTS

First and foremost, to the readers, whether you're just discovering me or have been there since the beginning, thank you. I started Dare's book about four years ago. It was the first thing I'd ever attempted to write, and I never thought it would see the light of day. So, thank you for wanting his story and helping make that dream a reality.

To my husband who probably wished he could divorce me while I spent hours upon hours writing, thank you for stepping in making sure the kids were fed, bathed, and happy. I love you.

Thank you to my amazing editor Paige Smith who deals with my crazy without complaint, and to Letitia Hasser for spending 2789423050 years on this cover. I'm sorry. You love me. Remember that for next time.

Hey Leigh, remember when Defy was almost called Dare, but then you changed it because you remembered Bad Intentions was titled Dare back then? Also remember how you forced me to write it so you didn't change the title for nothing? Thank you for believing in me even when I didn't. Love you.

Ella, you da real MVP. Thanks for always keeping it real. Serena, thank you for everything. You're irreplaceable. Bex, Melissa, and Melanie, thank you for stopping everything to help me. Love you guys.

To the bloggers, thank you for busting your asses all day every day. I appreciate you. <3

Lastly, Charleigh's Angels, my reader group, I fucking love you. You're my happy place. Thank you for all your support.

Read on for a sneak peek of *Yard Sale*, coming in May, plus excerpts from *Bad Habit*, the first standalone in the Bad Love series, and *Misbehaved*, a student/teacher standalone romance!

ABOUT THE AUTHOR

Charleigh Rose lives in Narnia with her husband and two young children. She's hopelessly devoted to unconventional love and pizza. When she isn't reading or mom-ing, she's writing moody, broody, swoony romance.

Stay in touch!

Facebook page:
www.facebook.com/charleighroseprose

Facebook group:
www.facebook.com/groups/1120926904664447

Instagram:
www.instagram.com/charleighrose

Newsletter: https://bit.ly/2hzVQy4

CPSIA information can be obtained
at www.ICGtesting.com
Printed in the USA
BVHW042012141121
621645BV00024B/900